the colossus

ranjini iyer

ASTOR
+ BLUE

THE COLOSSUS
Astor + Blue Editions
Copyright © 2014 by Ranjini Iyer

All rights reserved, including the right to reproduce this book or portions thereof, in any form under the International and Pan-American Copyright Conventions. Published in the United States by:

Astor + Blue Editions
New York, NY 10003
www.astorandblue.com

Publisher's Cataloging-In-Publication Data

IYER, RANJINI. THE COLOSSUS.—1st ed.

ISBN: 978-1-938231-85-8 (Paperback)
ISBN: 978-1-938231-92-6 (epdf)
ISBN: 978-1-938231-86-5 (epub)

1. Mystery—Thriller—Fiction. 2. Woman discovers mysterious document—Fiction 3. Cozy mystery—Fiction 4. Ancient civilizations—Mystery—Fiction 5. Health & Medicine—Fiction 6. Pharmaceutical mystery—Fiction 7. Chicago, London, Pakistan, and India I. Title

Jacket Cover Design: Danielle Fiorello

For Amol

असतोमा सद्गमय, तमसोमा ज्योतिर्गमय ।

मृत्योर्मा अमृतंगमय, ॐ शान्ति शान्ति शान्तिः ।।

From ignorance, lead me to truth;
From darkness, lead me to light;
From death, lead me to immortality
(from Brhadaranyaka Upanishad—I.iii.28)

PROLOGUE

Mohenjo-daro—"Mound of the Dead"
Site of the 5,000-year-old Indus Valley civilization
Around 400 km from Karachi
1935

Dr. Samuel Rosen opened his new leather-bound diary. The rich brown cowhide smelled raw and earthy. He unscrewed the top of his fountain pen.

About fifty yards away was the Colossus's tomb.

Samuel wanted to recreate what might have happened in that tomb over two thousand years ago.

He began writing.

> The artist mashed lumps of red clay into the water, dipped his brush into the paste, and painted the branches of a banyan tree with broad strokes. The foreman dozed beside him.
>
> Sunlight streamed down through the stairwell and lit up a column of fine dust. The pungent odor of dried cow dung and lime that covered the walls hung heavy in the air.
>
> Fifty men had spent the past two months digging out the tomb, carefully watched by the head priest who had supervised every minute of their work, their meals, even their sleep. Today, miraculously, the priest had left them alone.

There was some writing on the east wall. The artist went over to it. He and his kind would never know the divine power of the god men— to read and write. He touched the curves of the beautiful symbols. The wall felt cool. His fingers tingled as he thought of the secrets it held.

The foreman raised himself up on an elbow. "Is the demonic priest back?"

The artist shook his head. "Tell me," he said, "why was this man called the Colossus?"

The foreman looked at the artist's painting and frowned. "You've made him too short. He must be taller, bigger."

The artist went on, "And is this his story written here?"

"Yes."

"That's unusual, isn't it?" the artist said. "These murals, this writing, that priest watching us like a hawk?"

The foreman sighed. "You've kept your lips sealed long enough, I suppose." He picked up a brush and started to clean it. "The Colossus's name was Soodhanta," he said. "He was a rich trader. About ten years ago, he visited a faraway island, Ikaria. He found an unusual tribe living there. He was the first from these parts to trade with them."

"Unusual how?" the artist asked.

"People in this tribe had wrinkled faces, their skin hung loose all over their bodies, and they had lost most of their hair."

The artist's eyes grew wide. "Were they diseased?"

"They were old," the foreman said. "How long do our people live? Thirty-five, forty summers? These people had seen more years than we can ever hope to. And their bodies had shriveled up as a result."

The artist gasped.

"The tribe refused to sell Soodhanta their secret." The foreman paused for effect. "And so he stole it."

"What was the secret?" the artist asked.

"A concoction of vegetables and herbs, rolled into little discs." The foreman held his forefinger and thumb slightly apart to indicate their size. "About this big."

The artist's jaw fell open.

"Soodhanta stole urns full of them," the foreman said.

There was a rustle above ground.

"Did anyone here eat them?" the artist whispered. "Are there any left?"

The foreman stretched his arm and pointed to the large urns lining the back wall.

The artist put a hand to his chest and with a sharp cry, rushed to the urns and tugged at the sealed tops. He couldn't pry them loose.

"Stop!" the foreman cried.

The artist picked up a sharp rock.

The foreman was panic-stricken. "They will cut off your neck and not even bother to wipe the blade before they get to mine. Listen to me—"

Footsteps could be heard near the mouth of the tomb.

"They're coming!" the foreman said in a frantic whisper.

But the artist paid no heed.

The priest descended the narrow steps leading to the tomb, his elaborate jewelry jangling with his every step.

And yet the artist was too fixated on the urns to notice. He brought the rock down hard on one of them. It cracked. Little green pills spilled out. The artist grabbed a handful and swallowed them.

Samuel put down his pen. Beside him sat a vial of the same green pills. What a wonder that they had stayed intact for centuries. Were they just an early multivitamin? No, surely they were a lot more than that. The pills extended lives, the locals said. But something in them choked life away, too. The pills were cursed.

Samuel Rosen didn't believe in curses. He was a scientist. And he was determined to unlock the secret this little pill had held for so very long.

CHAPTER ONE

Maxine Rosen's apartment
Lincoln Park, Chicago
June 2000

The alarm went off. The first few bars of "Metamorphosis" began to play. For the sixth time.

This time, Max raised her groggy, disoriented head from her pillow. Her long curls were plastered about her head and face. She brushed some stray hair out of her eyes. A power nap had turned into a two-hour-long siesta. With a grunt, she turned the alarm off.

Even though it was Philip Glass, at this quiet twilight hour the soft piano notes felt like a grater against her nerves.

Max threw her legs over the side of the bed and looked down. Bare thighs stared back at her. One of these days, she promised herself, these soft thighs would not rub. No sir. They would stand taut and firm, with that fashionable gap between them. She'd finally start wearing mini skirts that would ride up, revealing—

Max jumped off the bed before her mind could race off to unpleasant places.

She set a pot of coffee to brew and looked out the window at the lake. Her condo, inherited from her late father, was a large two bedroom with a magnificent view of Lake Michigan and the curving Lake Shore Drive. Joggers were moving up and down the running path parallel to the lake, their rhythmic movement taunting Max for her lethargy.

Why couldn't they stay in just once? Watch TV or something.

The aroma of coffee slowly filled the room. Max poured herself a cup. It was almost 8:00 pm. Late, but she could still go for a run. She should go for a run. Well, more of a lumbering jog, really, one that would have her looking like she was about to keel over with every step. Unless she kept at it at least twice a week, her happy size ten would be quickly left behind. Going up half a size over two weekends was not unusual for Max. It was a battle she had grown up fighting, and one she felt herself losing at every turn.

Her phone started to ring.

She answered it. "Maxine Rosen speaking."

"Front desk, Miss Rosen. Good evening. There's a visitor for you. A Mr. Lars Lindstrom from London."

"Who?" Max rubbed her eyes.

"He's been calling for you all day. He's finally here now. He says he knew your grandfather Samuel in Germany. It's urgent, he says."

Max yawned. "How's he dressed? How does he sound?"

"Impeccable."

"Okay, send him up, please. Uh…in about ten minutes."

Max pulled on a skirt and scrubbed the sleep off her face as she went over her schedule for the next day. At noon she was seeing the principal of a private school about catering their lunches. After that, she had meetings with her accountant and two organic meat and produce vendors. Her accountant was insisting that it was time she mastered QuickBooks. He would send her into a dizzy spell with lengthy discourses on cash flow management. Bargaining with the vendors would feel like a fencing duel. Max wondered, not for the first time, why she had taken all this on.

Because I love to cook and this is the best way to do what I love and make money, she told herself. It was an oft-repeated mantra.

She went to the kitchen and looked over her tasting menu for the school. Ravioli, check. Chickpea salad, check. Sweet potato fries, and yes, the hummus and the peas curry. She had prepped some of the items. She could do some more tonight and finish first thing tomorrow morning.

An unwelcome pit formed in her stomach. She shouldn't do the fries. They would turn soggy. In fact the entire menu she had planned was child unfriendly. She began twirling a lock of her hair, slowly at first, then at a more frantic pace.

Calm down, she told herself. Hadn't they asked for healthy, and if possible, vegetarian food? Well, that was what she was giving them.

There was a knock at the door.

It would be fine, she thought as she undid the various locks. The school would hire her. And there was that one lead to cater board lunches at the Jewish Students Awareness Association. They might want kosher though. With a sigh she opened the door.

A man, probably in his late seventies, stood in the hallway, wearing an expensive-looking charcoal suit. He was slim. His head was covered with thinning white hair and his eyes were dark behind rimless glasses.

"Mr. Lars Lindstrom?" Max said. "I'm Max Rosen."

He took her hand and held it in a firm, almost desperate grip. Max winced.

"You...you look like your grandfather," he said in a polished but shaky voice. "The same large brown eyes, blemish-less skin. He was a handsome man."

Max blushed, not sure how to respond.

"Seeing you reminds me of times I have done my best to forget. Still, it's nice to meet you," he rasped.

Max stood aside. "Uh, come in, have a seat. I don't have much time, I'm afraid. I have several meetings tomorrow that I must prepare for."

"I'll make this brief. Let's see, what time is it now?" He glanced at the cuckoo clock by the door and started.

Max laughed. "That clock has never told the right time."

It was her 11:32 cuckoo clock. Or rather, her father's. The cuckoo clock's needles were frozen at 11:32, had been for years now. Since just before Papa died, actually. Every time she was tempted to throw it out, she stopped. She and Papa had laughed about the fact that the clock, which had never told time correctly, would now at least tell the right time twice a day. It had been one of their last happy moments together.

"Would you like some coffee and a sandwich, Mr. Lindstrom?" Max asked, moving towards the kitchen. "I was about to have dinner."

"Call me Lars. Just coffee sounds wonderful."

"Please make yourself comfortable," Max said, motioning toward the living room. She made a sandwich with leftover chicken and homemade red pepper paste, poured two cups of steaming coffee, and settled down in a chair facing Lars.

"So you knew my Opa—my grandfather," she said.

"I knew Samuel well, yes, but I'm really here to talk about your father."

Max took a sip of coffee and bit into her sandwich. "Hope you don't mind if I eat while we talk. I'm famished."

"Oh no, go ahead," Lars said, his voice and manner tense. "Now, before I say what I must, I need you to trust me. I'm one of very few people that have an ancient seal from the Indus Valley. Samuel gave it to me when he returned from his visit there. Do you know about this seal?"

Opa's Indian seal.

Yellowed memories began to grow vivid in Max's mind.

When she was about ten or eleven, she had stumbled upon her grandfather's diary. Not long after she'd turned to the first page, where she saw a bright red seal's embossment looking like a melted piece of candy, Opa had found and scolded her. Her tears had softened him, and he told her that the mark was made by his lucky seal. "This seal is from the Indus Valley, formerly in India," he had said as he showed her the seal. "An advanced civilization lived there thousands of years ago. This is a copy of a real seal. The original belonged to a man they called the Colossus. An archeologist friend gave it to me when I was in India visiting the Colossus's tomb."

His face and voice had taken on a somber tone. Max had wondered why was he so sad talking about it, if it was his lucky seal. He didn't offer any more stories, and asked her not to mention it to anyone else. It was to be their secret.

A few months later, Opa died. And with him all his stories.

Max put her sandwich down. "I do know about the seal, but—"

Lars Lindstrom held up his hand. "Hiram—uh, your father—was doing some research before he died. It was work he took over from Samuel. I knew this work too. You see, I was Samuel's assistant in his lab at Berliner Pharmaceuticals. In Germany."

A knot formed in Max's stomach, its grip slowly growing stronger. She drew back a little.

"Oh dear, I've upset you," Lars said gently. "This must be so unsettling. A stranger comes to your door and starts yammering about your father and grandfather."

Max shook her head. "It's fine," she said. "I'm just—" She gave a little laugh. "I've had a harrowing day, that's all."

They sipped their coffees.

"So you're from London," Max said at last. "I'd love to visit someday. What brought you to Chicago?"

Lars smiled. "I came here to say goodbye to some old friends at the French pastry school. And I thought it was time that I see you." He let out a loud sigh, rubbed his hands together, and put them on his thighs. He looked at her with melancholic eyes. "Five years ago, following your father's death, I received a package from him, sent by his lawyer."

Max raised her eyebrows. "Oh?"

"It contained a coded research document and a letter." Lars handed her a sheet of paper.

Max recognized her father's handwriting.

"Go ahead, read it," Lars said.

CHAPTER TWO

"Dear Lars," Max read aloud, "You are in possession of my most important work. I have not been able to show it to the world and I'm no longer around to do so. You should know that for the past several months I have been receiving threats from our former employer, Berliner Pharmaceuticals."

Max let out a stifled cry.

"Steady, child," Lars said.

She read on. "Consider it a dead man's last wish to make sure this research sees the light of day. I'm arranging to send you two packages. As a precaution, this package with the coded research will be rerouted prior to reaching you.

"The other package contains a sheet of paper with the key to decode the research, and a vial. The vial contains the health pills my father got from the Indus Valley dig in India. These are the pills you and he worked on at Berliner just before the war.

"Since you are familiar with the origins of this work, I am making a huge assumption that you might still have an interest in it. If not for my sake, do this for my father's. But please do not involve my daughter. I want to spare Max any pain associated with this work. I trust you to do the right thing. Call my lawyer at 773-555-8327 if you need to.

"Yours most gratefully, Hiram Rosen"

Max gripped the arms of her chair. The room began to blur. *Don't faint,* she told herself over and over. She put down the letter, moved unsteadily to a corner of the living room, and threw up all over a pot of pink begonias. Memories of Papa began playing like a movie in her head, and she broke into heaving sobs.

Lars went to her and held her shaking shoulders.

"That was insensitive of me," he said in a pained voice. He handed her a large white handkerchief and led her back to her chair.

"You think this means Papa didn't commit suicide," Max whispered. "These threats from Berliner...you think they were carried out? Is that how he died?"

How angry she had been with her father. And now, this...this meant she had been unfair to him for years, even if it was only in her thoughts.

But how was it possible? *Scientist and researcher Dr. Hiram Rosen's death was caused by alcohol and aspirin poisoning, accidental or self-inflicted,* the newspapers had reported. There had been no doubt in the police's minds about that, she remembered.

"Perhaps they drove him to suicide," Lars said with some hesitation.

Max tried to suppress the pangs of grief filling her chest.

"But how? Why?" she cried. "I mean, what is this research about, anyway?"

"I must give you some background. About me, about this whole business. I'm going about this all wrong." Lars pursed his lips and pressed his hands together. "But first, a glass of water for you, my child." He went into the kitchen.

Max took the water from him and sipped slowly. They didn't speak for a while. Max stared at the floor, her mind numb, her body drained of strength.

"Let's see," Lars said slowly. "I was a student at Berlin University when I worked with Samuel. This was in the mid to late thirties. During this time, Samuel was invited to India on an archeological dig. They had found some mysterious little green discs in the Indus Valley—medicinal pills—that the locals claimed was the pill of immortality."

"Really?" Max said.

"Well," Lars said with a wave of his hand, "they were health pills that helped the ancient Indus people live longer lives, a potent combination of herbs and vegetable matter. But because of its legend, Samuel was excited."

"What happened then?" Max refilled their cups with fresh coffee.

Lars smiled gratefully. "Samuel brought some back to Germany. We found that the pills did prolong life by reducing metabolic rate. My memory fails me now as to the details. But I do remember that we found a contagious bacterium in the pill. In 1939, the war began. As a Jew, Samuel's heritage became an issue when the Nazis came to power. When Berliner couldn't protect him anymore, he was sent off to Krippenwald labor camp. We were unable to finish our work."

"So Papa presumably took over the work you and Opa had left unfinished," Max said. "But Papa worked in genetics. What's the connection between your work and his?"

"I don't know," Lars said. "After Samuel was taken away, I couldn't bear to remain in Germany. I went to London. There I met my future wife and took over her family *patisserie*. It was a good life and I lost all interest in returning to a career in pharmaceuticals. Samuel and I stayed in touch off and on, but we never met again." Lars stared out the window, eyes unfocused. "Samuel once mentioned to me that Hiram was interested in our work on the Indus pills. I didn't know the extent of Hiram's involvement in Samuel's research until after your father's death. But by the looks of it, he unearthed something about the pills that made Berliner nervous." Lars turned back to face Max. "I called on you because I thought you might have some relevant papers Hiram or Samuel may have kept."

"I have nothing work related of Papa's," Max said. "As for Opa, he burned almost all of his papers in a fit of rage one evening. All I have left from him is his seal and a diary, but most of it is torn and burned."

"Why don't you give this some thought?" Lars said. "Perhaps you might be able to guess the key to decode Hiram's research."

"It's a really, really long shot," Max said. She put her hands over her thighs to stop them from jiggling, picked up her sandwich, and stared at it. Gosh, she was hungry. How morbid that she would want to eat despite their conversation, despite throwing up, despite feeling such raging sorrow. Disgusted with herself, she took a defiant bite.

"Of course, once we crack the code, if we ever do, we'll need the actual pills," Lars said, his face somber. "For peer review, et cetera. Otherwise Hiram's findings, whatever they are, will make a weak case."

Max stared at Lars. "Papa arranged to send this to you five years ago. Why did you wait this long to—?"

Lars turned away. "My wife was ill at the time. She died, but there was our daughter. I didn't want to put her in danger." He paused. "In case Hiram had been—well, if Berliner Pharmaceuticals had in any way been involved in his passing. Besides, the second package containing the key to decode the research and the vial of the pills never arrived. All I had was his research, but it was coded and therefore gibberish. I called Hiram's lawyer and told him that I would protect the research but would do nothing with it. It was a coward's act, but…" Lars shrugged.

"What did the lawyer say to that?" Max asked.

"What could he say? He agreed that without the key, the research was useless. He asked me to let him know if the key ever surfaced. But it never did. He was rather puzzled that I had received the package containing Hiram's research. Hiram had rerouted it several times and sent it to a post office box in London addressed not to me, but to Dr. Klein, about which I received detailed instructions."

"Who's Dr. Klein?" Max asked.

"Me! Your grandfather called me that. *Klein* means "little one" in German. I was rather young then, you see."

"All right, what about the second package?"

"That had been sent directly from the lawyer's office, also to that same PO box. But it didn't reach me. Possibly mislaid. Or, more likely, stolen."

"By Berliner?"

"Only they would have known Samuel's nickname for me," Lars said. "So yes."

That her father had been involved in all this intrigue stunned Max. It was as if she hadn't known him at all.

"What changed your mind?" Max said with a frown. "Why now?"

"I needed to do it," he said tightly.

Max was surprised at the calm she was starting to feel. Lunches delivered late were usually enough to leave her in a cold sweat. Maybe this was how numbing fear felt.

"I called Hiram's lawyer again a few days ago and asked him for your contact information," Lars said. "And well, here I am."

Max tried telling herself that knowing the truth about Papa was better, even if it burned a hole inside her that might never go away.

"Hiram's lawyer had asked me when I first called him five years ago if Kevin Forsyth was involved in Hiram's work in any way," Lars said. "Do you know him?"

"Kevin Forsyth is father's former business partner." Max said sharply. "I don't know him and I don't trust him. Papa and he started a business years ago. It failed. Papa never told me the details, but he hinted that Kevin Forsyth cheated him somehow. Papa was bitter about it for a long time." She shifted in her chair. "He started drinking. It was bad."

"I'm sorry," Lars said softly.

"So is Kevin involved?"

"Not to my knowledge or the lawyer's," Lars said. "But apparently, despite everything, Hiram admired Kevin, which is why the lawyer mentioned him."

Max closed her eyes. Her shoulders slumped forward. "This whole thing is as hopeless as it was five years ago."

Lars stood up and went to the windows facing the lake. "Remember I said I was here to say goodbye to some friends? Well, a few weeks ago, I found out I had stomach cancer. Stage three."

"Oh no—I'm so sorry," Max said.

She had seen death at close quarters. Papa's death had been a shock, but it had made her angry more than upset. Mama's passing had been different. Her mother had died of lung cancer when Max was ten. She had watched helplessly as her mother suffered through the intense pain of her disease, seen her smile through it all until the very end.

Lars took a deep breath. "I thought about Hiram as I sat making plans. I thought I'd destroy his research. Years had passed. No one was asking about it. But I couldn't. And since I didn't have Hiram's help in the form of the key, I'm taking the liberty of asking for yours. Despite his wish that I keep you out of this."

Max didn't know how to respond. She was still smarting from the shock of Lars's revelations. "What sort of code is it?" she asked.

"I was told it's a substitution cipher—using one letter for an-other—or a book cipher where the substitution is based on a portion of text. Or it could be a more complex one."

Max turned to her enormous movie collection. "I saw a documen-tary about complex coding once. About the Enigma machine. It was used to send secret messages by Germans." Max realized her voice had grown animated.

Lars smiled.

Max was embarrassed. "Papa and I loved movies. We'd watch our favorites over and over again. Sometimes I wish I could watch movies all day," she said wistfully. "Whether I am stressed or happy, I watch movies. Or I eat." She looked away, upset with herself for being so candid.

"Well, I hope it isn't coded like your Enigma machine," Lars said. "You said you still have Samuel's diary. Is it here?"

Max walked over to a small safe and opened it. After looking through it for a few minutes, she said, "It must be in the safe at my catering kitchen. Sorry, I'm horribly disorganized."

"Can we go look for it now?" There was urgency in Lars's voice. "I leave for London tomorrow."

Max had never before felt more exhausted. It was as if the last hour had torn her into ribbons. And she had so much to do for tomorrow.

She looked at Lars's desperate face. "Sure," she said.

CHAPTER THREE

Lars opened the cab door and followed Max into the back seat.

"Randolph and May please," Max said to the driver.

They stared ahead in silence, listening to the lilting beats of middle-eastern music as the streetlights zipped by.

"Do you think *we* need to be afraid of Berliner?" Max asked.

Lars scratched his chin. "This is probably a forgotten matter." He paused for a second. "But it wouldn't hurt to be careful."

Max wasn't sure if she ought to feel reassured or frightened. She glanced at Lars, but his face remained impassive.

Lars went on. "The person who must have engineered the theft five years ago—of the key and pills Hiram sent me—is Peter Schultz. Peter was heir apparent to the Berliner throne when Samuel and I worked there. He was ruthless and ambitious. He's as old as me, late seventies. Retired now. I checked. Only he would remember me after all this time. Only he knew that Samuel called me Dr. Klein."

An old memory surfaced in Max's mind. "Oh my goodness!"

"What is it?" Lars asked.

"Some months before Papa died, he received a job offer from Berliner. The offer was coming directly from Chairman Peter Schultz, they said. I remember Papa being part amused, part disturbed. When I asked him why, he told me Opa had once worked for Schultz. Might that have been their first threat to him? A veiled one?"

"It's the sort of thing Peter would do," Lars said drily. "Try and buy Hiram off. And when the bribe of the job didn't work, they probably made stronger threats."

"Are you sure they didn't…well, I mean can we be sure my father committed suicide?" Max said.

"Peter Schultz is ruthless," Lars said, "but murder is beneath him."

"One other thing," Max said. "How did Berliner even know that Papa had arranged to send you the document in the first place?"

The cab lurched to a halt at a stoplight. "Once Hiram died, they must have figured I was the only one Hiram could trust that knew about this research and about the Indus pills in particular."

"Hmm. But what was—or is—Berliner afraid of? What does Papa's research contain that is enough to scare such a powerful company? This contagious bacteria you found in the pill?"

"I'm not sure," Lars said. "I left Berliner as soon as Samuel was sent to Krippenwald. I do know that Berliner continued working on the pills even after Samuel was taken away. Maybe they found something awful and eventually realized that Hiram had discovered it too."

They arrived at Max's kitchen in the West Loop area. The streets were deserted. The only place with some life was an edgy new Chinese restaurant about a block away. It glowed under the light of bright red lanterns.

"Oprah's studio is there." Max pointed. "The area is not the safest at night, but the rent is affordable." She unlocked the door to her kitchen.

Lars walked into the simple but immaculate space. "Very nice," he said. "You run a catering company, then?"

Max nodded. "Max's Lunchbox and Catering," she said. "We provide gourmet lunches to executives in the Loop area. It's a struggle sometimes, especially since the severance from my old job is dwindling."

Lars smiled. "How long have you had this company?"

"Over a year. Before that I was a senior research associate at Granger Foods. Fiddling in a lab with chemical-laden cream cakes became meaningless. Sensing my lackluster attitude, they promptly laid me off."

"Samuel was a good cook," Lars said, turning the pages of a cookbook. "Did you study at culinary school?"

"I have a masters in food chemistry and an associates degree from the Chicago Culinary Institute. Papa wanted me to study science. I love food. So I combined the two!"

Max opened a safe in the matchbox-sized office area she had cordoned off in one corner of the kitchen.

An almost hysterical laugh escaped her. "Before you knocked on my door today, I thought I had problems! Well…here goes nothing." With a growing sense of anxiety mingled with anticipation, she reached into the depths of the safe and pulled everything out. A mass of papers tumbled onto the cement floor. She and Lars began going through them.

"Question is," she said, "is Berliner still keen on hiding this? I mean if we manage to decode the research, can you be sure we won't be in danger?"

Lars made circles with his forefinger on a sheaf of invoices. "I don't know," he said. "All I know is that I cannot die in peace knowing I let my friend's son down. If you'd rather not pursue this, it's all right. But if you do, together we might be able to crack this. After all, I knew Samuel well. And you know your father best."

Max felt a gush of affection for Lars. He had said *know*, not *knew*. Perhaps it was a slip of the tongue, but he truly seemed to care. She gave his hand a little squeeze.

"I don't see anything resembling a journal or diary," Lars said at last.

Max cursed. Might it be at home after all?

The door opened with a loud crash.

There stood the oddest-looking man Max had ever seen. He was short and heavyset, like someone who lifts weights but also eats too much bad food. His hair, which stood up in tufts, was sort of blond, well, yellow really. His face was jolly, even a bit stupid. He looked like a dull but sweet school principal.

He shut the door, bolted it, and came closer.

"*Wei geht's,* how are you, Herr Lindstrom," he said in a soft voice. Max let out a gasp. Lars turned pale.

"Looking for something?" the intruder went on in broken English. He collected every single sheet of paper Max had pulled out of her safe and made a small pile. He went through them with care, grunted with satisfaction, and poured some liquid on them from a small bottle. Then he lit a match and threw it on the pile.

"What are you doing?!" Max leapt forward to rescue some of the papers, but the intruder held her away with an outstretched arm and smiled, his eyes crinkling up in amusement.

They watched the flames go up, consume the papers, and die down completely—all in a few seconds. A small pile of smoldering ash was all that remained.

The blond dusted off his hands.

"Do I know you?" Lars asked slowly.

"My mistake," the man said with a small bow. "I represent old friends from Germany."

"What do you want?" Lars asked.

Max watched, horrified, as the man pulled Lars toward him.

"You're trying to be brave, Herr Lindstrom. That isn't good for anyone's health. I want the research. Where is it?"

Lars didn't speak.

The blond pulled out a small, shiny pistol and attached something to its end. Max felt the room start to swim about her. She opened her mouth to scream, but no sound escaped her.

The blond put a finger to his lips. "*Nein, nein, Fräulein,* we must make no noise." To Lars, he said, enunciating every word, "Perhaps I wasn't clear the first time. Where is the research?"

"In London," Lars said, his voice quavering.

"Where?" he pressed.

Lars hesitated. "In a locker," he said.

"I shall have the key to that locker, *bitte,* please." The blond extended a large hand toward Lars.

"I don't have it," Lars said.

"Of course you do. You told Hiram Rosen's lawyer that you were going to give her the research." He pointed to Max. "That ash there isn't the research. So either you have the papers or you have the locker key. There's nothing in your hotel room or her place. I checked."

Lars winced. Max let out a cry.

"You of all people should know that we mean business." The man checked his gun and caressed it with his left hand. "Beautiful weapon, no?"

"Berliner," Lars whispered.

The man chuckled. "Your disease hasn't affected your brain. So how brave are you really?" He held the gun to Lars's neck.

Max staggered back.

"The locker key," the blond said. The gun made a clicking sound. "The safety is off now."

Max began to sink to the ground.

"Or maybe she has it." The barrel of the gun moved toward Max.

"All right, all right!" Lars yelled. "Here. Take it. It's the key to locker number 53 at Waterloo Station. Now leave us alone." He rushed to Max.

"What do you think you're doing?" the blond demanded.

"She is not well." Lars held a very grateful Max in his arms and smoothed her forehead. Max had lost all feeling in her limbs.

"Lars Lindstrom, leave the girl alone and come back here," the blond shouted. "Now!"

Lars moved back to where he had been.

Max watched as the German meticulously searched every part of Lars, checking his briefcase, his pockets, his mouth, everything.

"I hope you aren't trying to trick me, Herr Lindstrom." The blond held his gun at Lars's neck and pulled the trigger. There was a *pfft* sound like a champagne bottle being uncorked.

Max put a hand over her mouth. Why was she incapable of screaming the place down? Not that there was any point. There was no one close enough to hear.

"If I find out that you have tricked me, my aim shall improve next time."

Max felt like she was being held under water. Lars put a shaking hand to the side of his neck and bent forward. Thin trickles of blood flowed down his hand and arm.

The blond strolled over to Max and brushed her cheek with a light sweep of his gun. "Consider this visit a warning to you too Fräulein," he said.

The world around her went black. Max fell to the floor with a thud.

CHAPTER FOUR

Max opened her eyes. She was sitting on her bed with her back resting against several pillows. Lars was waving a white bird in front of her face. Her vision slowly cleared. Lars was fluttering his handkerchief at her. The side of his neck was bandaged.

"What happened?" she said drowsily. "Didn't that beast shoot you?"

"He did, but it was meant to scare, not kill. The bullet grazed my neck, that's all."

"Did you call the police?"

Lars shook his head. His face was drawn. "I didn't see the point," he said. "That man is probably on a plane to Germany right now and I don't have the time or patience to deal with the bureaucratic engine of the local constabulary." Lars's eyes were bloodshot. There were purple shadows under them. "Anyway, it's done. I gave him a locker key."

Max sighed. With relief or disappointment, she wasn't sure. Some of both, she guessed.

Lars laced his fingers together. "You know what I think, given what happened tonight?"

Bile made a quick ascension up to Max's throat. She swallowed it down and counted to ten. Twice. "What?" she said hoarsely.

"Hiram may not have committed suicide after all. In fact, I am convinced that he may have been killed for whatever it was that he was about to reveal in his research. I'd suspected it, but I thought

Peter Schultz would never stoop to murder. Now I'm not so sure."
Lars's head dropped to his chest. "I'm sorry, Max, so very sorry to
have dragged you into this."

"It's all right." Max shrugged. "We tried and we failed."

Lars went to the window. "I said I gave him *a* locker key, not *the*
locker key."

Max blinked a few times as if it would help her fully comprehend
what Lars was saying.

"I never intended to just hand you the papers. I told Hiram's lawyer I would like to give them to you eventually. It was in the back of
my mind the whole time that there might be trouble brewing. And
so, before leaving London, I opened a second locker and filled it with
some papers that looked similar to the ones Hiram had sent me."

"Will they fool him?" Max asked. Every bone in her body felt
rattled, shaken loose.

"The blond perhaps, but not Peter Schultz." Lars went to her and
took her hands. "Remember how I held you right before you fainted?
In that commotion, I slipped the key under a shelf in your kitchen.
That man searched you and the kitchen too before he left, but luckily
he didn't look too carefully." Lars handed her a locker key. "This is
the key to the locker where Hiram's papers are. I've written the name
of the bank and the locker number here." He pushed a folded piece
of paper into her hands.

"What now?" Max was feeling like she might faint again.

"I'm going back to London. We have two, maybe three days at
most before Berliner realizes what we have done. Here's the difficult
bit. For you, I will remain in London three days—no more. I do need
to finish the sale of my business and wrap up my life there. I've made
plans to leave for France to be with family."

Max looked at him with wide eyes.

"It's going to be up to you now," Lars said. "I've lost my nerve, I'm
afraid. I plan to die fighting my disease, not by a bullet. I'm so sorry."

"You're abandoning me?" Max asked.

Lars squeezed her hands. "I wish it hadn't been like this. I wish
I could have been the one to take the lead, but I can't. You have a

choice. You can let it sit. I'll add you to my will so you get Hiram's papers when I'm gone. Or in the next three days, do some digging. If you find something useful, come to London. We can talk. And even then, if we decide to do nothing, I can add you as a joint holder so you can access the locker without me whenever you choose."

Max let out a sob. This was so unfair. What the hell did she know about decoding research papers and dodging clichéd blond German villains with guns?

"You keep the key." She shoved it toward him.

Lars shook his head. "Bring it with you. That way I'll be forced to help. It sounds awful, but that's the way it is."

He stood up. "Now, do you think Samuel's diary might be here after all?" He was suddenly all brisk and business-like. "It's just as well that it wasn't in your kitchen, otherwise that monster would have burned it too."

Max slowly slid out of bed. She went to her living room. The door of her safe was still open from when the German had searched it. There were books everywhere, papers strewn all over the floor, drawers open and emptied.

Dully, she began picking books off the floor and putting them back on shelves. One was a red notebook. It was her mother's journal. Max opened it. She sometimes thumbed through it when memories of Mama threatened to fade. She opened it now and felt her throat tighten at the sight of her mother's flowing handwriting. On this page she had written about the blueberry pie she had made to celebrate Max's birth. Max turned a few pages. There were recipes and drawings. She had written about her routine with a young Max, games they had played, crafts they had done. There were tidbits of gossip about neighbors and friends. The handwriting began getting illegible as her mother's illness progressed.

"Samuel's diary, do you see it?" Lars's voice was laced with impatience. He pulled a few books off a nearby bookshelf.

Max put her mother's notebook away. Her eyes stung with the promise of tears. She pulled out a few books that sat askew on the shelf.

And there.

Buried between two thick pastry books, she found it. Opa's thick, brown, leather-bound diary. The one she had found as a child.

"It's here," she said.

Max opened it, her unsteady hands fumbling with the sepia pages.

A plastic bag was taped to the back of the diary. In it was the ancient Indian cylindrical seal Opa had shown her. On the front page was the seal's embossment—looking as red and candy-like as ever. Below the embossment was some text in Sanskrit—written like a verse. No translation was provided.

Max turned the page.

Opa had started journaling in India. Max read the first few entries about his role at Berliner and his trip to India.

There must have been something heavy bearing on Opa's mind around the time he had burned his papers. There were days Max remembered Papa and Opa having heated discussions. Some days there had been triumphant smiles accompanying their discussions—they had filled chalkboards with flowcharts and frenzied writing that she had looked at with detachment. But more often, there had been arguments and sulking sessions.

Once Opa's health deteriorated, the discussions had stopped. During his last days, Opa's seal had often been in his hands. She could see him now, turning it over, looking at it as if he was willing it to speak to him. Console him. Poor Opa had spent those days lying on the couch, staring out at the lake alone. Whatever was burdening him, he had kept it buried inside.

"If this diary has nothing, we have nothing to go on," Max said. She took the Indus seal out of the plastic bag. Why was it Opa's lucky seal? The pills were from the Indus Valley. The seal was from the same place. Did that mean something, or was the seal simply an old souvenir?

"I must go now." Lars touched her arm. "I cannot stay and read the diary with you. I'm done in." He tried to laugh. "Besides, my flight leaves first thing tomorrow."

Max looked at the floor and nodded.

"Read it, give this some thought. Then decide if you want to come see me. Remember, three days from now I'll be gone."

"Okay," she managed to say.

"I hate leaving you here by yourself." Lars squeezed her shoulder. "Can I drop you off somewhere before I return to my hotel?"

Max started to shake her head no, then stopped. "I should probably see Uncle Ernst and tell him about all this. Maybe he could help us, too."

Lars frowned. "I didn't know Hiram or your mother had siblings. Wait a second, not Ernst Frank."

Max looked at him. "Yes. Opa's old friend from Germany."

Lars's eyes widened. "They were at Krippenwald concentration camp together. Goodness, Ernst must be well over eighty! How is he?"

"Ridden with problems, sadly—Parkinson's, senility, paranoia. He's the only family I have left. He's the only one I can tell." Max's voice broke.

"I'll take you to his place. He lives in Chicago, I take it."

Max wiped her eyes on her sleeve. "When the liberation happened, Opa and Uncle Ernst came here together."

"I'll get a cab."

"No need. He lives on the fifteenth floor."

They walked to the elevator together. Lars and Max stood side by side, not speaking.

At the fifteenth floor, the elevator doors peeled open.

"Max, one other thing. The only way these people would have known my intentions about coming to Chicago is by tapping my phone. We must assume they may have tapped yours, too. So don't call me. I'll contact you."

With a dull nod, Max started to get out.

Lars put a hand on her arm. "I'm so very sorry, child," he said. "About everything."

CHAPTER FIVE

Max walked down the corridor and slammed her fist against the familiar door of 1502 once, twice, her head hanging down, her throat ready to explode, eager tears waiting to spill.

The door opened tentatively. "Is that you?" Uncle Ernst said. "So late?"

Max took one look at his dear, ruddy face and could hold back the tears no longer. He took her in his arms and rubbed her back.

Dear Uncle Ernst. With his soft, watery brown eyes and sagging cheeks. Snug in his faded yellow sweater and moss green pants. Max had often begged him to wear different colors, offered to buy him new clothes—all to no avail. "But I like zis," was his response every time.

Max couldn't imagine life without Uncle Ernst. He had become a father figure to Papa after Opa's death and to her, after Papa's passing. Uncle Ernst had one daughter, Sally. Once a successful entrepreneur, founder and owner of a weight loss company, Sally had committed suicide many years ago. The reasons for her death were still a bit fuzzy to Max. All she knew was that Sally had suffered from paranoia. Towards the end, she had feared that her company was in danger of going under. And she couldn't handle it.

Above all others, this was the bond that held Max and Uncle Ernst—the untimely death of a fiercely loved one.

Uncle Ernst held her face with his trembling hands. Max closed her eyes. His touch felt like cheesecloth swaddling her cheeks. "You work too hard. Come with me to the driving range tomorrow."

Max put her hands on his shoulders. "I need to speak to you about Papa—"

"Your father," Uncle Ernst interjected, his eyes animated, his voice growing unnaturally high. He was going swiftly into the past as he often did these days. "His shots improved after he had a few drinks under his belt." Uncle Ernst shook his head with a brittle laugh, then instantly, as if he had been slapped, his expression changed to one of dismay.

Max was torn between screaming in anguish and shaking him out of his reverie.

Uncle Ernst began spluttering through bubbles of saliva. "I'm so sorry, *liebchen,* darling." He slurped and swallowed. "Hiram and his golf clubs were inseparable. And the drink…oh dear, I'm an idiot." His hands were shaking more than ever. His head began bobbing. His face had turned pale in places and bright crimson in others. "I cannot believe he is gone. I sometimes wake up thinking he will knock on my door, asking me to hit a few buckets of balls. Or invite me to breakfast…make his delicious poached eggs."

Max raised her hands with a cry and settled down on the couch. Her tears had miraculously stopped. She waited for Uncle Ernst to be done.

"*Mein Gott*, my God," he cried, "I'm a *schwein*. I should just—just stop talking altogether. I have become a fool." He turned away.

Max hated it when Uncle Ernst got this way. Maybe it was senility. Or maybe it was how *he* coped with her father's death.

Uncle Ernst was watching her from the corner of his eyes like a chastised child, holding one shaking hand over the other.

He went into the kitchen and returned minutes later with a cup of hot chamomile tea. He handed it to Max and sat beside her. "You came here to see me and I'm going on like an idiot. Tell me love, what's the matter?" He widened his eyes and pursed his lips like he always did when she had a story to tell.

Max took a deep breath to gather strength. "Today I met Lars Lindstrom, Opa's former lab assistant."

Uncle Ernst looked puzzled for a moment, but quickly his eyes brightened. "Oh yes, Samuel mentioned him a few times."

"He told me—" Max stopped. "How did Papa die?" she asked softly after a while.

Uncle Ernst's shoulders shrank, his cheeks sagged. The bags under his eyes seemed to grow larger than ever. Tears gathered at the corners of his eyes. Max bit her lip, regretting her abruptness.

"Oh darling," he said. "He committed suicide. Just like my foolish Sally. Sure there had been the threat that her company might have to shut down or change direction. But it was all in the future. Nothing was going to happen right away. I had been assured. I told her the same, but she was afraid of things all the time. And so she went and killed herself. She was sick and a fool! But she was my daughter. My only baby, and I could do nothing for her. Nothing!" Uncle Ernst's voice was angry, but his eyes had a glazed look about them. "But now Alex, my grandson, you know, he runs her company. I'm so grateful he took over—"

Max pressed her temples with her forefingers. "Yes," she said, "I know all that. But Lars said...he said Papa might have been pushed to commit suicide, maybe even killed. Because of some research he had done based on Opa's work."

Uncle Ernst turned pale, his jowls shook, his lips quivered. Max thought he might collapse onto the floor. He merely turned his face to the ceiling and said something she didn't understand and smacked his lips a few times. He kept shaking his head, looking like a large, wrinkled child who has been told his toy is broken and beyond re-pair.

Max leaned forward and told him about Lars, the Indus health pills, Papa's research, and its possible connection to Opa's work dur-ing the war. Uncle Ernst seemed to get more and more befuddled as she spoke. She decided not to mention the visit by the German or her home being searched. For now.

"I need to find a way to decode this research," she said.

Uncle Ernst got up and began dusting bookshelves with a bare palm. "I wish I could help. But my body has become a trap, my mind lets me down when I need it most." He sighed.

"Did you know about Papa's research?" Max said.

"Not much. But *I* was supposed to take care of it," Uncle Ernst said in a fierce voice. "Hiram didn't trust anyone else."

Max rubbed his back. "I think he wanted to protect you and me."

"Yes, yes."

"I have to look into this. I thought I'd start by reading Opa's diary. Do some digging at the university library." Max wondered if she should ask Uncle Ernst to go with her.

Uncle Ernst's bushy eyebrows bunched up like a small hairy animal on his forehead. "I could go with you," he said.

If he went with her, despite him being so feeble, she would end up depending on him to take charge of the situation. Besides, it would be cruel to take him along.

She shook her head. "I must do this alone."

"Ya," he said. His eyes had a faraway look.

Max picked up her bag. She shouldn't have come here. It had done neither of them any good. No, that wasn't entirely true. Telling Uncle Ernst had made her feel, if not better, at least not all alone in her adventure.

"Whatever you do, be careful," Uncle Ernst said unexpectedly. "If Berliner is involved, they will make sure they get what they want. They're probably watching us, even me. Samuel told me all about them." Max frowned. He sounded quite lucid. It was rare these days, but she could imagine how sharp he might have been as a younger man. "And if you want me to go with you, I will. I wasn't there for Sally when she needed me, but for you I'll be here. You know she called me right before she took those damn sleeping pills. She asked me to help her. She begged me. I thought it was her paranoia talking and I did nothing."

Max hugged Uncle Ernst tight. His soft warmth was so comforting, she wanted to never let him go. Without him, she wouldn't have survived Papa's death. Uncle Ernst had become her emotional support then. Her rock. And his love was unconditional, a ferocious, duty-bound love.

He went to his refrigerator. "I bought your favorite snickerdoodle cookies from Bittersweet bakery today," he said, handing her a white paper bag.

Together they walked to the elevator.

As the elevator doors began to pull close, Uncle Ernst waved with plump fingers. His sweet, lopsided smile was laced with concern, and it stayed with Max even as she felt herself alone once more.

Max had some strengths, and one was the ability to compartmentalize. Right now, she needed to make a plan. She opened the package of cookies Uncle Ernst had given her and bit into one.

As if in a dream, Max went back into her apartment. In an hour, she brought her home back to normal, making sure she'd put every strewn piece of paper, every book, every little meaningless tchotchke back where it belonged. After, she went to her desk, sat down with a sigh, and opened the top drawer. There sat a copy of the Gita, an ancient Hindu book of scripture. Opa's last gift to her.

She took it out and held it against her chest. She had promised him that she'd read a verse whenever she needed solace. The Gita isn't about religion as much as it is about self-realization and the art of living a life of truth and integrity, Opa had said.

She opened it to the first page.

> *Dearest Max, my visit to India introduced me to this great book. Your mother and I often had heated discussions about the wisdom presented here. I trust that it will give you the* <u>*peace*</u> *it has given me,*
> *Your loving Opa.*

Opa had not underlined the word *peace*. Her father had done that, a month or two before he died. On her twenty-second birthday, Papa had taken her copy of the Gita and made sure she saw him underlining that word. She had asked him at the time why he was doing it, and he had smiled. It hadn't been a happy smile.

"Hopefully you'll never find out," was all he had said.

Had he known then that he was going to leave her and wanted to give her a means to heal?

Max touched the page with a renewed mixture of anger, loss, and sorrow. She turned to a random verse, stared at the words for a while, and closed the book. A mere verse couldn't help her today.

She walked over to the window and looked at the lake. A sense of clarity seemed to descend upon her. If she went though with this, if she went on to decode her father's research, she would be bringing a part of him back to life.

But that would mean taking on danger of a magnitude that she couldn't possibly fathom. She hung her head down to her chest, relishing the sweet pain of her tense neck muscles stretching.

She *could* try and pretend she had never met Lars. Her home no longer looked like it had been violated. She could try and put this out of her mind forever. Of course, she'd have to figure out how to live with herself knowing she had taken the easy way out. Truth was, she wasn't very brave. No sense in pretending otherwise. Besides, Papa hadn't wanted her to be involved anyway.

All right.

She would spend one day reading the diary. If she found something worthwhile, she'd decide what to do next. She was convinced that the Indus Valley and the seal played a significant part in Papa's research. If so, she would need help. An archeologist or a historian to guide her.

First thing tomorrow, she would go to her alma mater—the University of Chicago. They had a strong history department. There, surrounded by the university's resources, she'd read what was left of Opa's diary.

Bone-crushing exhaustion hit her. Before getting into bed, Max took a large butcher knife and placed it under her pillow.

In one short day, life had changed forever. *What next?* she wondered as she stared at the inky, starless sky.

CHAPTER SIX

Berlin, Germany
Headquarters of Berliner Pharmaceuticals

Former chairman Peter Schultz entered his old office and made his way slowly across its polished marble floor, remembering with fondness the days he had spent there. Now his son served as chairman. Today, with his son away in Antwerp, Peter Schultz was going to address the board. He checked himself in the floor-length mirror by the large walnut desk. His hair was thinning, but elegant. Silver. His figure was lean, his skin wrinkled, but tan. Vanity remained one of his vices, but the years *had* treated him well. Schultz still felt handsome, energetic, and ambitious.

Ambition was a great driving force in old age, Schultz had always maintained. In one's youth there was time to procrastinate. At his age, he hadn't a moment to waste. And he wanted, more than anything, to leave behind as glorious a legacy as his father had left him. He straightened his navy blue jacket, turned, and swept the agenda for the morning off the desk's mirror-like surface.

There was a knock on the door. It opened and Hans Altgeld strolled in. Schultz smiled at the sight of his faithful man of action. Thickset, with bleached blond hair of an almost comical shade of yellow, Hans carried his fifty-odd years well. Hans did work for Berliner of the white-collar and semi-white-collar crime variety. Low-level

espionage and sophisticated threats were part of Hans's daily respon-
sibilities. Stopping research from appearing in scientific journals in
order to keep Berliner's stock high was another asset he provided.
Usually it involved arranging expensive gifts and lunches for editors and eminent research scholars and making sure various bits of
research in question were debunked or talked up—whichever was
more useful. There had been a few incidents where physical violence
had been necessary to encourage some people to see things from
Berliner's perspective. But Hans was always up for a challenge.

Hans glided toward the desk and stood beside it with hands folded
behind his back, managing to dwarf it with his demeanor.

Schultz extended his hand. Hans engulfed it in his beefy one. "*Wie
geht's*, Hans?" Schultz said. "Surely, you aren't here to see me." He
chuckled. "The chairman is out of town."

Hans's work at Berliner had remained unchanged under Schultz's
son. Without speaking, he set a key on Schultz's desk.

Schultz raised an eyebrow.

"Lars Lindstrom is dying," Hans said.

Schultz put both palms on the desk and leaned into it. An enormous weight had been lifted off his being with those few words. Lars
was the last remaining link to Hiram Rosen, Samuel Rosen, and the
Indus pills. With him gone—soon, hopefully—he was free. Berliner
was free.

"Finally we can bury the past," Schultz said. "Once I'm done addressing the board," he pointed to the room next door, "I'll drink
some champagne. A lot of champagne!" He rubbed his hands together. "This is excellent news!"

Hans's expression remained impassive.

Schultz recognized the look in Hans's watery gray eyes and picked
up a phone. "Start without me," he said to his son's secretary and
settled into the worn leather chair. "I haven't been in this room much
since we last met. Five years ago, wasn't it?" He waved Hans to a chair
in front of the desk.

"Five years ago, following Hiram Rosen's death, we intercepted
two packages from his lawyer's office," Hans said in a dull monotone.

"One addressed to a Dr. Klein, care of a London post office box, the other to a Dr. P.S. Oup, care of a PO box in Manhattan. Both packages contained a sheet of paper each and a vial of pills. We burned them." Hans pointed to a fireplace at one corner of the room.

"A moment of triumph," Schultz said, wondering what Hans was getting at.

Hans nodded. "Since the packages contained the key to decode Hiram's research, we surmised that Hiram had sent his work in coded form to Lars Lindstrom and Dr. Oup, whom we haven't yet identified. We hired a company to monitor Lars's phone after Hiram died. We also monitored Hiram's old business partner Kevin Forsyth, Maxine Rosen, and Ernst Frank. A software tap that would send me text messages every time one of them made a phone call and used words such as research, tablets, India—"

Schultz gave an impatient wave. "I remember all this! I'm old. Not gaga." He turned his eyes toward the boardroom. He ached to celebrate the decades of work, the frustrating, humiliating hours spent with the FDA, the Euro Medicines Approval Board, and all those in power, to get their assurance that Berliner's two new drugs would receive the adulation they deserved. Brocarax was Berliner's soon-to-be-launched miracle cholesterol drug, and Janperin was a revolutionary anti-obesity drug. He should be talking about them to the board right now, not reliving the past with his old henchman.

Hans went on as if he hadn't heard. "When Lars received the research, he informed Hiram's lawyer that all he would do about it was keep it safe. True to his word, he did nothing. We considered the matter closed." Hans took a breath, shifting in his seat. "Now Lars has developed a conscience, I'm afraid."

A point made at last. Schultz let out a soft curse. "Even if Lars is suddenly interested in fulfilling Hiram's wishes, without the key to decode it, the research is still useless."

Hans didn't respond.

Schultz's brain kicked into problem-solving mode. It was what he had been raised to do, and did well. This matter would have to end with him.

"What is Lars doing about it? And what is this key? Obviously you've been up to something." Schultz picked up the key Hans had placed on the table.

"It's the reason I'm here," Hans said. "Lars went to Chicago to see Hiram's daughter."

"Does Lars think she has the text to decode the work? I thought she knew nothing of the matter."

"It would seem that she knows nothing. Lars merely wanted to hand over the research to her since he's dying. I tried to check with you about going to Chicago, but you weren't available. You did say I could take action if needed."

Schultz nodded.

"I managed to get this locker key from Lars and frightened him a little. Heavy-set men speaking English with a German accent can be scary."

"I didn't know you had a sense of humor, Hans," Schultz said with a small smile.

Hans continued. "Anyway, I used this key to access the locker where Lars said he kept the research." He pulled a sheaf of papers seemingly out of nowhere and placed them on Schultz's desk.

Schultz's eyes scanned over the documents. "I cannot be sure if this is Hiram's work or not. Get these looked at by an expert. At any rate, we must get all copies of the research from Lars, once and for all."

"Ya, *mein Herr*."

"Drink?" Schultz opened a small cabinet by the desk, considered its contents for a while, and took out a bottle of Pierre Ferrand cognac. "I don't usually drink cognac at this time of day, but it is what calms me." He offered Hans a glass.

Hans began sipping his drink.

Schultz considered his glass. "Can you taste the anise, sense the sandalwood?"

"Years of eating bratwurst and sauerkraut have dulled my taste buds," Hans offered.

Schultz put down his drink. "How about the person who has the second supposed copy of the research?"

Hans shook his head. "The action has all been on Lars's end. There may not even be a second copy."

"Let's not underestimate Hiram," Schultz said. "Continue the taps on everyone's phones."

Hans agreed with a tilt of his head. "What if the Rosen girl gets involved?"

"We wait and see what she does," Schultz said. "Find someone in Chicago to keep an eye on her." He swirled the golden liquid in his glass, stood up and paced the room. "We have too much to lose if Hiram's findings about the Indus pills see light. I hope you know that." Schultz held out his hand for Hans to shake and end the meeting.

Hans didn't move. He said with some hesitation, "*Mein Herr*, five years ago, we didn't speak much about this."

Schultz looked askance at his faithful man.

Hans's father had worked for Berliner on an assembly line after the war. During the war, he had been a young SS guard. When all former SS were being prosecuted and jailed, Schultz had used his influence and given Hans's father and a few other low-level SS guards jobs at Berliner. In the process, he had saved the Altgeld family and won their undying loyalty.

Schultz clenched and unclenched his fists. His arthritis was acting up. "I hoped this old wound would never have to be opened again." He paused before continuing. "Samuel Rosen was once head chemist at Berliner. A brilliant man. He passed on his research on some health pills from the Indus Valley to his son, Hiram."

For an instant he could see his old friend, dark and intense, perched on a corner of his desk, staring down at him, giving *him* orders. Only Samuel had ever dared to talk straight to Schultz. He had admired him for it.

Schultz stared into his glass.

1943. Schultz could see Samuel being dragged away to Krippenwald labor camp. He had made a decision then to continue Samuel's work—it was far too important to be left unfinished. Schultz set up a lab to continue Samuel's research on the Indus pills.

The scientists at the lab made a discovery—one with disturbing implications. It might have been prudent to take the discovery public, make reparations, and be rid of the whole business. But Berliner was not the pharmaceutical power in those days that it was today. The negative publicity in the fifties, when German companies were only just picking up the pieces after a devastating war, would have dealt a fatal blow to Berliner.

It had been a grave error of judgment.

Schultz put his hands in his pockets. His voice dropped to a whisper. "Hiram found out what damage the Indus pills could do. What harm they had already done."

Hans's eyes narrowed.

Schultz settled back in his chair. "I have destroyed all the pills. The last few were in those vials we intercepted. However, if the scientific community embraces Hiram's findings, even without the pills for proof, it could be catastrophic."

Schultz wondered if his eyes betrayed his fears. "Along with his findings, Hiram will reveal our association with Nazis and concentration camp workers!"

"But Bayer had strong Nazi ties, too," Hans said indignantly. "They were part of IG Farben—and Farben created Zyklon B! Bayer even used Auschwitz inmates for their rubber works. No one cares about the Nazis anymore."

Schultz leaned forward, his long arms nearly spanning the width of the desk. "Very well," he bellowed. "*I could lose everything. Berliner's reputation and my life as I know it. Is that reason enough for you?*" He took a giant gulp of cognac. The drink burned through his chest.

Hans stood up. "It is, *mein Herr*."

"No Rosen will stand in my way again," Schultz murmured. "Do what it takes and bury this matter. But no blood. From now on, Berliner's name must remain unsullied." He breathed in deeply, lifted the drink to his mouth, and drained the last drops of cognac from the glass.

CHAPTER SEVEN

University of Chicago
History Department

"An archeologist?" the librarian mused. "Let me see if I can unearth someone to help you." She suppressed a laugh at her pun and picked up a phone.

Max looked around. Fresh-faced students buzzed about, sipping steaming coffee or nibbling on donuts and bagels.

Being here felt almost normal. The incident at her kitchen and her apartment, the whole business with Lars and Papa's death seemed eons away. She had stepped back into a less troublesome time. At least she hadn't felt in mortal danger back in those unsure undergraduate years.

She turned around suddenly. Was she imagining it, or was someone following her? She decided not to think along those lines, or she'd go totally mad. The shot fired at Lars, the same gun touching her skin—they had done their job. She *was* scared. Terror stricken, more like. And yet, here she was. It didn't mean she was brave. It was just that the previous day seemed so removed from her present sense of reality. Standing here amidst these students, surrounded by stately, old, comfortable-looking buildings, it felt almost absurd thinking on those lines. She decided it was a good thing. For now anyway. All she was going to do was some harmless research. How threatening could that be to anyone?

A slim young woman wearing pencil jeans that looked sprayed on walked up to the desk. Max tried to smooth the front of her wrinkled cotton skirt with her palm.

Dr. Julian McIntosh leaned back.

Classes were over, exam papers corrected. Why was he not feeling the sense of accomplishment he normally felt at this time? His choices for the summer were not unexciting. Dr. Jackson had requested his help to conduct research for a textbook he was writing on religion and related architecture, with a focus on Vietnam and Cambodia. A trip to the Angkor Wat was in order. Dr. Jackson was a brilliant man, if tedious at times. Still the work would—might—make up for that. Julian rubbed his eyes. And he mustn't forget the paper he had started working on for the conference in Prague next summer—use of Japanese iconography all over the world. With a special focus on Japan's Buddhist iconography. Fascinating subject.

He suppressed a yawn. He wasn't bored, surely. No, what he was was tired. He had been up late keeping Raquel company while she worked. My Raquel Stanton, he thought with pride. Girlfriend, banker extraordinaire, beautiful beyond compare, independent. And yet somehow, horribly insecure.

Raquel was the kind of person who liked to make and check off lists of high-powered weekend activities—sky diving, hot air balloon rides, jet skiing. She compared notes with colleagues about what everyone had done over weekends. "Did you check out the new jazz club on Huron? Tim Robbins played there last night," some colleague might say. And Raquel would spend all her free time trying to get tickets to some other frou frou show to compete, with the expectation that Julian would join her regardless of the event. All *he* wanted to do was sit in a coffee shop with a nice book and—

Stop, he told himself. He always philosophized when bored.

The phone rang. He grabbed it. "McIntosh here." He listened for a while, "Sorry, my area isn't South Asia but—pardon? Yes I know a little about the Indus Valley. Sure, I'll see her now."

The distraction would be a welcome one.

Julian walked over to the washroom and splashed water on his face. He returned to his desk and clicked on email. Dr. Jackson had some questions about an ancient Vietnamese text. The second was from Raquel—would he be coming over for dinner to her place tonight? She was going to try and make it an early night. She had a ton of work to do.

Julian sighed.

Max stood outside Dr. Julian McIntosh's office. It was a tiny room with one small window facing 59th Street. The door was slightly open.

As she was about to knock, her cell phone rang. It was Kim, her assistant.

"Hi," Kim said, "You wanted me to remind you about the sausage-making class at the Butcher and Larder at 11:30. Oh, but you're busy today, aren't you?"

Max put a hand over her mouth. She had rescheduled all her meetings for the day but had forgotten about the sausage class. She had been wanting to go for weeks. Maybe she could start her research after...but the class would last two hours.

"I forgot," she said, her voice a disappointed croak. "Do you want to take the class?"

"I'd love to!" Kim said. Max felt a surge of envy burn through her chest. "And don't worry," Kim went on, "our handsome interns have the deliveries covered." A bell rang in the background. "Oh, that must be the free-range meat guy you asked me to meet."

Max fought an urge to run to the market to shop for fresh vegetables, head for her cozy kitchen after, and start cooking, never to stop. She wanted to go to Dirk's Fish and Gourmet shop and talk about the day's catch. She wanted to do all this so badly that it hurt. She hung up. Tears sprang into her eyes. She wiped them with a vigorous palm and knocked on the door of the professor's office.

"Come in!" a friendly voice called.

She walked in. "Hello, I'm Maxine Rosen. Err...Max." Max's cheeks felt hot. She knew she was blushing and she wished she wouldn't. Blood rushed to her cheeks, giving her a patchy, wine-stained look.

But it couldn't be helped. Dr. Julian McIntosh was very, very good looking. His eyes were somewhere between green and hazel, and they were large. His mouth was full, and yet there was nothing feminine about his lips. He had a bluish shadow of stubble on his chin, and his auburn curls were unruly. Just begging to be played with. Max felt her breath catch at her throat.

He got up from behind his computer, leaned back against his desk, and smiled. His slender body was dressed in a crumpled white linen shirt and narrow chocolate corduroy pants. On any other man, his slight frame and narrow pants would have looked silly. But given his professorial aura; his deep, rather unexpected voice; and his office decorated with haphazard piles of books and papers and a half-dead potted plant, it was rather perfect.

"You have questions about the Indus Valley," he was saying. "My area of expertise is East Asia." Max suppressed a groan of disappointment. "But as it turns out, the Indus Valley is an area of private interest—a hobby, if you will. Oh, sorry. Julian McIntosh." He extended his arm. When he said "Julian" in his rather unusual accent, Max blushed once more. What a wondrous name, she thought. What a glorious accent! What a killer smile!

Max managed to take his warm grip and gave his hand a good shake despite her ruminations. She opened her mouth to say her name once more, but that ground had already been covered. She was glad she could recall that much, despite the tingling sensation in her ears.

She gave her head a quick shake to clear it. "Thanks so much for seeing me. Um, I was hoping you could take a look at this." She opened her grandfather's diary and showed him the embossment.

"Is this an imprint of a seal from the Indus Valley?" he asked eagerly.

"An imprint of a copy of an Indus seal. It's amazing that I remember, since my grandfather told me all this years ago," Max added with a laugh. "The original belonged to a man they called the Colossus.

My grandfather was given a copy when he visited a dig at the Indus Valley." She took out the plastic bag the seal was in and handed it to Julian.

Julian pulled out the seal and studied it. "When was he there?"

"1935."

Julian turned his eyes to the ceiling. "The first expedition when they discovered the Indus civilization was in the early twenties." He wrinkled his nose. Max noticed a dusting of light brown freckles on the bridge of his nose and cheekbones. "He was there not long after. How interesting." He went to his bookshelf and pulled out a book. He flipped a few pages and handed it to her.

Max looked at the picture of the seal in the book.

"The picture in the book is of the most common type of seal found in the valley," he said. "Your grandfather's seal is similar—it has the unicorn. Well," he smiled, revealing dimples. Could he be any more perfect? "We call it that. But it's most likely an ox."

Max peered at the picture and the Colossus's seal. Julian stepped closer to show her the unicorn in both. He was wearing a glorious cologne that was soft, peppery, and yet so masculine. She found herself sniffing at his curls.

"Look," he said. "The second horn is probably just behind that horn there—one-horn unicorn, hidden horn—voila, just a plain old ox." Julian rubbed the space between his eyes. As if addressing a class, he went on, "Indus seals were usually square, about three-quarters of an inch to an inch and a quarter. Yours is unusual—it is round. Most have animals—oxen like this one or elephants, tigers, crocodiles even. What else…hmm…some have shown prototypes of the Hindu God Shiva—the Indus Valley may have been the cradle of Hinduism. There are usually inscriptions on seals, but we don't know what they say, sadly. Some say the script is Dravidian, but…." He shrugged. "No one knows for sure."

Max nodded doubtfully.

"Not helpful?" he said, his eyebrows raised.

Truth was, she didn't know what was relevant and what wasn't. Her fingers went up and down the length of the cylinder of the seal.

It was smooth all over, but her fingers landed on one rough portion near the end of the cylinder. Something had been drawn there. She looked at it closely. Drawn close to the bottom of her grandfather's seal was a small broken type of square divided into four quadrants, and there were dots in every quadrant. It was unmistakable. A soft moan escaped her lips.

It was a Swastika. She looked at it closely. It wasn't tilted like the Nazi version. And the dots? What did those mean? The Swastika looked like it had been made using a penknife or some sharp object. Had Opa done it? But why? He was Jewish! He had been put in a concentration camp, for God's sake.

"Find something?" Julian McIntosh took the seal from her.

"A Swastika!" he said. "How interesting."

Max felt a chill seep through her. Had the swastika always been there? Was there one in other Indus Valley seals? She started to ask Julian when suddenly she was in no mood to learn any more. No mood to read the diary. Perhaps Opa had revealed something in it that was so distasteful that he had torn and burned away much of it in shame.

Max bit hard on her lip, wondering what to do.

CHAPTER EIGHT

There was an awkward silence for a few seconds.

Julian McIntosh sighed and folded his arms. "So how can I help?"

Max put her finger on the Swastika. "This doesn't disturb you?" she whispered. "My grandfather must have carved it there."

Julian looked at the Swastika and made no comment. He turned the seal back to its face, glanced at it, and looked again at the picture in the book.

"It isn't like any of the other Indus seals, is it?" Max said sadly.

Julian's face grew animated. "It isn't and that is odd." His eyes were doing a little dance. "Clever of you to spot such a minute difference."

Minute. Really!

"The Colossus's seal is different in a very intriguing way." Julian gave her a delighted smile. "I almost missed it." He dashed to his desk and returned with a magnifying glass, which he handed to Max.

She looked through it. The seals looked identical. Except for the Swastika.

"Ms. Rosen, how very rude of me. Please do sit down."

"Max," she said softly.

Julian went to his chair. Max sat opposite him.

"Not many experts would have noticed the difference," Julian said. "The Colossus's seal has a giant urn in front of the animal. Not this incense burner as is in the seal in the book. Whoever was the owner of this seal—and yes, all Indus seals had unique owners—was probably a maverick of some sort; that urn probably was significant to him, which is why he put it on his seal instead of an incense burner." Julian ran his fingers through his curls. "Very unusual!" he murmured.

Max looked at the pictures. The urn and incense burner did look kind of different. But not much. "How do you know it's an urn and not just a different type of incense burner?" she said.

"The commonplace urns of the period are exactly like that," Julian said, sounding a tad pompous. "Archeologists found dozens everywhere. Squat ones, plain. With those small handles. Look at the incense burner—they rest on a pedestal, they always have markings or decorations. Urns are jars. No pedestal, plain. Different? Absolutely. Significant? I don't know. But I believe that image on your Colossus's seal is an urn, unless I'm quite mistaken, which I am usually not."

He gazed into the distance and continued. "Question is, why did he make his seal so subtly and yet obviously different than the ones of his time? This is a true copy of the Colossus's seal, isn't it?" He examined it once more.

"Opa Samuel—my grandfather—told me it is a true copy."

"Sounds like there's a story here." Julian looked at her with great expectation.

Max lifted her palms, "Well, there's a journal. My grandfather's."

Julian's eyebrows rose a little.

Max sighed. "I wanted to research the seal before I read it. I also thought it would be better to have an expert around to ask questions once I read it. Now that I've found the Swastika, I don't feel like touching the journal. But the truth is, I *have* to read it." She turned away. "It's very involved…" She pulled on a lock of hair. "I'm sorry I'm taking so much of your time."

Julian waved at a clock behind him. "It's not a problem. I'm expecting a call in a bit, but right now it's fine. Please go on."

Max gave a little cough. "My grandfather was a chemist. He worked for a German pharmaceutical company in the twenties and thirties. He was even forced to do work for the Nazis while he was there. Then suddenly, he was sent away to a concentration camp. He was Jewish. That's why I was so shocked by the Swastika. I only noticed it today."

Julian gave her a wry look. "Your grandfather did work for the Nazis, but not willingly, right? Besides, the angle of this Swastika isn't right for Nazi symbolism. Those dots in the gaps are very Hindu. I believe some Indus artifacts have been found with Swastikas on them. It wasn't unreasonable for him to put it there, given where he got it."

Max was not convinced. "But—"

Julian held up his hand. He pulled out a thick red book from an over-burdened bookshelf, checked the index, opened it, and handed it to her with a flourish.

Max began reading aloud. "*The Swastika is an ancient Indian symbol of prosperity. Su means "good" in Sanskrit. Asti means "to be." It is widely misunderstood the world over due to the fact that it was adopted by the Nazis. The symbol has been in existence for over 3,000 years.*" She looked up, gave Julian a relieved smile, and continued reading. "*Widely used to signify prosperity and goodness in China and Japan, even in Judaism! Indians use it in several places.*" Images of garments, paintings, and drawings followed. Max closed the book. "I feel like an idiot," she said softly. "He *had* said it was his lucky seal. I should have trusted him."

"He couldn't have chosen a better symbol." Julian leaned forward, touching her hand. "And I'm willing to bet that your grandfather added the Swastika for another reason. The Nazis polluted it with their ideologies. He added it for its purity. I would. And yes, of course—for plain old luck."

Max leaned back in her chair, fighting the urge to reach out and smother this beautiful man with a hug. With a few casual sentences he had dragged her out of her misery. "You must think I'm a fool," she said. "My mother was Indian and Hindu. I remember learning about Om from her. But she died when I was so young." Maybe she taught me about the Swastika, too, I don't remember. I sometimes read from the Gita, and yet I know little about the significance of what is obviously a ubiquitous Hindu symbol."

Julian smiled. "You can always claim that you read the Gita purely as a philosophical text—thus keeping your mind untarnished by religious beliefs and imagery that might hinder your appreciation of its true meaning." He twirled a hand in the air.

Max blushed once more. "I try to read a verse as often as I can." She tried to sound nonchalant. As if remembering her grandfather's words, she added, "It's not a holy book but a spiri—"

"Spiritual dictionary," Julian finished. "Gandhi called it that."

Max looked at Julian as if seeing him for the first time, except with even more admiring eyes.

Julian nodded. "What's the matter?" he said.

"Uh, nothing." She looked at the floor to hide her embarrassment.

Max looked at the diary in front of her. She ought to read it now and see if there was anything in it related to Papa's research. *What a long, long shot*, she thought wearily.

Julian picked up the diary and stared at the first page with the embossment of the seal. "Do you mind?" he asked. Max shook her head. He read the verse written below the embossment.

"You know Sanskrit?" Max asked. Was there no end to his talents?

"Enough to be dangerous," he said in a distracted voice. "I studied Sanskrit for a year when I was considering majoring in South Asian history. A million years ago." He reread the verse. "My Sanskrit is rusty but—"

"Yes?" Max said eagerly.

"There is something familiar about this particular verse. *Kalosmi* meaning 'I am time.' That reminds me of something. I think this verse is from the Gita." He drummed on his temples with his fingertips as he tried to recall the reference.

Max hadn't quite gotten to this verse yet and even if she had, all she did when she opened the Gita was choose a random page, pick a verse, read its translation, and imbibe some strength from it.

"Never mind," he said with a sigh. "So the story here has to do with the seal?" His curiosity quickly seemed to turn to discomposure. "Or am I asking too many questions?"

"I am on a quest, I suppose," Max said in a more dramatic voice than she had intended, and at once regretted her colorful choice of words.

Julian remained unfazed. "What kind of quest? I'm sorry. It's none of my business." But he didn't mean it, Max could see. His eyes were gleaming, his lips pursed in anticipation. If he needed strangers to bring excitement into his life, perhaps he needed to get out more. She should know. The sight of fragrant chives and fresh-picked tomatoes at the farmer's market were enough to make her dizzy with excitement. Kim would turn to her, aghast, at such times. "Don't stay in yet another Friday night planning menus and getting high sniffing cilantro and mint," Kim would say. "It isn't healthy. Come have a martini with me."

"I must go," Max said. "Once I read this diary, I might have more questions. May I come to you then?"

Julian nodded. On his face was an expression so kind, so very full of concern that Max blurted, "Or would you like to read it with me? It's disjointed since Opa tore a lot of it out. But it might be interesting."

Julian's eyes grew animated. "Sure," he said.

Max felt an ache in her chest. Was he being kind? Or was he truly interested? She looked around and let out a nervous cough.

"Would you like some coffee?" He leaned forward.

"Please." Max stared into his eyes. There were flecks of dark brown in his greenish hazel eyes. Or were they flecks of a green so dark that—

Silly Max, what are you doing? You're not a teenager, so stop acting like one, she scolded herself.

"Is there something—" Julian vigorously wiped the end of his nose. "On my nose? You keep staring at it. So where were we? Ah, coffee. I have a fresh pot here somewhere." He looked around and found his coffee machine. "It keeps moving." He poured out two cups and offered her cream and sugar.

He dragged an enormous chair close to his own and invited her to sit. He spent a few minutes clearing his desk and sat down beside her. They looked at each other for a second. Their noses were almost touching. Their chairs were too close. The room was too small. Max felt like she might swoon, overcome by the romantic intensity of the moment. She tried not to look too deep into his eyes.

"The diary," Julian said, all business-like.

Max jerked her head away. There was an awkward pause. "Uh, I'll paraphrase what I've already read," she said. "My grandfather was head chemist at Berliner AG. Berliner was one of the fastest rising pharmaceutical companies in Germany. Their main competitor, Far-benfabriken Bayer, had risen to great heights following the release of aspirin in 1900. Um, what else…after that, Berliner and the other German pharmaceutical companies raced against each other to find the next miracle drug."

Max glanced at the diary. "When Opa started making entries here, many of his colleagues were also on hunts for obscure cures and medicines in Africa and Asia. The idea was to try and translate them into modern drugs."

Julian nodded.

"My grandfather's good friend Bernard Baston was in India at the Indus Valley. He was an archeologist. My grandfather was in Bombay visiting a former colleague at the same time, so Baston invited him to visit the dig site. Clear so far?"

"Yes ma'am," Julian said.

Max turned the page and began reading aloud.

CHAPTER NINE

From Samuel Rosen's diary

Mohenjo-daro—"Mound of the Dead"
Site of the 5,000-year-old Indus Valley civilization
January 6, 1935

2:00 p.m.
    Arrived a few hours ago. Hot as hell. Red dust everywhere.

3:00 p.m.
    At the Colossus's grave site.
    Abdul, the almost hundred-year-old chief of the Chapar tribe,
was our guide. The Chapars have lived in the nearby village of
Hakkra for centuries. Abdul was putting me to shame, standing
bent but energetic, unaffected by the sun, his piercing dark eyes
tucked away in a face that was a mass of leathery wrinkles.
Our group today comprised my friend Bernard Baston (head of a
team of archeologists from the Dresden Museum), Abdul Chapar (our
guide), Abdul's great grandson Fardoon (our interpreter). And me.
    In the distance stood the remnants of the homes of the Indus
Valley peoples. Immaculate brick structures surrounded a citadel,
which may have been used as a granary. The bricks were all even,
identical, and surprisingly, largely intact.

I followed Bernard to a small hill. There was a doorway in its side. We made our way down mud steps that ended suddenly, opening into a grave about 20 feet by 14 feet and about 6 and a half feet high. Bernard said 11 skeletons were found in the grave.

I walked around, feeling the rough walls under my fingertips, when I spotted some writing. Rows upon rows of beautiful symbols. I asked Bernard what the writings said. He said no Rosetta stone had been found yet. So an accurate translation isn't possible. But, Abdul could read some of it.

I must have looked skeptical, so Bernard explained. Apparently, Abdul has managed to find quite a few treasures based on other written material. Before he was shown this tomb, Bernard said, Abdul had talked about what they might find in it. And he had been right.

Bernard signaled to Abdul. Abdul began to speak in Brahui, a local dialect. Young Fardoon translated. The underground tomb was built for Abdul's ancestor Soodhanta—the Colossus of Mohenjo-daro. He was powerful, both in physical stature and status.

I spotted a large collection of urns stacked against the east-facing wall. I asked Bernard what they were. He said they were the reason I was there and handed me a few flat, round green discs, about two centimeters across. Their tribe has long life spans, even to this day, because of that pill, Abdul said.

The Indus people lived thirty to forty years at most. This I knew. So a life span increase even of ten years was a huge leap. It must have seemed as close to immortality as they were going to get. The pill must have worked like some sort of multivitamin, a combination of potent herbs that helped organs thrive longer.

The Chapars were appointed to guard the Colossus's grave when it was first created. They were given the authority to kill anyone who tried to desecrate it. Bernard told me that Abdul's family probably saw the futility of holding on to age old, irrelevant secrets. And they saw the power of money. Bernard's people had offered quite a lot.

Bernard said they probably agreed to give them access after all this time because of a supposed curse. For years the Chapars had argued over whether or not to reveal the Colossus's grave. These days, excavations here have trickled down. Seems Abdul's people decided to accept the offer on the table before all interest in this place wanes away.

9:00 p.m.

Had fantastic roast lamb for dinner. Must ask for recipe.

It was a cool evening. I leaned back in my chair, and over a glass of red wine, I asked Bernard to tell me about the curse of the pill. The pill was a blessing to some, Bernard said. The blessing has kept Abdul's tribe well and living long, but the curse is why the other tribes, perhaps the entire civilization, died. But the experts still have no idea why the civilization ended. Drought, flood maybe. Anemia, some experts have said.

I asked him where the Colossus got the pill from. Ikaria, the Greek island, most likely, Bernard said. (N.B: Research the fact that people still live exceedingly long lives in Ikaria. Possible connection to pill since it was acquired there.)

Bernard said the story was that the Ikarian people had refused to sell Soodhanta the pills. He was told that the pill had been beneficial to the Ikarians but had proved fatal outside their land in the past. Soodhanta ignored the warning and stole several urns of them. The curse must be superstition. Why else did Abdul's tribe live such long lives?

Perhaps it's like the curse of Tutankhamun's tomb, Bernard said.

If someone reading this (when I'm dead perhaps!) doesn't know about the curse of King Tut's tomb, here's a short history lesson. In 1922, Howard Carter discovered King Tut's tomb. Seven weeks later, his sponsor Lord Carnarvon died suddenly. Some say his dog died, too. The writers of the time had a field day with it. Arthur Conan Doyle called it the Pharaoh's curse. A few years later, others related to Howard Carter's work also died.

Coincidence is what I would say.

Bernard then said that the Colossus's grave had other mysteries, too. The first being that one of the people in that grave had been killed. Beheaded. And the second being that tombs in the Indus Valley usually have families buried together—husband, wife, children added to the tombs later. This tomb had eight men and three women, more or less of the same age and, according to the personal objects left there, of different social standing. Siblings, was the presumption. One of them was the Colossus, I supposed. Bernard agreed.

He said the grave is also unusual because of the writings and drawings on the walls. Seemingly only about the Colossus. Other mass graves in the valley found so far have shown no elaborate writings or drawings. This grave showed no signs of a massacre either, which is one reason for a mass grave with unrelated people. So perhaps a mass grave such as this one means they all died of a boring disease.

I asked Bernard what happened when the Colossus returned to India with the pills. To test his claim, he was asked to eat the pills himself and give some to a handful of people who were about forty years of age, ones who weren't terminally ill but were nearing the end of their natural lives.

Some years passed. Suddenly, Soodhanta disappeared. In time, the elders announced that he had died and decreed it illegal to mention the pills or Soodhanta's name. Banishment or beheading awaited those who disobeyed.

So what happened to the Colossus?

The story and pictures on the wall seem to indicate that the elders kept him prisoner in his home. But no one knows why, Bernard said. I asked if we know what happened to the others who ate the pill. Sent into the jungles or put to death, Bernard suggested. Most likely because of the curse. The Indus people, likely ancestors of early Hindus, were a superstitious people.

Bernard has given me a copy of the Colossus's seal and another for my assistant, Lars. It will remain a cherished possession.

Bernard of course had to turn the discussion to Hitler and German politics, much to my irritation. Many Jews have left Germany, he said pointedly. I told him I'm not an everyday Jew, even in the present Germany.

I don't want to appear arrogant, but I run Berliner's labs. I am respected. And I'd like to believe that there are some decent Nazis, too. And in case anyone thinks I am naïve, I do also realize that what keeps me safe is the fact I make Berliner a lot of money.

None of that matters, for I am now starting to feel a familiar tingle of excitement. The Indus pill is a sign. Scientist I may be, but I believe in signs. Let the Nazis do what they want. This little pill might, just might have the power to keep my beloved Martha and me safe. Even in Nazi Germany.

CHAPTER TEN

Max stopped reading.

She ran her fingers over her grandfather's writing and caressed the embossment of his seal, wondering what it might have been like on that hot day in India, all those years ago. Her eyes stung as she thought about her young and ambitious, blind and foolish Opa.

She turned the pages. "The next few pages are torn," she said, trying to keep her voice steady. She turned some more pages. "There's some writing about his work on the pills. Maybe there's something about the time he was sent to the concentration camp—"

She set the diary down and looked away.

"Let's stop here while I have some time," Julian said, "and see what I can find about that dig, perhaps."

He pushed back his chair and began looking through the books piled in disarray on his floor-to-ceiling shelves. He plucked out a few from the floor, one or two from under his desk. He shoved aside a large pile of exam papers to make room for them. He opened one book and put it away. He opened another and, with an irritated grunt, tossed it aside. He picked up a third. A leather-bound book titled *Ancient Civilizations: Archeological Dig Data.* "This is a chronicle of who did what and where," Julian said. A cloud of dust rose from the book as he set it on the desk. With his palm, he wiped the book clean and sat down with a contented sigh.

Julian laid the book flat on the table. "In '35 to '38 there were five recorded expeditions. Lets see. Dr. Bernard Baston's group is listed here." He read some more. "Nothing else." Julian scowled and muttered something Max didn't catch. Suddenly his face brightened and he dashed out.

"Wha—?" Max began. But he was gone. She got up and stood at the door for a few minutes. Should she go look for him?

She went back into his office. Such a cozy space—filled to the brim with musty books, the aroma of fresh coffee still in the air. Through an open window, she could hear the pleasant murmur of passing students on the street a couple floors below. With a sigh, Max returned to her chair. The headrest popped up. Perfect. She let her head fall back.

"Maxine Rosen," a voice called.

She jumped up, disoriented for a second or two. She had fallen asleep! How awful. She turned. Julian was at the door, holding the doorway with his hands, leaning in. A rascally grin played on his lips.

Max felt moistness on her chin. Drool! She turned away and wiped her mouth with the back of her palm. She should tell him how she had been up curled up in a ball all night trying to be brave. She should tell him everything she had been through the night before. She wanted desperately to prove to him that she wasn't the sleepy oaf she appeared to be.

She turned back to face him with a forced smile and was about to pick up her bag when Julian took her hand in a firm grip. "I think I may have found something," he whispered.

They went back to the library area. Julian opened the door to a room at the back of the library with a brass plaque labeled *Microfilm Area*. It was air-conditioned as cold as a winter day in Greenland, Max thought.

"There's a book," Julian said. "People laughed at it when it was released. It has been out of print for years. We had one copy but it's long lost." He pulled out a chair in front of a microfilm viewer. "Luckily, it's here. Look at the screen."

Magnified on the screen in front of her was a yellowing sheet of paper. *Indus Valley*. Sub heading: *Societies and Clubs*. Max's heart began to race. She glanced at Julian.

"Read," he commanded.

She read aloud.

"*No fewer than six known groups, perhaps many more, were formed by people who had visited the Indus Valley, an advanced civilization.* Blah blah. How do I turn the page...okay, got it." Max pressed the turn button.

"Go on, go on," Julian urged. He began to pace.

"I'm trying," she said. "Okay, *Indus Religions, as the name suggests, was a club whose focus was religion as pertained to the—*"

"Not that one. Go to the end of the page," Julian said, still pacing.

"Okay," Max said, exasperated. "*A group called Umrit was in all probability formed following an expedition in 1935 headed by Dr. Bernard Baston. This author speculates that the club might have been formed to celebrate or record something special they found at the valley.*

"*The term* Umrit *means 'the nectar of immortality' in Hindoo mythology. It is a tantalizing idea that what they may have found may have inspired the intriguing name given to the club. Inevitably, the club became legend and stories about an Indus pill of immortality began appearing in newspapers. Baston used the limelight to direct attention to his more important work on the dig. He was eventually awarded a Chancellor's medal for his work.*

"*Names of members: founding member Bernard Baston, Andre Georges, Ulrike Johannsen...*" Max went down the list. "*Honorary members: Abdul Chapar, Fardoon Chapar, and Dr. Samuel Rosen.*" Max swallowed hard and looked up at Julian.

He was looking at her with palms turned upwards, as if expecting her to cry "Eureka" or something.

"Any current members?" she asked.

He shook his head. "I checked these names. They're archeologists and all dead. The two Chapars are the guides mentioned in the diary," Julian said. "Look at the very end."

At the bottom of the page was the symbol of the seal from her grandfather's diary. Below it was a Swastika—Opa's lucky symbol had been this group's symbol, too.

"This doesn't tell us anything new," Max said glumly.

Julian looked askance at her.

Max didn't want to appear like a complete idiot to this crazy cute, brilliant professor. "How about descendants?" she said, working up some enthusiasm. "Like me."

Julian looked unimpressed. "They key takeaway here is that since Bernard Baston was awarded the Chancellor's medal, there might still be papers relevant to the dig."

Max looked puzzled.

"He was German," he said, impatience creeping into his voice. "So?"

Julian looked positively irritated. "*Ai, yi yi*, Ms. Rosen, Germans those days were obsessed with preserving records. Probably still are. And if he won a medal, I bet his records are archived somewhere. A good place to start might be the Archeological Society at the DANK Haus—German American Cultural Center. The chaps there might know something. Let's go back to my office."

Back at Julian's office, Max felt drained. This wasn't what she did well. Legwork. And research! She had detested doing it for her job at Granger Foods.

If there had been doubts before, there were absolutely none now: she was a cook and nothing but a cook—heart and soul, every sinew, every cell of her being. She felt a gush of warmth and possessive love for her fumbling little catering company, her demanding clients, her elaborate, labored-over menus, her barely affordable employees.

Julian got busy investigating the DANK Haus website.

The reality of her situation suddenly struck Max. Memories of the state of her apartment from the night before flashed in front of her eyes. Followed by an image of Lars being shot.

This was a huge mistake. She was not qualified to do any of this. Max touched the arms of her chair and got up. It was time to put an end to this madness. She was faced with the very real possibility that Papa had been killed. This was a job for the police. Certainly not for catering company owners with anxiety issues. She should go to the cops. She would explain everything and they…they…

They would sit back and laugh.

She shivered and collapsed back into the chair. Truth was, the people who had caused her father's death were out there somewhere. And they were possibly watching her.

"Someone from DANK Haus emailed me right away!" Julian almost did a little jig in his office chair. "He has found information about Baston's club. He's going to make some calls. There's a place in Hamburg that houses archeological records. He bets they will have Baston's dig records. He'll fax them over to me once he gets them faxed from Germany. Because of Baston's medal, they preserved almost every single sheet of paper they could find on the guy. Max? Ms. Rosen?"

"Huh?" Max looked at Julian. He was eager to help and so interested. *And* he was smart and resourceful. Of course it didn't help that her entire being ached just to look at him.

A phone rang. Julian answered it. "Yes Dr. Jackson, I got the email. Now? Well, all right. Be there in a bit." He hung up and made a face. "I'm sorry. I would have loved to read the rest of the diary with you, but I have to see someone right away." He rolled his eyes. "I'm really sorry." He picked up a smart-looking tan briefcase and moved to the door.

He looked at her with an expression of…was it regret? Max squared her shoulders. If she left now, she would not see him again. She held on to that thought for strength. "Would you like to have dinner with me tonight?" she asked, her voice turning hoarse.

Julian seemed taken aback.

"As, as a thank you," Max spluttered. "I'm an excellent cook—and maybe we can read the rest of the diary, too. If you like. Not like a date or anything…" She gave a weak laugh and trailed off.

A second later he broke her heart. "That's sweet of you. But Raq…" He hesitated for several seconds, his eyes searching her face. "I have, uh, to work," he stammered. He looked flustered. His cheeks had turned pink.

Max managed to keep a straight face. All she wanted to do was turn around and run. She steeled herself. There was a lot more she wanted from this nice guy than a fun evening out. He probably had a girlfriend, maybe even a wife. And four adorable kids. But she wanted to see him again. How was that for conflicting feelings?

She needed to make her offer enticing enough. She tried to be breezy. "It's just that I realize you are far more capable of doing this than I can ever be. If you're willing, this could be an extremely interesting historical problem." She ran her tongue over her dry lips. This was urgent, important, and she didn't have many choices. "Not to mention it involves a suspicious death," she said. "But you're busy. Never mind. Thank you so much for your time."

Julian, it seemed, had finally been stunned into silence. His jaw went slack. He started to say something, but his phone began to ring again.

Max picked up her bag as nonchalantly as she could. Julian stood speechless, his phone still ringing. Max worried that she had frightened him. Oh well, it was too late now to change tactics and not look stupid. She had started the drama. She had to finish it.

She took a few baby steps toward the door, hoping he'd stop her. But he didn't. She turned. Julian had picked up the phone and was speaking in urgent whispers. He raised his arm and waved. Tentatively she waved back. His back was turned to her now.

Inspiration struck. She took out one of her business cards, scribbled her home address and phone number on it, and placed it on his desk in a spot where she knew he wouldn't miss it. She watched him for a while more.

Then she left.

CHAPTER ELEVEN

Max hung up her cell phone and pinched herself. She wasn't dreaming. He was coming. Here, to her apartment. To drop off the papers the DANK Haus people had faxed over. But he was coming and that's what mattered. And he wasn't opposed to eating, but only if she was going to cook anyway.

Max rushed to the kitchen. She was going to cook a simple meal. The urge to go overboard was strong, but she would resist it. The last time she had cooked for a date had been over six months ago. Not that this was a date, but still.

The last time a truly attractive man had stopped by for dinner had been well over a year ago. A blind date set up by Uncle Ernst with a nice Jewish boy, a gentle soul whom Max had really liked. But at the end of a wonderful dinner he had blurted that he was gay and cried for an hour on her shoulder.

Kyle, Max's boyfriend of three years, had left her eighteen months earlier. She was getting heavy, he had said. And *he* was no Cary Grant to start with. Still, it wasn't as though the relationship had ever been wonderful. Even on the best days it had been just about adequate—the affection, the sex, the conversation.

Max had begun to suspect that after the first year, Kyle had stayed on because she had cooked him delicious breakfasts, lunches, and dinners. Every single day. His leaving had been a bit of a relief, for she had tired of playing cook, mechanical lover, and cleaner. And so when Kyle hemmed and hawed about her weight, she felt a release of tension she hadn't known she had been harboring for so long. She let him leave, much to his surprise. And after, she had a nice cry, took a shower, put on her best dress, and went out.

Anyway, this was not a date and Julian wasn't Kyle.

She made pasta primavera, with veggies slightly crunchy and the pasta—farfalle—just a little *al dente*. She baked a few mini loaves of crusty garlic bread. To go with those, she made a spicy, tomato-based dipping sauce seasoned with mint and a dash of chipotle peppers for smoky heat. For dessert, she made a butternut squash flan. It was a simple recipe that came out looking like a much labored upon dish.

She set the oven to warm and kept the food inside. The table was set with her grandmother Martha's German crockery. No wine. Wine would give the wrong impression. But she was serving Italian food. Damn.

There was a knock on the door a few minutes before seven. Gorgeous *and* punctual. *I like*, she thought. She pulled up her obscenely expensive Spanx underpants, sucked in her belly, went to the door, and opened it with a bright smile.

There stood Uncle Ernst with a small bowl. Matzo ball soup. His weeknight special. "Expecting me?" He smiled.

Max put her head out the door for an instant. The corridor was empty.

"Hmm." He entered the kitchen and sniffed the air.

Max looked horrified.

Uncle Ernst patted her cheek. "I'm not staying. Take this. I made it from scratch!"

"Thank you." She gave him a quick kiss on his cheek.

"Someone special coming, eh?" He leaned towards her.

The explanation was too long for her to get into now.

"Yes," she said with a shrug, which was true. Ernst shook a finger at her. "Don't do anything I would." He laughed, probably thinking about his own days of wining and dining young girls. He had told her many stories. "Have you lost weight child, you look positively skinny!"

Max grimaced.

"I'm going…going, I'm gone."

Max watched Uncle Ernst amble toward the elevator.

It was 7:15. No Julian.

At 8:00p.m. there was a knock on the door.

"I'm so sorry, so very sorry." Julian handed her a small bouquet of tired-looking white lilies. Funereal flowers.

Max took the flowers with a gracious smile. Julian set a large manila envelope on the coffee table and turned to face her, his hands clasped in front of him in apology. "I was held up." He sounded out of breath and sincere.

Max held the flowers away from her. She was trying to say they looked lovely, but that would be a lie. They looked half dead and were scaring her. "Thanks for these," she managed.

Julian glanced at them. "They look more horrific than I thought." He let out a nervous guffaw.

He looked like a sad puppy. Max wanted to hug him.

"But I have this to make up for the flowers," he said brightly. "It's only sold at a small French bistro in London that I like." He handed her a bottle of wine.

Max took it from him. "Thank you and relax, its okay." She started to take the food out of the oven. "Hope you're hungry," she said.

Julian walked toward the large windows facing the lake. The sun had set, but a pink glow of light remained. "Oh yes, I only had a light supper ages ago," he said. "What a view!"

Max checked the flan. It was a deep burnt orange color with a light brown layer of caramelized sugar on top. Perfect. She put the pasta and garlic bread on her grandmother's serving dishes. "Dinner is served," she said gaily.

Julian looked at the dining table. "You made all this?"

Max looked at the food. "I left it all in the oven and forgot I had put on a timer so it wouldn't dry out. Now I don't think it's very warm." She wrung her hands. How did people give effortless dinners? How did food stay hot for guests who arrived late?

Julian walked into the kitchen, opened a few drawers, and found a corkscrew. Max pulled out two dusty wine glasses and gave them a good wipe down while Julian uncorked. He poured the wine and handed Max a glass. "*Sláinte!*" He raised his glass, checked the bouquet, and sighed with pleasure. He took a sip.

Max did the same. The wine smelled of the French countryside— she had never been there, but she was sure this was what it would smell like. She closed her eyes and in her mind saw Julian and herself cavorting on lush green fields in some vineyard in the Mediterranean somewhere, on an isolated island perhaps, with indulgent workers looking on and giggling.

Julian touched her arm. She snapped back to the present. They began eating.

"Delicious," Julian said.

"Thank you. Uh…I've been meaning to ask," Max said, "hope it's not rude. Your accent is so, uh," she could not say delicious or sexy. "Interesting."

Julian threw his head back and laughed. "I grew up in Northumberland County. In Berwick upon Tweed. It borders Scotland. Father Scottish, mother English. Bit mongrel now, my accent, with English and American influences."

"Long way from East Asia," Max said with a smile.

"I loved Asian mythology growing up. Mum was a bit crazy about pho, the Vietnamese noodle soup, while pregnant with me. The interest must have been passed on that way!"

Max laughed. They talked a little about his family and the beauty of Northumberland. Finally Julian put down his fork. He studied his plate for a second and turned to Max with a satisfied smile. "Thank you," he said. "That was excellent."

Max felt her heart swell with pleasure.

"Dessert?" she offered.

"Sure," he said.

She got up, brought out the flan, and served him a slice.

He took a bite and considered it. "So," he said, "I have the papers from DANK Haus."

Max sighed. It was as though Julian had just put out the romantic candles she had lit in her mind with one single blow, and turned on a harsh florescent light.

Julian pushed back his chair and picked up his wine. "Did you read any more of the diary?"

"No. I was hoping maybe you might have some time, but if you don't, it's fine."

Julian didn't speak. Max sat on her couch. Julian seemed to hesitate, but sat down, too. The diary was on the coffee table. He gestured for her to open it.

Max started reading.

There was one entry on the work Opa had done upon returning from India. Dull stuff. Drugs he had worked on, accolades he had received. Then there were some pages about sending his wife Martha to Geneva.

Opa had also written at length about realizing the harsh truth of being a Jew—even a privileged one—in Nazi Germany. The realization had finally hit, it seemed, after *Kristallnacht*—Crystal Night—happened. It was a horrific anti-Jewish directive Propaganda Minister Joseph Goebbels had called for. Numerous synagogues were set on fire and Jewish businesses and homes looted. Thousands were arrested and sent to concentration camps, and all Jewish pupils were expelled from public schools. It had finally dawned on Opa that Germany had become hell for his people and that it was too late for him to leave. But he had held on to the hope that at Berliner he was still safe.

All of this was written without sentiment, but Max could almost feel the searing pain of her poor grandfather's comprehension that he had been a fool to consider himself immune.

As for the Indus pills, he had worked on them, run numerous tests. *Nothing but vegetable matter content*, the tests had shown over and over. No unusual ingredients, nothing of note.

"Not much of use here." Max got up. "Would you like some coffee?"

Julian nodded. "So does a pretty lady like you have a boyfriend?" he said out of nowhere. "Many boyfriends?" he added with a wink.

Max shook her head, wanting to sink down to the floor. Was he making fun of her?

"I cannot believe it," Julian said.

Max frowned. He wasn't being sarcastic. He actually seemed puzzled that she didn't have a string of boyfriends. Boy, he was so darling.

"Well, if you want the ugly truth, my last one left because he thought I was getting heavy. I was with him for too long. He left me with a rather distorted sense of self." She wished she could rid herself of his disapproving glances. His barely hidden grimace every time he saw her naked. Holding her breath and sucking in her belly until she was blue in the face in order to look more attractive to him.

She closed her eyes. She shouldn't have opened herself up like this to a stranger.

"A dreadful man," Julian said sharply. "Been hit by a bus since, I hope."

Max focused on getting coffee.

Julian was silent for a while. "I read an interesting research paper not long ago about beauty standards over the centuries and in different cultures," he said slowly. "You know if you had lived one century ago, you'd be the belle of the town."

Max returned to the couch with two steaming cups.

Julian took a sip. He looked deep into her eyes. "Magazines, the media have conditioned us to think the way we do. So think of it this way. In those days Twiggy or whoever the latest supermodel is would be considered not beautiful at all. Too boyish. Not feminine enough. Too many angles, not enough curves."

"Twiggy, huh?" Max tried not to laugh. "You *are* a historian, aren't you? But point taken."

Julian put down his cup and leaned toward Max. His hand was close to hers. She could feel warmth emanating from his fingertips, willing hers to move closer. "In the Kayan Lahwi tribe in Myanmar, women lengthen their necks by putting on these rings. It's very painful. In China they used to tie women's feet to make them smaller. The ideal foot had to fit into a four inch shoe."

Max winced.

"The bindings were so tight, they could lead to gangrene and blood poisoning. Women couldn't walk because they'd keel over and fall. The practice lasted a century. Today, women subject themselves to liposuction, breast enhancements. My point is—"

Max looked at her hands and inched them closer to his. Their fingertips were touching now.

"You are beautiful if *you* think so. Why does *Vogue* or whatever airbrushed magazine get to decide? You decide." Julian turned his attention back to his coffee.

Max looked at Julian wanting to ask, *and what have you decided?* But she couldn't. And she shouldn't.

Julian glanced at her, a sweet expression filling his eyes. *"Yer mair bonny than ye wull ever ken,"* he whispered.

"What did you say?" Max asked, her heartbeat quickening.

"Nothing." He turned away quickly. He looked angry.

"Perhaps we should read on," Max said, swallowing hard. She picked up the diary and turned to the next entry.

CHAPTER TWELVE

From Samuel Rosen's diary

Berlin, Germany
January 1938

> *Lars asks me over and over again if I have found a way to leave Germany. And I snap, as I seem to do a lot these days. With a resounding no. Martha I managed to send to Geneva. No one was going to take the risk of helping me leave Germany. Not now. I am too visible, even well known in Nazi circles.*

> *Peter Schultz came to the lab today. Tall, lanky, egotistical Peter. Head of operations, son of current chairman Leopold Schultz. Lars leapt to his feet. The idiot. Peter sat at the edge of my desk and asked if I had an answer for him. He was being so tedious. So grown-up.*

> *Peter had been a mere teenager when I first met his father at a conference. Leopold had convinced me to work for him instead of Bayer. Peter started spending a great deal of time with me at my lab, asking questions, assisting me whenever he wasn't at school. We had become friends, despite the fact that I was more than a decade older.*

> *I waved Lars back to his chair and told him not to be so intimidated by Peter. He is non-lethal, like the crowd control gases you're concocting for the Nazis, I said. My first joke in weeks. Schultz let out a booming laugh.*

Just to torture Peter Schultz, I asked Lars to recapitulate our work on the Indus pills.

Here are the details of our experiment so far in layman's terms.

Three years ago, we first got the pills and started preliminary tests from which we were able to determine its vegetable content.

We commenced animal testing with monkeys. We had two groups of monkeys. All were offered normal nutrition. One set, the test group, was given the pill. The other set, the control group, was not. The monkeys on the pill ate less and less over time. Tests showed decreased thyroid activity in these monkeys.

Note 1: *Something in the pill lowered the monkeys' thyroid levels, giving them lower metabolic rates. A few studies have shown that lowered metabolic rates indicate higher life expectancy.*

We also found a protein element in the pill. However, incubation of the pill didn't result in any development of microbes. We concluded that the protein element was probably vegetable or animal protein.

A big mistake.

One **month** *into testing, the test group—the monkeys on the pill—developed fevers. The ones in the control group showed no symptoms. We ran blood cultures of the affected monkeys' blood and found a fully formed bacterium, of the sporohalobacter genus. This bacterium was similar in composition to the protein element that we had found earlier in the pills.*

Now for a fantastic find. The protein element in the pill was an endospore—which is a dormant bacterium that can survive for even millions of years in dormancy. Mummies, fossils, etc., can harbor endospores that can revert to their active state when conditions are perfect for them.

Note 2: *This endospore probably used components in the monkey's cells to convert to its active state.*

Conclusion 1 and 2: *Since the fevers disappeared, we concluded that the bacteria had caused the fevers in the test group monkeys.*

The bacterium is likely the reason for the decreased thyroid activity and metabolic rate reduction.

Now for the odd bit. The control group, the monkeys who had not had the pills, got the fevers, too, but two months after testing began. And as Lars likes to point out—so did we. We thought we caught it from the test monkeys. However, the control group had been isolated, so why did they develop the fevers? And also, why after all that time?

Conclusion 3: *The bacterium is possibly contagious and takes about two months to synthesize in a mammal and release toxic enzymes, which causes the fevers.*

Interestingly, six to ten months after testing began, the control group of monkeys started to show elevated blood pressure. In humans, high BP is a primary condition, but when an animal shows it, there is almost always another underlying reason for it. In the monkeys, routine blood tests continued to be normal. We were unable to identify the reason for the rise in BP. The question was, why was the test group not showing elevated BP? After all, the control group had not even taken the pill.

Conclusion 4: *Since the control group had not ingested the pill, the increased BP was most likely random and unrelated to the pill.*

We spent a year running the same tests on a second group of monkeys. It was a repetition of the first time.

Conclusion 5: *Since our findings have been observed twice, we decided that the elevated blood pressure had something to do with the pill, most likely with the bacteria in it. But we have no idea how or why.*

Note 3: *What is puzzling are unrelated symptoms exhibited by the control group. Some monkeys developed high cholesterol, others showed slight increases in blood sugar levels.*

There is a link between all of this, but we haven't been able to find it.

Schultz of course was hopping mad by the time Lars was done with the recap. He hates it when I tell him things he already knows. He has heard us talk about the Indus pills and our inconclusive results dozens of times. And yet he wants to start human trials.

I told Lars this for the first time today. Lars was shocked and stated the obvious. The pills were nowhere near human consumption. I looked at Schultz.

Schultz stood up and put his enormous hands on my shoulders. They felt like dead weights. He had never touched me before. The Nazis are excited at the prospect of a drug that can extend lives, he said. His hands gripped my arms. They want to include our pill in their medical experiments, he said. To his credit, he said those awful words with a degree of contrition.

But I jerked him away. Schultz tried to sound sincere. If we want to stay alive, we must do as the Nazis ask, he said. He told me Hitler had heard stories of the immortals of Indus Valley. Lowered metabolic rate is the answer to living longer, Hitler and his cronies have decided.

And because we have concluded lowered metabolic rates twice over with our pill, that mustachioed idiot, that failed artist wants a piece of this immortality!

The Indus pill, Schultz informed me, is the main thing—perhaps the only thing—keeping me in my lab and Berliner still in business. That and Lars's crowd control gases, he said, glowering at poor Lars.

Schultz moved closer, towering over me. I was this close to being put away myself, he said.

Today for the first time, I felt real fear. I staggered toward my table and let my forehead hit its hard, cold surface. Over and over again. And I'm not one to display emotion freely.

Schultz touched my shoulder. Never in over a decade and now twice in one day! He told me about a labor camp for skilled workers based on the 'Hofjuden' portion of Sobibor starting at Krippenwald. Skilled Jews who aren't part of the Hofjuden will be placed there, he said.

Sobibor is a death camp, of course. And Hofjuden. Privileged court Jews of the old times. Even as they kill us, they mock us. They strip us of our dignity.

Schultz then tried diplomacy. The Hofjuden have slightly better living conditions, he said. And at Krippenwald, they want to keep the inmates alive. But what they also want is to spend as little on nutrition as possible. I knew the Nazis were conducting medical experiments at Krippenwald, among other places. Schultz said he had met with some top Nazi officials last week. They would like us to conduct our human trials at Krippenwald labor camp.

The final straw is that he has told the Nazis the pill works. So of course, they are eager to test it. I remember letting out a moan, like the cry of a lamb about to be slaughtered.

Schultz persisted. With this pill, the Nazis will get workers to live on reduced nutrition and live longer. And you get to continue working, he told me.

I have said nothing so far, but I could not hold back any longer. I lashed out at Schultz. How can I do this to my people? I asked him. Aid in experiments with my brethren? I have been blind and arrogant, but I cannot unleash an unknown compound on anyone, let alone my own people who are suffering simply because they are Jewish.

Schultz slammed an enormous fist against the table. In the quiet of the lab, it sounded like a cannon going off. Again, to his credit, Schultz did try to send me away when the Nazi propaganda began years ago. He begged me to leave. A thousand times. But I didn't listen.

I was a fool.

I could tell that Schultz was upset for me. But he was also excited for the possibilities that lay ahead with the Indus pills. And no matter how hard he tried, his voice betrayed it.

I am trapped. I am at young Schultz's mercy. I know this now.

Schultz tried to tell me that the inmates at Krippenwald are skilled workers, useful to the Nazis and therefore being kept alive, but in the end, they will die. We cannot help them get out. We are extending their lives. They can survive on lowered nutrition because of our pill.

Schultz was succeeding in making his point without raising his voice. It was a practiced art. He had often practiced it with me before addressing meetings. And today he was using it on me! Keeping calm, his voice modulated as if he were talking about gardening tips. I tried telling him that I need more time.

All Schultz did was sit down and cross his long legs. All those unexplained symptoms must be because of contaminants, he opined, calmly examining his manicured nails.

It's true. Lab animals are notorious for having unexplained symptoms. We have to ignore that which is unrelated and work with what we know. The good results triumph over the bad side effects. We say that to clear our conscience, but this time, it's different.

He asked me to start work on a composition profile for the pill so we can manufacture them. Hitler is going to start a war. He wants enough pills to dispense to every single soldier. If this pill works in their camps, we need to be able to produce them.

I've been asked to find out how much we have in stock. We have quite a lot, and a trip to India should be enough to take care of us for a while. I know Schultz will send a team to India to clean out the grave. I wish I could go, but my passport was confiscated years ago.

April 1938

Thousands of pills have arrived from India and will be dispensed as the Nazis choose. Manufacturing will begin in a year's time, Schultz has informed the Nazis. I have been assigned a team of scientists and a superb new lab. We have commenced work on a composition profile. The active bacteria will be included in the manufactured pills.

All aspects of its contagiousness, the fevers and other unexplained symptoms in the monkeys, are to be kept secret, Schultz has warned—known only to Lars, himself, and me.

December 1939

> *Germany attacked Poland three months ago.*
>
> *In a listless bleeding of one miserable day into another, I go on. The Nazis have spared me for now, perhaps because the Indus pill seems to be working. The bacteria is seemingly lengthening the life spans of Krippenwald's inmates, since with slower metabolisms, they can survive on lowered nutrition. No problematic symptoms have been reported so far.*
>
> *The Indus health pills have passed the human trials test.*

CHAPTER THIRTEEN

Max put down the diary. A dull ache had started at the nape of her neck. She massaged it. When she realized that it was moving up to her temple, she went into the kitchen. A bottle of aspirin stood on the counter. Max took out one tablet and swallowed it.

"My grandfather was so hard on himself." She stared at the label. "He punished himself by keeping a bottle of aspirin near him always to remind him of what he couldn't achieve."

"Which is?" Julian said.

"Discovering an aspirin of his own."

Julian raised his eyebrows. "That is a rather lofty goal for anyone."

Max smiled lightly. "My Opa wasn't just anyone."

Julian laced his hands behind his head and put his feet up on the coffee table. "Is that why he went to India? To look for exotic remedies to turn into drugs? Isn't that how aspirin came to be?"

Max ran her fingers over the words on the aspirin bottle. "Yes, from willow bark—salicylic acid. Berliner wanted to be a powerhouse like Bayer. So Opa was quite the globetrotter—Malaysia, Thailand, parts of Africa. Over the years, he became desperate to find something as miraculous as aspirin. It became an obsession with him. Then he went to India and found the Indus pill."

"So aspirin is the elephant in the Rosen household," Julian said. He poured himself another cup of coffee.

"It's more like an appendix we cannot get rid of," Max murmured, almost to herself. "I take it so I don't ever forget how Papa died. He overdosed on it and alcohol. Morbid, I know. But I cannot help it. It's as if—"

"Max," Julian said gently. "You're starting to frighten me."

"I'm sorry." She gave him an apologetic glance.

Julian tilted his head. He looked tired, but he smiled. Max's heart did a quick somersault. Julian had dark rings under his eyes, but he looked positively alluring—could 'alluring' be used to describe a man? Max leaned forward to get closer to him.

"Did you know Bayer was also the company that came out with heroin and initially sold it as a pick-me-up? Heroin comes from the Greek word *heros*, so the user feels like a hero when he takes it."

Julian gasped. "What a colossal blunder!"

All at once Max felt like the air had been sucked out of the room. The happy air. And taking its place was cold, gloomy air. Cold, like being in a house in winter without the heat turned on. A coldness that was worse than being outside amidst the elements. A cold that permeated every bone and made its home there.

"Perhaps Opa found heroin in his quest for aspirin," Max said, picking up her grandfather's diary. "Perhaps what he found is the reason he died a broken man."

CHAPTER FOURTEEN

From Samuel Rosen's diary

Krippenwald special labor camp
About 90 kilometers west of Berlin

January 6, 1942
 This is my fourth week at Krippenwald. I haven't felt like writing so far but I must. It's a miracle I still have this diary. That must be considered a gift. I have found a cleaning job in the kitchen and am staying focused on getting through one day at a time.

 After the successful human trials of the Indus pills, the Nazis asked me to work on chemical warfare. Invisible gases that are undetectable, but lethal—not just to those directly under its onslaught, but for miles around. I finally took a stand. Schultz pleaded with me not to. But I had had enough. The Nazis have raped my country and my people. I had been a coward so far. But I decided not to be anymore. Once I refused to do as I was told, I was sent away.

 Here at Krippenwald, the inmates—semi-skilled jewelers, shoe makers, tailors, and cooks—are kept barely alive and working, sometimes on projects that utilize their skills,

sometimes in the nearby stone quarry. But people keep con-
tinually disappearing.

Krippenwald has gas chambers, too.

A few days ago, Lars managed to smuggle a note into the camp.

Herr Dr. Rosen,

I trust you are keeping fair health.

I was banned from entering our lab the minute you left. But I have found out that the scientists have succeeded in completing the composition profile that you started, with the bacteria included.

The pill will be mass-produced. The initial plan is to dispense to minor soldiers on the front. After, it might be marketed as a wonder drug. All I know is based on rumor. I'm not even allowed in the building anymore.

I'm leaving for London next month. I'm sick of this place.

I promise to get in touch with Frau Rosen. We will pray for your release and the end of this horrific war.

Yours sincerely and gratefully,

Lars Lindstrom.

I may not see Lars again. It's hard not to grieve.
I wonder if my team at Berliner have found the answers Lars and
I didn't. Have they figured out why the animals developed all the
unexplained conditions? And why is the contagious nature of the
bacteria being ignored?
Forget it, I tell myself. The past is gone.

February 10, 1942,

Today as usual, the shrill whistle woke me at 6:00 a.m. I
reached for the aluminum bowl by my sliver of a pillow. Clutch-
ing the bowl to my chest, I stepped out for roll call into the
bitter morning. We lined up for breakfast. I got my morning
ration—watery turnip soup and a two-inch long piece of hard,
yellowing bread.

Lowered nutrition is key to the Indus pill experiment.

I walked to my usual spot, from where I have a clear view of the SS clubhouse.

"You're not on the membership list this month, either," a boyish voice said.

Ernst. Dear Ernst Frank, my constant companion and comfort these days. He plopped himself beside me and smiled through the grime and dirt that lined his handsome face.

Ernst Frank is a happy-go-lucky man-child, barely twenty. A peddler of dubious herbal cures during peacetime, Ernst managed to convince the SS that he had a marketable skill, and was therefore allowed to stay alive at Krippenwald, where he quickly charmed a shoemaker inmate into taking him on as an assistant.

His honest manner and ability to laugh at his circumstances won him my friendship. But it is his willingness to suffer through painfully detailed stories about Berliner and my work that has endeared him most to me. That and his unconditional camaraderie.

Poor Ernst lost his wife and two-year-old daughter to the gas chambers a year ago. He spent months after their deaths trying to kill himself. Following a third attempt involving a makeshift noose that broke before it could do harm, Ernst had a change of heart. The best thing he could do for his beloved Inge and baby Sophie was to go on, he decided. Now what Ernst yearns for most is to have a child, hopefully a daughter, who will become the center of his life. Never again will he find himself helpless as he did when his loved ones were carted off in front of his eyes to the gas chambers, he rants and swears.

Ernst took a whiff of his bowl and declared the toilet water in it to be delicious. How I envied his ability to smile through his pain.

A whistle sounded. The soup guard called out, "Herr Doctor!" I didn't respond. Why would I? I wasn't Herr Doctor or Herr anything here. "Doctor Rosen," the guard called in a singsong voice. He was smiling. Had Peter Schultz been able to exert some influence? Were they going to release me? I stood up and went to him.

The idiot asked about my Indus pills and congratulated me on their success. When I turned away, he struck my cheek with his leather whip, called me a Jew swine, and dismissed me.

I returned to Ernst, lowered myself to the ground, and raised my bowl to my lips to finish the last dregs of the tasteless soup.

Ernst put a hand on my injured cheek. He looked livid, but only for an instant. He asked why the guard had called me. I told him the guard had asked about the pills my company had made. I would tell Ernst the truth. I just didn't feel like it yet. I was too ashamed.

Ernst tore off a piece of bread with his teeth. He said they call the pills the "profit maker." And asked me if I knew why the camp inmates' nutrition had been reduced.

Ignoring his question, I asked him when he had taken the pill.

A year ago, he said. And his fever occurred a month after he took it. I asked him if he knew if the others who had taken the pill had gotten fevers. He said that fevers and colds occurred in many inmates. But disease isn't uncommon here.

I asked if they had been given more than one dose, and he said they had. But the fevers had only happened the first time. It was obvious he wanted to know why I was asking all this. I promised to tell him, but right then I wanted to think.

Presumably the bacteria had caused the fevers once. The fevers didn't recur because the body now had the bacteria protecting it, acting like a vaccine possibly. I asked him if people had developed any other symptom than fevers. Other ailments.

"A few have died of unknown diseases," he said. "Others..." he pointed to the gas chambers.

I wonder if I needn't worry, since the symptoms of fevers came and went like in our lab monkeys. No one was being carted away with strange symptoms. But our test group monkeys hadn't shown any symptoms after their fevers went. And their nutrition had been much below normal. Like the camp workers' here.

The control group, on the other hand, showed the odd assortment of symptoms. And they had normal nutrition—like the guards here. How would I know if the guards had developed anything? Besides, even if one of them had any issues, how could we attribute it to the pill? Plus how was I to know if the guards had been given the pill or not?

One thing is certain. The bacterium is now free to spread, potentially infecting anyone who breathes it. It is contagious among humans. That's one thing Lars and I have proved.

I am unable to put my mind at ease these days. What I have helped do is unconscionable. Of this I am certain. Will I ever be forgiven for it?

Will I ever forgive myself for it, I wonder.

CHAPTER FIFTEEN

That was all that remained of the diary.

"Opa burned the rest." Max held the diary close to her chest.

Julian picked up the envelope he had left on the coffee table. "These are the papers the DANK Haus people faxed me. Copies of everything they got from Germany on Bernard Baston. It has details about the dig and names and addresses of those involved. Irrelevant, most likely. I wasn't much help after all. I'm so sorry."

"No!" Max touched his hand. "You've been very helpful. And kind. Thank you so much."

Julian waved away her gratitude. He didn't make a move to pull his hand away, and she didn't remove hers either. "You're welcome," he said. "I rather enjoyed chatting with the guy at the DANK Haus. But Max—"

"Yes?" Her hand was growing warmer by the second.

"You haven't told me the whole story." His soft voice turned Max's knees to Jell-O.

"What do you mean?"

"The bit about the, uh, suspicious death." His eyes were shining.

Max pulled her hand away, nauseated by his transparent interest. But she had no right to be mad at Julian. After all, she had used her poor father's death as the carrot to entice him.

Max decided to trust Julian. She had trusted him this far.

She told him about Lars and the package her father had sent him, in as impassive a way as she could manage. She ended with how the man from Berliner, most likely, had attacked Lars and threatened her. She felt such relief after telling him.

Julian sank into the couch. His eyebrows were furrowed. "Your father," he said softly. "How awful. You must think me callous coming here looking for a juicy mystery." He jumped up and took her hand. "Did you go to the police after the incident with this man, especially since he had broken into your home?"

"I was frightened. Besides, this man is probably in Germany now. And how do I explain his attack? Say that my father may have killed himself or been killed over some pills my grandfather found in India decades ago? Nazi Germany, India, ancient civilization. It's all too out there for a police complaint!"

Julian's eyes softened. "But I'm a stranger," he said. "Is there no one you can confide in?"

There was pity in his voice. Max thought of the few friends she had, who for one reason or another had all left town. They were married and tied up with kids and families, living a life that was alien to her.

She missed them terribly, especially now.

Truth was, she had no one. Except Uncle Ernst.

"Uncle Ernst knows some of this, but I haven't spoken to him since I met you," she said flatly. "Talking about Lars and Papa upset him. I didn't even mention the attack on us. He is old and unwell and he is all I have." She was getting flustered. "If something happens to him because I involved him in this, I'll never forgive myself. So yes, I suppose I have no one to tell." She added with an air of defiance, "Unless you count my assistant, Kim!"

Max cleared the table and began noisily stacking the dishes by the dishwasher. Julian gently pushed her away and loaded the dishwasher while she wiped the counter and put away the leftovers. She covered Julian's unfinished slice of flan with plastic wrap and put it in a box for him to take home.

When the kitchen was clean, Julian re-filled their wine glasses and led Max to the couch. They sipped their wine in silence.

Max stared into her glass, wanting to drown in its intense burgundy. "I'm sorry I got angry earlier," she said.

"No worries," Julian said. He turned to her. "Max, I'm not a criminal expert and I know nothing about chemistry. But I want to help. So tell me, how can I?"

Before she could answer, the phone started to ring.

Max answered. It was Lars.

"I'm calling from a neighbor's phone," he said. "Best if you call me back from a different phone."

Max asked Julian if she could borrow his cell phone, and seconds later she had Lars on the phone again.

He spoke in choppy sentences. "I wanted to tell you something before you decide what to do."

"Is it that yellow-haired beast again?" Max felt an icicle of fear run down her back.

Julian stepped closer and put a hand on her shoulder.

"Maybe," Lars said. "My computer hard drive has been wiped clean. My place torn apart, my safe broken into. It has begun, Max. They probably know I gave them the wrong key. Have you found out anything? Are you coming to London?" It sounded like Lars was pacing, out of breath.

Max put a hand over her mouth.

"What is it?" Julian asked. Max held up a palm asking him to wait.

"I'm ready to leave town, Maxine." Lars sounded close to tears.

Max tried hard to stay calm. "I have learned a few things from Opa's diary entries. But I don't know if they're relevant."

"Perhaps we should just let things be," Lars said. "It's safer that way."

Max felt like she could die with relief. Yes, that was the way to do it.

A thought nudged at her. What if Lars's disease progressed, and he was not around to help if she decided to do something? Then she'd have no one, absolutely no one to talk to who'd have any idea about her father's work.

"I agree. That's what we should do," Max said, but not as forcefully as she had wanted to. "This is getting way too dangerous."

She heard Lars exhale sharply. "If you change your mind and want to see me while I'm still healthy and useful, come. You'll have to decide in the next two days." With that, Lars hung up.

Max tried to smile at Julian. "Thanks for coming," she said in an unnatural voice and handed Julian his phone. "Hope that call doesn't cost you too much." That was all she was going to be able to say without breaking down and becoming completely incoherent. "I really appreciate it." She was starting to sound like a robot.

Julian took both her hands. "*What* is going on? Who was that?"

Max looked at the floor, pools of tears dangerously forming in her eyes.

Julian knew a lot already. What difference would it make telling him this, too? He would just be walking away after she told him, never to be seen again. She told him what Lars had said.

Julian's face turned bright pink. His voice took on a lower timbre. "I cannot believe this man. I understand he was shot at. That is enough to frighten anyone. But he was the one that got you involved. He ought to at least—" Julian shook his head.

Max felt grateful for Julian's support, but she couldn't blame Lars. She too wanted to leave the whole thing alone now. Behemoth corporate villains, bleached blond assassins, computer drive wiped out, homes ransacked. Watching such things in a movie was tense enough.

Living it was hell.

But she mustn't show her true feelings, for once the dam burst she'd be sniveling, snotty, and red faced like a small child. So unattractive. For once she was glad her shallow thoughts were helping her put on a brave front.

"If I were a stronger person, I'd go to London and do what it takes. For my father," she said. "A part of me feels I should."

Julian gave her an admiring look she didn't deserve and couldn't bear to face. She turned away.

They stayed holding hands, their faces lit by the dim floor lamp in her living room. Max wanted the moment to last forever.

She could almost sense a stranger's fetid breath on the back of her neck with Julian's sweet breath on her face canceling it out. These people were obviously keeping track of Lars's movements, maybe even hers. What was she going to do? That blond meant business. How dangerous was this whole thing anyway? Could they be sure it was Berliner? Lars was assuming it. It could be someone else from the pharmaceutical industry using Berliner's name. Goodness, could it be Kevin Forsyth?

Would she find a bullet in her mailbox like Russell Crowe had done in *The Insider*? News flash Max, you already got a bullet in your mailbox. Two in fact. One grazed Lars's neck. And the second had been aimed at her face.

This was all so unfair. And to add insult to already grievous injury, Julian was leaving now, probably for his wife or girlfriend's shapely arms. He hadn't mentioned one, so maybe he was single. She ought not to think too deeply along those lines. What was the point?

"I don't think I'm going anywhere," she said. "But I couldn't have done any of this without you. They're such inadequate words, but thank you. So very much."

"My pleasure," he said. "I suppose I should say good night." He gave her hands a little squeeze.

"Good night," she said sadly. She wanted him to go.

And she wanted him to stay.

He let go of her hands. They dropped to her sides, limp and lonely.

Max looked at the dim floor lamp. She should change the bulb. It made the place look so damn depressing.

CHAPTER SIXTEEN

Julian was unable to leave. He couldn't stand to see Max alone and sad, burdened by her family's past. He so wanted to do something useful for her.

But he had said goodbye. He checked his watch. It was past 10:30 p.m. He had told Raquel he'd be back by ten. He felt like he was being unfaithful merely by being here in Max's company.

Why had he not told Max about Raquel? What was wrong with him?

He didn't know how else to explain it, but being with Max was easy. Fun. It was like being home. Comfortable. He didn't want to ruin it by mentioning a girlfriend. Max seemed obviously attracted to him. That meant he was leading her on by not mentioning Raquel. Surely, though, it wasn't so wrong to enjoy Max's adoring gazes if he wasn't going to ever see her again, was it?

He looked at Max. She seemed mesmerized by the floor lamp. When she became thoughtful, like now, her flawless olive complexion turned transparent. It made her seem so much more delicate. Especially with those soft wispy curls around her face.

Stop! he almost cried out aloud. This was getting out of hand. He needed to walk out the door and go back to his life. To Raquel.

And yet in front of him was Max, temptingly Rubenesque. The generous curve of her chest, covered, with barely a hint of cleavage showing. So tantalizing.

Julian had tried telling Raquel not to obsess about her weight, which was a joke, since she weighed about a hundred pounds. Dining out was painful since she would only nibble at her food. If she did eat, it would be a salad. Julian had tried ordering foods he normally ate, but seeing her wistfully eye his juicy steak while she toyed with some greens had become too difficult, and they had started eating out less and less.

Max was pushing a curl away from her face. She turned to him, her eyes puzzled. Perhaps because he was still there.

Really now, he said to himself, *you have a gorgeous, fantastic girl-friend. A good life. You did this sweet woman a favor. This mini adventure was fun while it lasted. Time to bloody go home.*

He stepped outside. Max moved to the door and started to close it when Julian noticed that her eyes were glazed and remote, her mouth quivering. She seemed to be thinking a hundred thoughts, each jostling with the other.

"Max—" he began.

She looked at him. Expectantly, he thought.

He was about to open a door he had no business even touching. If what he desired was excitement, he needed to find another line of work.

But it was more than that, wasn't it?

Was he drawn to Max's innocent charm and vulnerability? Or was it simply that this woman actually needed him? With Raquel, he often felt out-loved by her laptop. He was being idiotic, of course. Stumbling blocks were part of any relationship.

But there was no denying that this whole business with Max had rejuvenated him in ways that he hadn't felt in years. That meant the attraction he felt toward Max was solely because of this journey she had embarked on. Or was it sympathy? Neither was reason enough to risk what he had with Raquel.

"If you go to London or…if you need anything, call me," he found himself saying. "I…I know London well. I went to university there." He should stop right now. He was making an utter ass of himself.

Max nodded absently.

And now that he *had* made an ass of himself, it was time to mention Raquel.

But the words refused to come out.

Julian had taken a few steps into the corridor when Max started to close the door. He turned, rushed back, and gave her a quick kiss on her cheek. Without another glance at her, he left, his lips tingling with the soft electricity of her skin.

CHAPTER SEVENTEEN

Pilsen neighborhood,
Lower West Side of Chicago

Aaron West was a slim man of about twenty-five. Five foot ten, with wispy reddish-brown hair, a waxy complexion, and a narrow, mousy face. He stood outside the new Big Bowl. The lunch crowd had dispersed. Aaron looked at the wallet he had just picked. Unbelievable. The guy had gotten out of a brand new BMW 7 series sedan wearing gold chains. Reeked of cash, too. Aaron threw the wallet away in disgust. Twenty bucks. One credit card—*check ID*, it said.

Plastic—the bane of his existence. And here in Pilsen! There used to be cash in this neighborhood, wads of it in every pocket, piles in every store. The business owners, mostly Hispanic, trusted only cash in their transactions. Aaron had friends who hit the ethnic grocery stores here and in other parts of Chicago—Indian, Chinese, and Mexican places—since these people kept so much cash around. But now, everyone was turning yuppie and the neighborhood was gentrifying. What a waste!

His cell phone rang. It was Geoff, the man who called himself Aaron's pimp.

Aaron answered. "Got something for me?"

Geoff let out a laugh. He sounded tipsy. Aaron rolled his eyes. Geoff was losing control. He was becoming useless.

"Where you at today?" Geoff asked.

"Pilsen," Aaron said tiredly.

"Dry day?" He laughed. "Not for me."

"A man has to do something in his off time, which I seem to be having too much of."

Silence.

"So do you have anything?" Aaron persisted.

"Well, it's slightly different than your usual," Geoff said.

Geoff brought Aaron computer hacking work. People wanting to get access to their ex-spouse's bank accounts, disgruntled employees itching to install viruses on former employers' mainframes. This paid well, but the work was starting to get sporadic. As a teenager, Aaron had picked pockets. He kept going back to it during lean times. He was constantly being tempted by Geoff to hold up pawnshops and grocery stores, but Aaron didn't want that kind of exposure. Still, he would need to do something if the computer business slowed down any further.

"Come on. My landlord comes after me with a shiv these days. I'll do anything, but no hold-ups, no guns." Aaron could hear Geoff take a swig of a liquid he guessed wasn't water.

"What a brave heart you are!" Geoff scoffed. "It's a traveling job."

Aaron was disappointed. "Traveling? Where?"

Geoff hadn't heard, it seemed. "I can't do it, Ricky and Nico are otherwise occupied right now, so all I had was you."

Aaron sighed. Ricky and Nico were doing time for a Mexican grocery store break-in gone sour. "Why can't you do it?" he asked. Geoff wasn't one to let go of plum assignments.

"Smart ass, aren't you? It involves going abroad." Aaron let out a moan of protest as Geoff continued. "Maggie is pregnant and it's not a good time."

Maggie was Geoff's self-proclaimed wife. But Geoff had another problem—one small matter of being an illegal immigrant from one of the numerous Russian republics.

"Where?" Aaron said.

"London, for starters. You'll need visas if—"

"How much?" Aaron interrupted.

"Twenty grand!" Geoff shouted. "All you have to do is follow this girl and grab whatever it is that she gets her hands on. Easy mark. Just a fancy pickpocket job."

"And your cut?" Aaron asked.

"A meager twenty-five percent."

Aaron inhaled through clenched teeth. "Ten is what you usually take. And for doing exactly nothing."

"You are being given an opportunity. I was asked to find a tough guy—a thief with serious skills. Not a soft computer hacker who snatches purses on the side. It's a gift. Take it or leave it."

Aaron sighed. "Where did you find this job, anyway?"

"Heard about it from the father of a friend. Why?"

"Nothing, I was just—"

"Ok. For you only, twenty-two percent," Geoff said with a tinny laugh.

A young woman with a large Louis Vuitton handbag walked by, looking confused. Her entire being screamed "tourist," with her Chicago Bulls cap, camera, and practical shoes. What the hell was she doing here? Sears Tower, Michigan Avenue—*that way*, Aaron wanted to point. He watched her fumble in her handbag, drop something, and bend down for it.

"So, what'll it be?" Geoff said.

The woman started to walk away.

Aaron needed rent money and he needed it now. "Expenses?" he asked.

"I negotiated a grand more," Geoff said.

The woman was hailing a cab. Aaron slid his phone into a deep pants pocket and glided up to her with practiced ease. There was no one around. He snatched her bag and started to sprint.

A police car turned onto the street a block ahead. Aaron felt his stomach tighten. The woman was screaming in a foreign language.

Aaron ran into an alleyway and entered a tobacco shop owned by his cousin Marco. From his pocket he could hear Geoff singing. He tossed the bag to Marco. "'Sup, brah!" Marco called and stashed the bag under the counter. Aaron took off his T-shirt and turned it inside out. It was white on the inside, black on the outside. He took off his baseball cap and tossed it to Marco, too.

The police car seemed to have taken off. Aaron's heart slowed to a steadier beat. He gave Marco a nod and went to the back of the store.

He returned the phone to his ear. Geoff was still there. He was calling Maggie vulgar names. Aaron winced. Perhaps this trip to London was his ticket to start a legit business—a liquor store, a donut franchise even.

"Oi, you there?" Geoff said. "Got some rent money, I hope."

"Yup, and yes, I'll do it," Aaron said.

Geoff let out a shout. "I told them you would. They won't tell us who they are—it's very hush-hush. But there's an emergency number to call in case of trouble."

Aaron's ears perked up. "Whoa! Trouble? What kind?" Aaron lived on the less-than-right side of the law, but he liked to avoid unnecessary trouble as much as possible. That and any job that might involve blood. Aaron considered himself strictly white collar—the pickpocketing notwithstanding. That was artistry. And desperation.

"More than a paper cut, less than a knife wound," Geoff offered.

Twenty thousand was not money to be easily refused, but Aaron needed some assurances. "You gotta give me more info than—"

Geoff sneered. "No pain, no gain, buddy." Maggie was shouting for him now. "One of these days I'm going to off this woman, I swear."

Aaron hung up.

CHAPTER EIGHTEEN

The Bengal Clipper Restaurant
Shad Thames
London

Max looked at her watch. 10:00 a.m. London time, but the middle of the night according to her body.

Lars had asked her to wait by this Indian restaurant. The place was closed, but her mouth watered as she studied the menu on the door. She would love to have dinner here. Maybe she and Lars could discuss the papers over the fish hara masala or, ooh…that beef bhoona sounded good, too.

Half an hour passed.

Where was Lars?

Coming to London was starting to look more and more stupid. Could this be an elaborate trick like those Nigerian email scams? Lure a gullible person away to a foreign land with an irresistible story and take them for all they've got. Could the German attacker have been an actor? She tried not to panic.

She tapped her feet until they started to hurt. *Lars, where the hell are you?* He lived near Tower Bridge, didn't he? He had said the Bengal Clipper was not far from home. Lars didn't own a cell phone, but she had a number to his apartment. She pulled out her cell phone.

But Lars had asked her not to use it. Letting out a groan of irritation, she looked around for a phone booth. There was none.

"I'm going to use my cell just this once," she said aloud and dialed Lars's apartment. Great. No answer.

Max was drained. She'd gotten less than an hour's sleep on the flight. Seated next to a talkative young man on his first trip abroad hadn't helped. Neither had her nerves about wandering around a strange city on what might be a wild goose chase. Her anxiety about flying was another matter altogether—something she solved with Xanax and a red wine chaser. The combination usually left her somewhere between calm and slightly overconfident for a day or so after. It was that feeling of confidence that was keeping her on her feet right now and her brain cells somewhat alert.

Poor Uncle Ernst, Max thought. She should call and tell him she had landed. He had tried so hard to tell her not to go. Why confront danger when she could avoid it? His eyes had teared up as he tried to tell her in a halting voice how important she was to him. Oddly enough, his dissuading had only served to convince her to make the trip. When she refused to budge, he finally relented. He even said he'd wrack his brain for anything important he may have forgotten. And before letting her go, he held her close and begged her to be careful.

She promised to keep Uncle Ernst informed about her movements so that he could call the police if needed. His face had drained of color. That was when she decided she had worried him enough.

Before she could change her mind, she told Kim she was going away for a bit and quickly bought a ticket to London.

It was done. Here she was. And there was no turning back.

Aaron West, who had taken an earlier flight, watched Max from about a hundred yards away.

Geoff had pointed her out to him in Chicago, but she looked different, her hair pulled back in a long ponytail. It made her look like a lost schoolgirl.

Aaron glanced around to see if anyone else was watching her. Someone would come, he had been assured. The thought made his stomach turn. Was he supposed to attack this person if he got in the way? All he was armed with was his trusted penknife. He had refused to carry a gun.

He saw a man rush toward Max. It was his secondary mark, Lars Lindstrom.

Lars reached for Max and gave her a hug. "Good flight, dear?"

She nodded. "How are you?" she asked.

"Not so good," he said, not meeting her eye. Lars's hair was uncombed, standing out in wild bunches. His shirt was untucked. The last time she had seen him, he had looked so calm, so dapper. "I'm sorry I'm late," he said. "I've just not been myself these past few days. And to top it all off, early this morning, someone called and asked me to 'back off.' His exact words. He even said my daughter's name. He spoke better English this time. Odd that." Lars considered it. "Or maybe I just didn't notice the German accent." He shrugged helplessly. "He didn't say 'or else.' Just 'back off' and my daughter's name. In an almost friendly voice. It was altogether more frightening than if he had said 'or else.'"

Poor Lars. Max squeezed his hand.

Fatigue began slamming down on her. Even intense dread would have to take a back seat until she was rested. It was an anesthetic, this intense sleep deprivation. All she wished for now was a nice long nap.

"Let's walk to the Little Tower Hotel," Lars said. "It's just around the corner. It's close to my place and the area is lively at all hours." He handed her a copy of a credit card receipt for the hotel. Two hundred and fifty pounds, it said. This was going to be an expensive adventure, Max thought wearily.

The Little Tower Hotel was a two-story bed and breakfast with large windows, facing the cobbled Shad Thames on one side and the river Thames on the other.

Lars helped Max check in. A bellhop opened the door to a charming little room furnished in sea blues and greens, with antique furniture and a view of the street below. From one of her windows,

Max could see the London Bridge and from the other, a flower shop bursting with color.

Lars settled into a sofa.

"Shall we have dinner at the Bengal Clipper tonight?" Max said. "We can talk about the papers then."

"It's best if we go to the bank right away."

Max shook her head. "I know we have to get to the locker, but I need a short nap or I'll drop dead."

"Very well. I have to see about a few things at my patisserie anyway." Lars scratched his forehead, a frown pasted on his face.

"What time shall I see you?" Max asked.

Lars looked at his watch. "Come to my apartment at two. We'll go to the bank and collect the papers. After, we can talk and you can decide what you want to do. We'll eat at the Clipper. Excellent food." There was a tone of finality in his voice.

Max felt like a child about to be abandoned.

Lars seemed to be steeling himself. "My apartment is a few doors down from the Butler's Wharf Chop House. There's a back door to the apartment compound. Not many know about it. Come in that way to be safe." He drew her a little map, pointed out to his place from the window, and gave her the entry code.

Now seated on the bed, Max was consumed by its incredible softness. She managed a small nod before Lars left the room.

She closed her eyes and let herself sink into the cloud of pillows and down.

CHAPTER NINETEEN

Aaron West was perched on a small, uncomfortable chair in the lobby of the Little Tower Hotel.

He saw Lars coming down the stairs.

"I hope your guest likes her room," the receptionist said.

"Oh yes, thank you," Lars said. "She's quite jet lagged from her flight. She's probably already fallen asleep!"

The receptionist smiled.

Aaron suppressed a grin. Lars had just saved him the trouble of finding out what Max was doing. Lars didn't even glance at him, despite the matchbox size of the lobby. But then, few ever noticed Aaron. It was a gift in his profession. And for his trip to London, he made sure he looked like the average broke, affable American student tourist—from his ragged jeans and faded blue T-shirt to his nondescript gray backpack.

Lars left the hotel. Since Max was resting, Aaron could keep an eye on him. He gave Lars a minute's lead. A surge of adrenaline ran through Aaron's veins as he got up and followed.

Lars walked with short, brisk steps. His breath was ragged, not wholly from exertion. He walked by a bustling café. It looked warm and inviting. He found a table in a quiet corner.

"A cup of Earl Grey, please," he called to a passing waiter. Lars picked up a newspaper from the chair next to his, unfolded it, and distractedly folded it back up again.

He thought of Max sleeping a few doors down and her palpable disappointment that he was no longer interested in helping her with a problem he had dragged her into in the first place. If only he had spoken to a psychiatrist to deal with the remorse he felt about ignoring Hiram's plea. Instead, he'd gotten impulsive and rushed off to Chicago, only to be attacked. His home had been broken into, his fragile sense of peace violated. Now Max was here. And of course, there was the small matter of his disease. Could things get any worse?

He grabbed his tea before the waiter could place it on the table. It was excellent. He stared out into the street and was jerked out of his reverie by a flash of bleached blond hair disappearing into the crowd. Lars strained to get a better look. He stood up. Now there was no one. He looked around. Where did the beast go? Or had he imagined it?

Lars sat down with a frown. If that German attacked him a second time, his aim would be more precise, wasn't that what he had said? He would tell the blond that he was done, that the whole thing was over. He no longer had any papers. Again he saw the flash of yellow hair.

Something snapped inside of Lars.

He jumped up. "You!" he shouted, "What do you want from me?"

Aaron was seated a few tables away, his face buried inside the pages of a book. At Lars's shout, Aaron jerked his head up. But Lars wasn't looking in his direction.

Perhaps the "someone else" he had been warned about was here.

Aaron slunk out of the café. Even if he hadn't been spotted, Lars was on the alert now.

Aaron walked briskly toward Lars's home—he had studied the maps and memorized all relevant addresses and the areas around them. On the way, he knew, was the patisserie Lars owned.

He tried the door. It was locked, but the lock was an easy pick. He glanced around. The street was deserted. Things had gone well so far. Why not look around while he had the chance? He took out a small wallet filled with surgical-like instruments. Geoff had given him his best tools and several hours of instruction.

The lock clicked open. Aaron went in, found Lars's office in the back, and began looking for anything resembling research papers.

At the café, Lars's exclamation had caused a small stir. A fork clattered out of the hand of an older woman sitting next to him.

"Sorry," Lars said, not looking at her. She muttered something about chivalry being dead.

Lars felt his heartbeat quicken. He felt light-headed and wondered if he had his nitroglycerin pills with him.

Was it the German who had called this morning? He clutched his teacup so hard, the handle broke. The cup fell to the table with a clatter.

Lars threw some money on the table and walked away. In the distance he saw a butter-yellow head bobbing in the crowd. That same large, square, leather-covered back. The man was built like a bus. It *was* his assailant. One part of Lars wanted to chase after him and confront him, another wanted to turn back the clock and shrink into someplace safe. He stood still, torn by both desires, and watched the man stroll away.

Lars walked with brisk steps. He wondered if he was safer at the patisserie or at home. There were people around the patisserie. And he had intended to check on a few things there before meeting Max. He unlocked the door.

People were strolling outside. There was an air of gaiety. Lars's breathing became easier. He didn't want to go over boring business papers. He needed the calm satisfaction of baking. A quick American special. Lars opened a bag of flour and started a batch of thick, chewy chocolate chip cookies. He decided to add some pistachio paste to make them interesting. He began pulling out the ingredients.

Aaron was in the back, in Lars's tiny office. He surveyed the mess he had made. Nothing here. Lars was well organized. There was no safe—just a desk with a couple drawers and a filing cabinet. Most papers were bills, business documents, and letters, some recipe notes. Aaron continued to rummage through a drawer and found a flash drive. He put it in his pocket. He should probably leave. If he had missed something, he'd just grab it when Lars handed it to Max.

At the very least, ransacking this office would scare Lars into handing over the documents to Max. Aaron got the feeling that Lars wasn't very brave. He started to leave when he heard a clatter of tins. He peered outside.

Shit. Lars was here. Now what? The only way out was through the front door. He'd have to walk by Lars to get there. Aaron began picking at a pimple on his chin as he watched Lars.

Lars put the tray of unbaked cookie dough balls in the oven and turned the timer on. He then collected his mail from the box outside his shop and began looking through it.

An uneasy feeling gripped at him followed by a wave of nausea. Those damn drugs. They would kill him before the cancer did! He took a sip of water and tried to steady himself.

There was a small noise close by, and Lars turned to find a young man trying to sneak out of the store. "Hey, hey, who are you!" he called angrily.

The young man was empty handed. Did that mean he was here not to steal but for the sole purpose of harming him? Lars reached for a serrated bread knife sitting on the counter.

At that moment, the blond stepped into the store. So he *had* been followed. Lars felt his heartbeat quicken. His nausea returned.

The blond was smiling at the young man. But the young man was looking at him with a befuddled expression. What did that mean?

Lars started shaking. Acid flooded his already weak stomach. His dizziness worsened. He clutched at his chest, and a shooting pain went up his arm. Whom should he attack? The blond hadn't drawn his gun yet.

The young man stood closer. Without another thought, Lars rushed toward him with the knife.

If Aaron waited a second longer, the knife would rip through his stomach. Here was a situation where he had to inflict violence on someone, and it was abhorrent to him. Lars had clearly become unhinged, but that short, heavy-set blond with the icy expression at the door was frightening Aaron even more. For some reason though, Blondie wasn't making any move. He seemed content to just watch.

Lars's knife was an inch away. He was clutching at his chest and letting out a loud cry like a deranged warrior. Aaron raised his backpack and brought it down hard on Lars's head. The clank of skull against the bag's steel buckles was sickening. Lars staggered back in shock. His knife clattered to the floor, and he sank down in a heap. Aaron felt his heart hammer inside him. Had he killed him? He looked up, expecting the blond to attack him now, but the man didn't move. Was he a cop? A customer? Why was he just standing there looking so damn pleased?

Aaron made a quick dash for the door past the blond who stretched an arm to stop him. He managed to push aside Blondie's beefy arm with strength he didn't know he possessed and ran out.

"*Schiese, schiese!*" He heard Blondie curse.

Aaron hesitated for a few seconds outside the patisserie before breaking into a run.

The blond was quick. He dashed outside and was able to keep Aaron in sight. Aaron started running helter-skelter, disappearing into side lanes and re-appearing again. He found himself in a narrow alleyway filled with trash cans. While the blond searched a nearby alley, Aaron managed to squeeze himself between two large trash containers and under a black tarp. A giant rodent began gnawing on his foot. He tried to ignore it. He could hear the blond closing in now, kicking trash cans, letting out a stream of curses in German. Aaron held his breath.

A second later, a foot came within an inch of Aaron's own. He could see the polished tip of a shoe, hear the man's heavy breathing. Blondie's foot was about to touch Aaron's when the rodent that had been gnawing on his foot grabbed the blond's. Blondie let out an angry roar and turned away.

Aaron stayed in his hiding place for several minutes more. Everything became quiet. Aaron waited until his heart rate had returned to normal and only then crept out.

CHAPTER TWENTY

Having lost his quarry, Hans returned to the patisserie, pulled down the blinds on the doors and windows, and hung out the closed sign.

He pulled on a pair of surgical gloves and checked Lars's pulse. It was slowing. He was near death. There was a trickle of blood running down Lars's head, and his eyes were starting to glaze over.

Hans had followed Lars from the café, hoping he would lead him to the papers now that the Rosen girl was in town. Instead, the idiot had decided to bake and now lay here dying.

Besides, there was this new fly in the ointment, the young intruder. Hans was livid at himself for having lost him. No matter. He knew what he looked like. If he was an adversary, he would return. If he was just a common thief, good riddance.

Hans watched Lars take his last breaths. Had this been a result of the blow, or had the man just suffered a heart attack? Hopefully, the question would baffle the police, too. He checked Lars's pulse once more. It was almost gone. A few seconds later, Lars's body was absolutely still. Hans wondered if he should move the body behind the pastry counter. Moving it would point to foul play.

He thought for a moment or two more, dragged the body around the corner, and left.

CHAPTER TWENTY-ONE

Max awoke with a start. Her temples were throbbing. She glanced at the clock by her bedside. It was past 1:00 p.m. Lars had said to meet him at 2:00 at his apartment.

Despite the gravity of her circumstances and the thick veneer of unease that had enveloped her entire being since this whole business had begun, the prospect of a delicious meal at the end of the day gave her goosebumps of pleasure. She put on a simple day-to-night sleeveless indigo dress that stopped at her knees, smeared on pink lipstick, and grabbed a pink and gold stole and her handbag.

She arrived at Lars's apartment and tried his doorbell a few times. No answer. Perhaps he had gone to the patisserie. Max walked that direction.

She peered in through the glass door of Lars's patisserie and tried it. It was open. "Hello?" she called.

No answer.

She really needed to eat. She should have raided the mini bar and eaten the minuscule bags of peanuts and cashews while she had the chance.

She inhaled—the smell of overdone cookies wafted toward her. Max checked the oven. There were cookies on a baking sheet inside.

Where was Lars?

The pastry counter beckoned. Surely Lars wouldn't mind her sampling one thing. Or two. Fruit tarts! How luscious those raspberries looked. She felt a sharp, sweet sensation in her mouth. There were the heavenly *religieuses*—brown for chocolate, lilac ones, lavender flavored most likely, and pink—raspberry or rose, perhaps. Choux pastry filled with flavored cream, topped off with a thin layer of fondant. She leaned forward to pick one of them. She'd have the lavender.

She raised her eyes a little.

Behind the counter, Lars lay on the floor. His face was frozen. Magazines and letters were scattered around him. With a cry, Max went to him. He didn't look at all well. He looked…he was…was he? He couldn't be.

Numbly, she pulled out her cell. 911 wasn't the number in London. She ran out. An elderly man was bicycling by. She almost pulled him off his bike.

"Oi, watch it!" he cried angrily.

"I need to call an ambulance, please!"

The man pulled out a phone. Max ran back to Lars. And she saw it. A trickle of dried blood formed a line from his temple to his cheek. Lars was dead! She staggered back and fell.

Clutching at the pastry case, Max screamed. Minutes later, an ambulance arrived. Paramedics rushed in. Questions were fired at her. The police were called.

There were people everywhere. Two police cars had arrived shortly after the ambulance. They had put that ominous yellow tape outside the patisserie.

"Who found him?" a voice was asking urgently.

What if Lars had been murdered, Max thought? She felt herself shudder as a man walked up to her. Dressed in a plain black suit, white shirt, and striped tie, his entire being screamed detective.

"Did you discover the body?" he said.

Max looked up at him. He had a lazy smile on his lips, but his eyes were alert. She nodded.

"Did you know him?" he asked.

"Huh?" She glanced at the case behind which poor Lars lay. "How did he die?" she asked.

"We're not sure yet. Did you know him, miss?" He was watching her closely, she knew.

Max had regained some control of her emotions. She made a decision. "Oh, no," she said as glibly as she could. "I just stopped by for some pastries."

She didn't look the detective squarely in the eye. Awful liars averted their eyes, poor liars stared too hard, she had heard in some movie. Good liars did neither. She glanced at the detective, held his eye for a second or two, then turned to look inside the bakery.

The detective glowered at her for a bit. He lit a cigarette and offered her one. She shook her head. He sat her down on a nearby bench and asked her a few questions about her stay, her plans, and how she had found Lars. She was a chef, she said, taking a holiday in London. She was looking for a nice place to eat. She had heard good things about the Butler's Wharf Chop House, she offered with last minute inspiration based on the directions Lars had given her. Seeing the pastry shop open, and overcome with hunger, she had stepped in. She did a brilliant job, she thought, of keeping the tone light and yet suitably horrified.

"Very well," the detective said. "Do you need someone to take you where you're staying?"

"Please," she said.

"We may need to speak to you again."

"Of course," she said.

"Let me get you an escort." He signaled with his hand.

A woman approached. "Excuse me for a second," the detective said to Max.

He turned to his colleague, who said softly, "Heart attack. He possibly hit his head on the pastry counter causing the wound to his temple. The body was moved…but why, and by whom?" She shrugged.

Max caught the woman's quick but obvious look in her direction.

The detective shook his head. "Maybe a customer found him and got scared. If it's only a heart attack, let's wrap this up quickly. I'll dig up his relatives. You drop her off at her hotel. Take a copy of her passport, just in case. And make sure she isn't suffering from shock."

The detective thanked Max and handed her over to his colleague. Max's escort left her at her hotel room and gave her the number of a hospital to contact if she felt unwell. She took a copy of her passport and left.

Max bolted her door and collapsed on the bed, hugging her knees to her chest. She was trembling. She kept picking up the phone, but wasn't sure whom to call.

Claiming not to know Lars had been deceitful and disloyal. But if she had said she knew him, she would have had to reveal so much more. What did one do in a time like this? She really needed to talk to someone. *Uncle Ernst...should I call you?* He'd be worried sick if she told him. Besides, he'd insist that she come back home. She had come too far now to return empty-handed. Friends? There weren't any she was close enough to for this kind of news. She dug her fists into her eyes. *Just admit it.*

You want to call one person.

He did say to call if she needed help. Hopefully he had meant it.

Max stared at the phone for a while more before dialing room service. "I'd like two scones and two sticky buns, clotted cream, jam and butter, some orange juice and coffee. Please."

Max stayed in bed and turned on the TV. She watched *Die Hard* in French. It was fascinating to watch a film she knew backwards and forwards when she could not understand a word that was spoken.

Her food arrived.

She turned off the TV and stared at the blank screen, wondering what she might cook for Bruce Willis if he accepted an invitation to dinner. Eventually, she slipped into an agitated sleep.

At first light, she glanced outside her window. A fog had seized the city in a dense grip. The Thames flowed in tranquil peace, but in the distance she could see the Tower of London, the place where Anne Boleyn and many others had been beheaded. Death seemed to loom everywhere.

But she had made her decision.

She dialed Julian. Their conversation was brief.

Max went into the bathroom and turned on the shower. Like a million tiny needles, she felt its force massaging some relief into her tense muscles.

"Lars is dead," she had spluttered to Julian. "Please come. Please. Please. Please."

And he had said only three words of immeasurable sweetness.

"I'll be there."

CHAPTER TWENTY-TWO

Max lightly knocked on the door of the room directly below hers. Julian opened it, looking scrumptious in dark blue jeans, a pale pink button-down shirt, and smart, new-looking suede shoes.

She threw herself into his arms. "Thank you for coming," she said into his chest.

He patted her head as if she were a puppy or a small child.

"There, there," he said.

"Someone was probably following Lars and me," Max said. "The German."

"Have you seen anyone?"

"No," she said, peeling away from him, "but isn't that the point? Anyway, I figured if these people—Berliner—want the papers, I'm the next lead. Since Lars died, I haven't had the courage to leave this hotel. It's been two days. Staying here is driving me crazy. I'm about ready to jump into the Thames."

She leaned against Julian's bed and stared thoughtfully at the ceiling. "It's probably safer for you if no one knows you are with me."

"Okay," he said. "So what do we do now?" He rubbed his red-rimmed eyes.

"You rest a bit," she said. "Then we can see about retrieving the papers. I have the locker key and the name of the bank." She didn't feel half as confident as she was trying to sound. And poor Julian was suppressing yawn after yawn, looking exhausted. She shouldn't have called him. It would have been best if she had just returned to

Chicago. With Lars dead, the whole business had become a mine-field, no place to turn without risking an explosion. Besides, what might she accomplish even if she had the papers? She'd just be a sitting duck for the Germans. Julian would be, too.

She turned to him, her guard slipping away. "Actually, I'm not at all sure what to do. I called you because I was frightened and still am. I'm sorry to have taken such a liberty—it was wrong of me."

"It's fine," Julian said, suppressing yet another yawn. "I did offer to help, didn't I?" There was an awkwardness about him now. Julian was keeping a respectable distance and his eyes averted, Max thought.

"This is a dangerous situation," Max said. "That sounds almost lame said in broad daylight. But it is."

Julian folded his hands. "Let's focus on the task at hand. We can always worry later."

Max tried to smile. She handed him a mustache and a hat. "I asked the hotel receptionist to give me the number of a costume shop. Luckily they deliver."

The ice seemed to have broken, for Julian let out a laugh. He took them from her and tried them on in front of a mirror. "I look ridiculous," he said. But Max was pleased.

Julian was looking at the bed fondly now.

"Crazy business, isn't it?" Max said. "Get some rest." And she left the room.

Two hours later, Max and Julian were in the hotel lobby.

"Lars's bank," Julian said, "is the Co-Operative Trust Bank, right? It's the bank of many minor members of the royal family—and of men hiding money from their wives. Beautiful building. Twenty-two Curzon Street. It's easiest to take the Tube. We can walk to London Bridge station. It's about a mile from here."

"I don't see the point of going there," Max said.

"What else is there to do? Perhaps we can talk to someone there."

"Hmm…okay. I'll find my way to the train station," Max said. "It's best if we go separately. Where will you wait for me?"

"By the ticket counter," he said. Giving her hand a tight squeeze, Julian left the lobby.

Max took a few deep breaths. She opened her purse to look for the locker key. She rummaged through it for a while as panic rose within her. It wasn't there. She pulled out receipts and papers until she was staring at the bottom of the purse. No key. Damn.

Perhaps she could simply tell the truth at the bank. Sad thing was, the truth was seldom appreciated or believed. She didn't know what they were going to do. She hoped Julian might have a plan. This dependence that she had developed on him almost as soon as he had arrived in London was typical of her. She always depended on whoever was available. Wasn't that another reason she hadn't gotten Uncle Ernst involved?

She went through her purse once more. Wait a second. She had given the key to Julian. Safer that way, they had decided. Exhaling with relief, she began putting the scraps of paper away. One of them caught her eye. It was the credit card receipt Lars had handed her for her room. A germ of an idea formed in her mind.

Max rushed out of the hotel and started walking along the river toward the Tube, keeping an eye out for anyone who walked too close.

Outside the bank, Max showed Julian the credit card receipt with Lars's signature on it. She asked him to practice copying it a few times.

"I think you have it," Max said. "Now, lets go over what we are going to do one more time."

At the bank, Max stayed in the waiting area. Julian went over to the lockers. A few minutes later, he returned.

"The person at the lockers is an old timer," Julian whispered. "He knows Lars. We cannot risk this with him. But his shift changes in ten minutes. David takes over then." Julian pointed discreetly across the room. "Him."

David weighed about two hundred pounds, sported a face sprinkled with pimples, and had greasy, curly hair. He looked young, oafish, and uncomfortable with himself.

"He is perfect," Julian said. With eyes on David, he put his hands on Max's blouse and undid the first two buttons.

"Hey!" Max cried. Her cleavage showed now. Julian patted her collar down, stepped back, and gave her an admiring grin. She wished she could give him a sultry smile. One of her advantages was a nice cleavage. But at this moment when she could show off something she was proud of, she knew her face bore not a seductive look, but schoolgirl gawkiness. She squirmed.

"Use all your charm." Julian's hands hadn't quite left her blouse yet. He fiddled with her collar.

"Yes," she said with a wry grin, "that is what we Americans are known for. Our charm."

Julian laughed, pulling his hands away.

"Ready?" Max asked.

"I have an idea. Just in case." Julian casually walked around the bank, then approached the desk of a stern-looking woman. Her nameplate said *Manager*. Max made herself comfortable on a sofa close by and watched David.

When David's eyes glanced toward Julian and the woman, Julian began to speak. Max couldn't hear what he was saying, but the woman seemed quite taken by him. She invited him to sit and started chatting freely.

David watched them for a while before turning away. He started descending the spiral stairs to take his place at the lockers. Max signaled as much by standing up and smoothing her shirt.

Julian quickly finished his conversion and went over to Max.

They waited until David was out of sight. Max started down the stairs, with Julian close behind. They approached the desk in front of the locker area as if in a great hurry, ran into each other, and apologized. With formal graciousness, each acted as if they ought to let the other go first.

"Please go ahead," Julian said with a wave of his arm and looked at his watch.

Max thanked him. David, who was sorting a lot of papers on his desk, stood up. Max leaned forward. David glanced at her face first and dropped his eyes to her breasts that were almost spilling out of her blouse.

"Hello," she said in a low, throaty, Lauren Bacall voice, attempting to sound sultry.

"Hello," he said, still looking at her chest.

Max touched her clavicle, a last minute inspiration from *The English Patient*. If Ralph Fiennes had found Kristin Scott Thomas's clavicle attractive enough to obsess over for years, surely hers was attractive enough to distract this boy-man for a few seconds.

David's eyes sought her hands. He licked his lips and swallowed.

"My grandfather owns a locker here," she said. "Can I open it?"

"Are you listed as a signatory?" David said mechanically. This time he looked at her face.

Max turned down her lips and brought a hand to her face. "Well, I have the key. My grandfather has had an account here for years," she said. "He was English. I'm American. He died recently. Now I want to open a locker in my name, but first I need to take some documents from his locker. It's such a bother." She wrung her hands.

"I see," he said. "You can open it if you're a signatory."

Max glanced at Julian.

"Please," Julian said to David, "I would like to access my locker. How long is this going to take?"

"Just a moment sir, let me help this young lady first," David said.

Max moved closer and began to stammer. "My grandfather died yesterday." Genuine grief for Lars brought tears to her eyes. She held out her arms, as if looking for comfort.

Max could tell that David had softened considerably. He had compassion written all over his face. The kid was probably a product of an all-boys school.

Julian threw up his hands. "Maybe I should see the manager. Some of us have work to do—"

"Or better yet, I'll go see her." Max glared at Julian.

Julian shrugged.

David looked at Julian. Quickly he said, "One moment, madam. I'll be with you shortly. Sir," he said to Julian, all business-like, "perhaps you'd like to sign here."

Julian huffed, shook his head, and grunted, grumbling all the while about being in a hurry. He signed the book, distractedly checking his phone at the same time. David opened a drawer and took out the signature card box. He pulled out the one for Lars Lindstrom and stared at the two signatures.

Max started sobbing even louder. "Maybe I should go to the manager right now," she said. "It's obvious you don't have the power to do anything."

Julian rolled his eyes. "This had to happen to me today of all days! I insist that you help me now." He slammed a fist on the table. A few papers flew down to the floor.

"Have some pity," David said angrily, bending down to retrieve the strewn papers. "She has just lost her grandfather. I'm trying to help her without breaking the rules." To Max he said, "Madam, one moment while I help this…this *gentleman*." His voice dripped with sarcasm.

"Can I get to my locker now?" Julian said. He dialed someone, went to a corner, and began speaking in urgent tones.

"Yes," David hissed, almost putting an arm around Max. "I tell you," he murmured into her ear. "I don't know what's wrong with that man."

Max nodded in agreement.

David went on, "Such men give Englishmen a bad name. He sounds Scottish, though, despite his name. He's insensitive and brusque. But we're all not like that. You please sit." He indicated a sofa away from the main desk. "I'll find a way to help you, I promise."

"No, I'd rather wait here." Max dabbed her eyes with a hanky and continued to sob.

Julian returned to the desk. Max stood close to both men, so they were all crowded around the tiny desk.

David glanced once more at the two signatures.

Julian was threatening to call the manager now. He insisted that she was an old family friend.

David bit his lip. His eyes showed fear. "I'll, uh, need to see some identification," he stammered.

At that moment, Max pushed her ample bosom at David and began to sob. David was startled, but immensely pleased.

Julian looked at his watch. "Unbelievable, this circus you people run here," he shouted. "Thanks to you, I have just missed an important meeting. The papers I need are in that locker. If I lose this multi-million-dollar contract, it'll be your fault, young man! I'll have you fired. As for ID, mine has been on your desk for ages now." David looked down and began searching through the scattered papers. Julian let out a groan. "Great, now where did it go?" He started shuffling through the papers, dropping some, moving others, and generally making an enormous mess.

Max turned toward the stairs. "Should I go see the manager?" she said.

"One more minute," David said to her in a pleading voice. "Sir, let me look please."

Julian grunted with displeasure.

"You're so nice," Max said to David.

David's expression was one of pure delight. He turned to Julian and said in clipped tones, "Do you have your key?"

"Yes," Julian snapped. "And you better find my driver's license."

David meekly led Julian toward the lockers, returned to his desk and resumed his search for Julian's ID. Max persuaded him to go and fetch her some coffee. On her way out of the locker area, she saw David silently debating whether or not to add sugar and milk to a steaming cup.

She stepped out of the bank. A few minutes later, Julian met her at the entrance. "I tiptoed past the poor kid. He's still looking for my ID!" He handed her a backpack. "Got them," he whispered.

Max pulled the backpack over her shoulders and gave Julian a high five. She then took out her cell phone.

"I thought you said it was tapped," Julian said.

"Lars was sure it was. I've tried not to use it. But sometimes it just seems like paranoia. Besides, looking for a payphone and change all the time can be very tedious!"

"All right." Julian pointed at her phone. "So what's going on?"

"I am going to call as many people as I can and tell them we have the papers," Max said. "The more people I tell, the safer we are."

"Brilliant!"

Max first told Uncle Ernst that she now had the papers and asked him to keep the Chicago police informed, for what it was worth. After, she called Kim.

If anything happened to her, it was most definitely connected to her father's work, she told them both. And therefore, to Berliner. Furthermore, they must look out for a bleached blond, heavy-set man, most likely Berliner's henchman. Peter Schultz's man.

CHAPTER TWENTY-THREE

Concealed behind the dark windows of his sedan, Hans watched Max and Julian, who were standing across the street and a few doors down.

He had followed Max to the Tube earlier. He had kept an eye out for the intruder from Lars's patisserie, but there had been no sign of him.

Max had approached a young man wearing a hat and false mustache at the ticket counter at the Tube. Hans had gathered that their destination was the Co-Operative Trust Bank.

Now, they were standing outside the bank making phone calls. So Lars had kept the papers in a safe there, most likely.

Neither Max nor her new friend had noticed Hans so far.

Max probably had the papers with her now.

Hans looked at his phone. He had several text messages informing him that Max was calling people from her mobile. She had seldom used her mobile until now.

He dialed a number and listened back to the calls she had made. He heard one she made to Ernst Frank. She was telling him that she had the papers. And to call the police. She mentioned Berliner, Peter Schultz, and Hans himself. Bleached blond indeed!

Hans put his phone away. *Smart girl*, he thought grudgingly. The good news, though, was that she now had what was probably the only remaining set of Hiram's papers.

He watched Max and her friend walk down the street. He started to follow them, wondering where he should confront her and relieve her of the papers, when he saw the thief from Lars's bakery approach Max.

The cheeky rat. So he was more than just a common thief.

Hans realized the thief was much closer to Max than he was. And he was an artist. Hans could only watch—half-helplessly, half-admiringly—as the thief waited until a small crowd formed around Max. He slid in, approached Max, and managed to neatly slice the backpack off her back.

The thief took a few slow strides away from Max then broke into a run. Max let out a scream. Her companion started to chase after the thief. Hans wondered if he should chase the thief on foot, but decided not to. He wasn't much of a runner. He started his car and wove through traffic, making sure he kept the thief within sight.

Hans managed to keep an eye on his target, who was now walking at a relaxed pace among the throngs of people on the busy Piccadilly Street. He had taken off his baseball cap and jacket and was barely recognizable. The backpack was hidden under the jacket. He looked like a student on his way to class.

The thief stopped at an intersection, waiting for the light to change. On the opposite side of the street, Hans parked his car and waited. The thief crossed the street. He was walking toward Hans.

Hans stepped forward.

"Excuse me," the thief said politely, not noticing Hans. Hans pulled out his .357 Magnum and stuck it at his waist.

"What the—"

Hans nudged the gun harder. "Turn around and get into that car."

The thief turned around with one frantic movement. He looked at Hans, and his expression changed from fear to recognition and utter terror.

"If it isn't the kid that murdered the old man in the bakery," Hans said calmly.

"I didn't kill him," the thief managed to say.

Hans shook his head and rolled his eyes.

The thief was stammering now. "He was already dying by the time my bag hit him. I...I'm not even sure my bag struck him."

"But it did, my friend. There was a trickle of blood running down his head." Hans indicated where by touching the boy's head with a forefinger. He clucked his tongue. "Very sad. The good neighborhood baker killed by a passing tourist. I even gave the police your description. American-looking tourist type left the area right around the time of the murder, I told them. Young, with greasy hair. Very suspicious."

CHAPTER TWENTY-FOUR

Aaron looked at the blond. He didn't sound like the joking kind. Aaron had kept an eye on the patisserie after he had seen Max leave the place looking pale, accompanied by a policewoman.

A stretcher bearing a covered body had pulled out of the store. This maniac had then appeared out of nowhere and started talking to the police. That meant Lars had died as a result of Aaron's unfortunate encounter with him. It was possible, Aaron thought now, that Blondie had killed the old man and had taken steps to pin the death on him! He tried to swallow, but his throat swelled. His breath came out in gasps.

Blondie went on. "I told them I didn't remember you too well. Just a vague idea. It all happened so quickly, I said. But a lineup might refresh my memory."

"What do you want?" Aaron said weakly.

"Get into the car."

"Not on your life," Aaron said.

"My life isn't the one in danger," Blondie said. "*Get in!*" Aaron got into the passenger seat. Blondie bound his hands with duct tape.

They drove for a while. His captor finally stopped on the side of a quiet street and killed the engine. "Hand me your bag, please."

"Not that," Aaron begged. "Please. It's for a job. It has nothing to do with the old man."

Blondie made a face and held the .357 up so Aaron was looking down its muzzle. Aaron promptly handed him Max's backpack.

Blondie asked him to open it. Inside were the research papers. He looked through them and put them in a nondescript black briefcase. Aaron glanced out the window. He watched longingly at a rattling truck laden with vegetables driving by. Other than that, there was no one, it seemed, for miles around. The sound of the wind broke the silence, slipping in through a small opening in the rear window with a low, ghostly whistle.

"What's your name?" Blondie said in a conversational tone.

Aaron hesitated. "Geoff."

Blondie tilted his head. "*Nein, nein.*"

He sucked at this stuff. "Aaron."

"Aah-run, who are you working for?" The blond looked straight ahead, his fingers drumming against the steering wheel.

"No one," Aaron said.

"*Ach!*" The blond held the gun against Aaron's head. "I have very little time for your nonsense. You have two choices. I can shoot you and toss you out there." He pointed outside. "And once the police find you, they will conclude that your accomplice killed you. They assume you had one. And besides, you are a killer—the unknown American tourist. Who cares if you were murdered?"

"My other choice?" Aaron was trying hard to keep his voice from sounding like a tinny squeak. For one horrible moment Aaron thought he might soil his pants. Thankfully, the moment passed.

"A flight back to USA. Now, who are you working for?"

Truth was, Aaron didn't know. Geoff had said he didn't, either. But this man wouldn't believe him. What should he say? He looked askance at the frightening, stocky man. A lie would buy him a bullet in his head. Better to stick to the truth. He tried to look sincere. "I really don't know," he said.

The blond struck Aaron's head with the butt of his gun.

Aaron touched his temple. It felt sticky. His fingertips were moist and bright red. "Listen—I'm so regretting taking this job, mister; you can consider me officially frightened shitless. I don't want to die. This was supposed to be easy money. All I want is to get away from London before you...they...pin the murder of the old fart on me."

"I'm getting tired of you." Blondie's voice was ice. The gun was at Aaron's temple once more.

It was the most terrifying object Aaron had ever felt against his skin. He closed his eyes, expecting his brains to splatter across the seat. He even started to pray.

"Last chance," Blondie said softly, "who hired you to steal the papers?"

Aaron threw up his hands. He was thoroughly ashamed, but he could do nothing to stop the wracking gasps of fear he was producing. "A contact brought me the job—I don't think even he knows who I'm working for. He couldn't do it, so here I am." He closed his eyes. Magically, his sobbing slowed. He felt calmer.

"Okay," Blondie said. "I believe you."

Aaron sensed the absence of cold pressure against his temple. He opened his eyes.

Blondie started the car. "Now I will escort you home." He sounded almost kind.

Aaron nodded. Visions of his big payday had disappeared into smoke, but at least it wasn't his life that had gone *poof*.

The blond took Aaron to his hostel, where Aaron packed in record time, then dropped him off at the airport. "Hope we never meet again," Blondie said. "Be smart and leave now."

Aaron wondered what he was going to tell his client. This might be a good time to call the emergency number. Between a paper cut and a knife wound, Geoff had said. Fuck it. This was now Geoff's problem.

He made his way to the check-in desk.

As he waited in line, he realized the finality of his situation. He was going home—alive—but he was also going to have to forget the big payoff, his ticket to a new life.

The brass ring that had dangled so close had been yanked away.

CHAPTER TWENTY-FIVE

Julian and Max sat outside the bank. Not speaking. They were both staring at the street. Max grunted and stomped her foot a few times, never as ashamed of herself as she was now.

Sure, the thief had taken her by surprise. He had cut her backpack and made off with it, sprinting like a pro. But they ought to have caught up with him. Julian had given chase for a while, but eventually his pace had slowed. Max had valiantly followed, but she could only run so fast.

"Why have you slowed down?" She had gasped, pointing in the direction the thief was going. In seconds, he had disappeared.

Julian had pointed to his new shoes. "I can't run any faster...I just can't," he cried. "These damn shoes have clasped my ankles and toes in a vise-like grip."

"Well, neither can I!" she had screamed, pointing at her quivering legs. "Oh damn, damn! He's gone, the thief is gone!"

She was too slow, too fat, and too foolish to even give decent chase to a stupid thief. What hope in hell did she have of finding her father's killer?

"That's it." She jumped up. "I need a donut or something."

"A donut?" Julian asked incredulously. "Are you kidding me?"

Max started walking toward a coffee shop.

Julian walked by her side, wincing with every step. "I'm trying to appreciate this urgency for the donut, but can we please slow down?"

"I cannot believe you wore new shoes for this trip." Max snarled. She tried not to think about how much she had admired them when he had first arrived.

"I wasn't aware I'd be expected to chase after goons on the streets of London," Julian murmured angrily. "Goddamn it, Max! Slow down."

"What *did* you expect when I told you about Lars?"

"I thought you were overreacting." He threw up his hands. "You are a bit emotional. Overwrought."

"Overreacting!" Max exclaimed. "Overwrought! Really?"

"Yes, yes, yes." His voice rose, his face turning red. "You have said so yourself. You're not exactly the bravest person. You didn't even want to do any of this. Forget it. I thought—" He clenched his fists and walked away.

They were at the coffee shop now. Max walked in, leaving Julian fuming outside. She stepped out with two glazed donuts and began eating one. The sugar calmed her nerves.

Minutes later, Julian said, "Look, I'm sorry I lost my temper." He didn't look at all sorry. "But I thought when you said Lars had died… well, I thought it was possible that maybe he just died naturally. You must admit you're very stressed."

Max let out a low groan. Her eyes bored into the ground. She sat down on the pavement.

Julian sat beside her. "I have no experience with people getting killed, so I put that bit out of my mind," he said. "I mean, who imagines murder and spy games when someone asks for help? I'm only an associate professor of history, not Indiana Jones, sweetheart!"

Max's eyes narrowed. "You think I'm exposed to murder everyday? I'm a cook. *Sweetheart*! Did you forget everything I told you about my father? And that German who attacked us? Or did you think I was making it all up in my hysteria?"

Julian grabbed the other donut from her just as she was about to eat it.

"Hey!" she cried, but let him have it. She stared down the street for a while. From the corner of her eye, she glanced at Julian. He was munching on the donut with ferocious glee. His cheeks were flushed an angry pink and his eyebrows were furrowed.

Max began dusting donut crumbs off her lap. It occurred to her that just by being here, Julian was doing her an enormous, totally unnecessary favor.

She touched his arm lightly. He turned to her, surprised. "I'm sorry," she said. "You have taken the time to be here for me, and look at how awful I'm being to you." What was wrong with her? She had no right to be mean to this man.

Julian's frown melted into a smile. He let out a laugh.

"What?" Max said.

He took out a handkerchief and wiped around her mouth.

"Stop taking so many liberties, friend," she said, not meaning it.

Making a peace sign with one hand, Julian took a big bite of his donut. Half his false mustache came unglued and hung along his cheek.

Max let out a giggle.

"What?"

She yanked the mustache off his face and threw it away.

"Ouch!" he cried. "I apologize too. Friends?"

Max nodded. "Did you get a good look at this guy?" she said. "We could give the police a description."

Julian shook his head and sighed. "He was dressed in jeans and a T-shirt. Very ordinary. Slim. Other than that, I have no memory."

"Do you think it may have been the blond?"

Julian shrugged. "He didn't look very distinctive. I'd say he was thin. You said the blond stood out—heavy-set, short, right? Maybe this was his associate."

Max shivered. How was she ever going to sleep at night again? Maybe not until this was over, whenever that might be. Over. How comforting that sounded. Finished, wrapped up. That's where she wanted to be. At the end of the line.

"Isn't it strange how adventures are wonderful when they are over?" Max said wistfully.

Julian stood up and held out his hand. "Come." Max started to protest, but he put a finger to his lips. She took his hand.

They walked for a long time, eventually crossing the Thames over the Millennium Bridge. At the end of the bridge, just below them, an accordion player was surrounded by a group of people. He was playing an upbeat tune. Some people clapped, a couple even danced.

Max and Julian continued to walk by the river toward the Tower of London.

"Do you want to tour it?" Julian pointed to the tower.

Max thought about Anne Boleyn. "Not today," she said.

A few dancers were breakdancing to eighties music on one side of the street. On the other were throngs of tourists posing for pictures or just hanging out. Beyond, not a hundred feet away, were the locals, seemingly unaware of the spectacular—if somewhat gruesome—symbol of history, the great Tower of London, that stood not far from them.

Julian checked his watch. "It's almost dinner time," he said. He led her to a French bistro on a narrow street.

The *maître d'* seated them at a table with a view of the river. Max studied her menu. Julian didn't open his. She closed the menu and smiled. "Okay what are we having?"

A waiter came by. Julian asked for a bottle of the house red and two orders of the beef bourguignon.

The wine arrived. Max picked up her glass and took a sip. She watched the sky turn from cerulean blue to a brilliant pink. Voices rose and fell around them. Julian drank the wine as if it were water. "I hope you don't mind." He slipped his feet out of his shoes and let out a soft cry. He took off his socks, too. His feet were covered with blisters.

Max watched him wince in obvious pain and started to laugh.

"You think this is funny! Look at my feet? They're bleeding!"

Before Max could answer, the beef arrived. The waiter fussed about their plates and served them with great care.

"*Bon appétit*," he said, and left.

Max took a bite. The meat melted in her mouth. The sauce was divine—velvety, peppery. *Mmm.* This almost made up for the bank fiasco.

Julian said, "One of the best-kept secrets in London—this bistro. The wine I brought over the other day? It's from here."

Max gave him a grateful smile. *Thank you*, she mouthed.

Julian ate slowly, savoring every mouthful. He sipped his wine and sent her a smile now and again.

But the magic couldn't last forever. She put down her fork. "What do we do now? Maybe you should go back. I'll just sit here and wallow in my shame."

Julian shook his head. "You give up too easily. We'll figure something out. Maybe Lars told someone else about all this. We just have to find out who that might be."

Max didn't think Lars would have told anyone. But it was adorable how optimistic Julian was being.

Max began to take another bite when Julian held her hand, not allowing her to bring the fork to her mouth. "Not so fast. Every morsel must be carefully considered. Do you Americans even taste what goes down your throat? Now we shall talk only about this beef for a while, and maybe dessert."

Max laughed and shook her head no.

"You have to have dessert." Julian winked at her. Max looked at him. He had a small dimple in his chin. She wanted to reach out and touch it.

"What is it?" He took out a handkerchief and began dabbing his face.

Max smiled. "You have a dimple in your chin, too. I didn't notice that one before."

"*Ah dinnae hae* any dimples," he said, putting a forkful of beef into his mouth.

"You do," she said with a giggle. "There, there, and there." she pointed to his cheeks and chin.

"Here?" he asked, pointing to the wrong part of his chin.

No, she kept saying and laughing. But he couldn't seem to find them. Finally she touched the three places.

"See, I got you to caress me." Julian raised and lowered his eyebrows like a clown. Max shook her head and laughed.

The waiter arrived and whisked their plates away. Julian asked him if they had the *Clafoutis aux Cerises*.

"Cherry custard cake," Julian said. "A trip to heaven."

"Really?"

"Yes," Julian said, "and when the bill comes, it's a quick trip back to earth."

Max giggled once more.

Dessert arrived and was polished off. The bill was paid. It was time to go.

"I want this moment to last forever," Max said wistfully. "Julian…" She pushed her chair back and stood up. So did he. She moved close to him.

Julian inhaled deeply. "You smell of strawberries," he said. "And some perspiration." Max giggled and punched him lightly. He was making her giggle like an idiot. It was too sweetly cruel. "And garlic and cherries," he whispered.

Max pursed her lips. "I'm sorry about yelling at you." She fidgeted with her hair. "I should never have even called you."

Julian put an arm around her shoulder and gave a little squeeze.

They held hands all the way back to the hotel.

Max wanted to ask Julian if he had a girlfriend. But he surely wouldn't hide that from her, would he? Would he be holding her hand this way if there was someone? Max felt an urge to strangle this mystery girlfriend. An image of a svelte female began to form in her mind. Part of her was afraid to find out if someone like that existed in his life.

Bet I could snap her like a twig, she thought.

***

Julian was wondering if he should call his girlfriend. Raquel had told him she was going to Mongolia to broker a deal with small village banks. Leveraged buyouts, mergers maybe—they all sounded the same to him. She was going to be "offline"—her words—for a week. "We can talk when I'm in Beijing," she had said. Still, perhaps he should call anyway, or she'd be mad that he didn't even try. Women. They tell you something. They expect something else.

He hadn't even mentioned Raquel to Max yet. And here he was, getting way too attached to Max. He shouldn't have come to London, but now that he was here, he really ought to tell her.

But first, he had to call Raquel.

"Might you know what time it is in Mongolia?" he asked Max.

"Mongolia!" she exclaimed. "You're crazy." Max burst out laughing.

CHAPTER TWENTY-SIX

Back at the hotel, they were at Max's door. It had been a long day. The weight of the day's events was thick in the air.

"Thanks for dinner," Max said. She opened the door and stepped inside her room. Julian almost followed, but she started to close the door.

"Good night," she said, turning away.

"Good night," he replied. And left for his room.

Max held on to the door, watching him go down the stairs, wondering if playing hard to get had been a good thing to do. She was exhausted. Still, it would have been nice to cuddle with someone who seemed to care. So much. With a sigh, she closed her door and bolted it.

The next morning, Julian knocked on Max's door. Max let him in just when the phone started ringing. Max answered it.

"Max?" A German-sounding voice said.

"Uncle Ernst?" she said eagerly.

"My name isn't important. But what I have to say is. Forget this whole thing. You know what happened to Lars, to your father. We have the papers now. From the bank, remember? Leave now, and we will forget you exist."

"And if I don't?" Max's voice rose.

"Oh Maxine," the voice said almost gently. He pronounced her name Mah-xine like Opa used to do. It was altogether frightening to hear it said that way by this stranger. "I'm sure you don't want to find out." The line clicked dead.

"Who was it?" Julian asked.

Max let the phone fall from her hands. She covered her face with her hands for a while until she found her voice. "Enough," she said. "We're going back to Chicago. I'm not getting us both killed over some stupid papers we don't even have now." She started throwing her things into her suitcase.

Julian followed her around the room as she gathered her stuff. "What did this person say? For God's sake, Max, who was it?"

Max continued to mutter, "I hate Lars for putting me through this. I had a good life! A lonely, sometimes pathetic life, but a safe one. Until Lars came into it." She picked up a skirt and flung it across the room at her suitcase. "And now I'm left with some ancient curse and the mystery of my father's death. I'm not Sherlock Holmes. No sir." She collected her toothbrush and toilet bag, "Coming here was a horrible idea." Holding up the toothbrush in her hand, she began to laugh hysterically.

"When you came along, I thought, 'Oh, with his help we can do this.' What an idiot I am." She gave Julian a harassed look. "We're ordinary people, you and I. We have no business being here. And so we leave tomorrow." She tried to close her suitcase, but it was too full. She slammed her fist against it.

Julian began to pace the room.

When the tiny suitcase sprang open for the fifth time, Max began to cry.

Julian watched her for a while. "What did he say exactly? Don't shut me out now, Max."

Max's tone softened. "He said he has the papers. Which means that our thief from yesterday must have been Berliner's man, too. 'Go home,' he said, just like someone told Lars. Yesterday, wasn't it? Feels like a lifetime ago. Maybe it was the same fellow, same gang of fellows. Who knows, Julian? My father is dead. Lars is dead. Let's leave before it's our turn."

Julian continued to pace.

Max felt like a volcano about to erupt. Her chest grew warm with rage at the man on the phone. How dare this stranger threaten her when they had managed to come this far? The gall of the man. She kicked her suitcase and tried to hide the searing pain that began running through her toes.

She stormed outside the hotel and looked around.

"Hey!" she shouted, "You…you fuh…fuckkking German…" She hesitated. "*Arschloch*!" she cried, "You Deutsch asshole. Where the hell are you?"

CHAPTER TWENTY-SEVEN

Hans was in his car. He had relayed his threat to Maxine not long before and now here she was outside the hotel, making a commotion. He rolled down his window. She stumbled on a step. Hans smirked.

"I know you're watching us!" she screamed.

People avoided her as they walked past the hotel.

"I'm not frightened. Not anymore. I thought I'd hide under my sheets until you went away, but I know you won't go anywhere."

Maxine's friend and an older man in uniform tried to bring her in, politely at first, then by force. But she was resisting them.

"How much time do you have for this, huh?" Maxine shouted. "I have my whole life. So kill me now if you like. Do it. Go ahead." She put her hands on her hips and growled. "Make my day."

The two men whisked her in right then.

Hans wondered what he should do. Had Herr Schultz known he might hesitate to kill in cold blood and therefore used someone else—a contract killer perhaps—to finish off Hiram Rosen? Had he thought Hans didn't have it in him? Was he testing him this time around? But he had also told him to exercise caution. For the sake of the company, he had said. Was he serious, or was it merely a round-about way to get him riled up enough to kill? Herr Schultz could be very cryptic at times.

If Maxine Rosen died now, the problem was gone forever, wasn't it? But there were those phone calls she had made. And this boy-friend. Killing her might make him even more determined to retrieve the papers. The old Jew Ernst Frank had known the family forever. He would be sure to name Berliner if Maxine was killed. And if that happened, Hans might be made the scapegoat.

It was apparent that she had no access to another set of papers, not at the moment anyway. And what she said made sense. He could not tail her forever. There was no need to stick around anymore.

After all, the job was done. Lars was dead. Hiram's last set of papers was safe with him. He had bugs on everyone's phones. He could travel at a moment's notice.

Hans started his car and drove away.

CHAPTER TWENTY-EIGHT

Julian led Max back to her room.

"I'm not sorry," Max said. "It felt good. Maybe the German even heard it."

Julian didn't respond. He closed Max's door.

"I'm so ashamed that we're going home empty-handed," Max said, fingering her bags.

"Don't be." Julian put her suitcase by the door.

Max grabbed his arm. "Julian, tell me, why are you here? Why do you make love to me with your eyes, your chocolate-covered Scottish words, your expressions, and your tantalizing little squeezes and touches? Huh? Why did you kiss me that night in Chicago?"

Julian turned away and ran his hands through his large brown curls. "I don't know. I don't know!"

Max touched his face. "Am I just a summer flirtation?"

Julian took her in his arms. "Would I risk my life for a summer flirtation?"

Max closed her eyes. In a few hours, they would be back in Chicago. She may not see Julian again. And he would have no reason to see her now that her quest had come to a whimper of an end. She leaned her head against his shoulder. "Thank you for coming," she whispered.

He brought his face close to hers. His breath felt warm and fragrant against her lips.

And then…it couldn't be helped. She leaned forward and kissed him. He hesitated at first, but slowly gave in to her lips. Reluctantly, they eased away from each other. Max ran her tongue over her mouth, savoring the sweet, salty taste of Julian.

Max took a deep breath. "James Dean said, 'live as if you will die today.'" She started to unbutton her blouse. "Since that almost became a reality for me this week, one thing I don't want to regret is not doing this."

Julian put his hand on hers, his eyes wide and mortified. "No!" he cried. He kissed her on her mouth, her eyes, her lips, and her forehead. "Not like this. I can resist anything but temptation. You are that, Maxine Rosen. And yet, no, not like this."

Max closed her eyes. He had quoted Oscar Wilde. She loved Oscar Wilde. It wasn't fair.

She let out a long, melancholic sigh. He was right. This was no way to start something with this lovely man. A man so darling that setting eyes on him caused an ache in her chest. Saying his name started a lump in her throat. Hearing him speak made her feel like she was sitting on a lush green hill listening to the lilting notes of a flock of bagpipes. Gosh, he had turned her into a total sap!

Julian pulled her close and wrapped his arms tight around her. Max nuzzled her face in his neck and tried to commit to memory the contours of his lean, sinewy body against hers.

"What happens when we go back?" she asked.

Julian pulled away from her.

Max felt a tightening in her chest. "I am the unluckiest girl in the world. I have failed my father and I'm going to lose you the minute we set foot in Chicago." Not that she ever had him, to be fair.

"You should be proud that you even came this far," Julian said. "We lost what we came here for, yes, but you took on some rather big guns. Your father would have been proud to know how hard you tried. Don't forget, he didn't even want you to be involved in the first place."

Julian hadn't said she wouldn't lose him.

And so, none of his words made her feel better.

The fact that she had failed her father, perhaps even her grand-father, was the bitter pill she was going to have to swallow and live with every single day.

That was the only truth she was leaving with.

CHAPTER TWENTY-NINE

Aaron's flight was indefinitely delayed. He was flying stand-by, thanks to Blondie.

This was the pathetic result of this sojourn. No papers. No pay. He would have to go back to working the rush hour.

This thing, whatever it was, was important enough to attract the German muscle in addition to bumbling Maxine Rosen and her boy-friend. That meant big stakes. Why should he not get a small part of it?

He sat in a nondescript coffee shop with a black coffee and a slice of cake for company. He had tried calling Geoff, but Maggie said he wasn't available. He had called the number he had been given in case of an emergency and left a message. No one had called back yet. He looked at his cell phone for the millionth time. Nothing. He played with some cake crumbs.

His phone began to ring.

"Aaron here," he said.

"You have a problem?" a metallic voice responded.

Aaron collected his thoughts. His initial plan had been to inform his unknown employer about his failure. But now that he had had time to reconsider…

Truth was, Blondie or not, the brass ring was too close to let go of so easily. After all, he had been kept alive. That meant he was small potatoes to these people.

Aaron hardened his voice. "I just spent the night in the airport after being held at gunpoint by a German psychopath. That wasn't part of the deal—"

The voice interrupted, "Do you have the papers?"

"I did, until Mr. Psycho took them."

"Explain," the voice said.

"He wanted to know who I was working for."

The voice chuckled. "I bet he did."

Aaron was glad the mood was light. "Of course I didn't tell him, since, well, I have no idea. But I want my promised wages for all my pain and suffering."

There was silence at the other end. "Where are the papers now?"

"I have no idea."

"What about the marks?"

"They're still here, so I'm thinking—"

"Don't think. They're going back to Chicago. You go back, too. And listen carefully—if you lost the papers, so did they, right? They won't give up without a fight. If you want to get paid, we want whatever they get their hands on. Wherever they get it from."

"Understood. And since the danger factor has gone up several points, I want double." Aaron bit his tongue. Had he gone too far?

There was a long pause. The man had hung up. Damn.

But the voice said, "Fine. But only if you get us what we're looking for."

Aaron put his phone away, got up, and stretched.

He walked around the terminal, unable to decide whether even double the money was worth taking on Blondie once more.

CHAPTER THIRTY

Max's apartment
Chicago

Max sat at her dining table, pen and pad in front of her. Usually the week's menus flowed out of her head like water from a tap, but today, every idea was frozen solid.

Pasta, she wrote, and promptly thought about the pasta primavera she had made for Julian not long ago. She wondered how he was.

They had landed in Chicago the night before and Julian had left her with a long, lingering kiss on her lips. *A goodbye kiss*, Max thought with a growing sense of doom.

Max took a cab home, burdened by the weight of exhaustion, defeat, and loss.

She had slept for twelve straight hours and was up now and trying to work. She ought to call Kim and tell her she was back. She found herself dialing Julian's number instead. "Please leave a message for Dr. Julian McIntosh," the message said.

Max hung up.

Julian had said he would be busy catching up on work since he had left some important things half done when she had summoned him to London.

Max called Kim.

"Welcome back!" Kim said. "Did you have a good trip?"

"Not bad," Max said, not wanting to get into it. "How are things here?"

"Excellent. We are good for this week's lunches, but I hope you're working on menus to email out. And we also need to prepare for the Jewish Students Awareness Association presentation."

"Great," Max said, trying to work up some enthusiasm.

"Sounds like you're jet-lagged. How about this? I went berry picking this weekend, and guess what, I have a ton of blueberries I'm going to drop off at your place. That should cheer you up."

Max smiled. "I'll make Mama's blueberry pie, and maybe a compote for next week's lunches. A blueberry gelato maybe! Can we deliver gelato?"

With a laugh, Kim promised to have the blueberries delivered to Max's front desk by one of their delivery interns.

Two hours later, Max was scrambling to find her mother's blueberry pie recipe. She knew she had it written somewhere. She was pretty sure about the proportions and method, but Mama had a few hints that Max didn't always remember. The recipe wasn't in any of her myriad of notebooks, not even with her precious cuttings.

When she couldn't find it in the usual places, she opened her mother's journal. Mama had mentioned the pie there as something she made on special occasions. Maybe she had written the recipe, too.

She carefully began going over every entry.

The entries began to get less and less legible as Mama's illness grew worse. Max squinted, unable to make out many of the words. She turned to the last entry, planning to work her way backwards. She glanced over it, then turned to the previous one.

Wait a minute, something wasn't right. She flipped back to the last entry in the book. It was dated November 1982.

How could that be? Mama passed away in September. Max started reading the notes her mother had written that day. There was a list of hospital expenses. *Large bills will follow when I'm gone. Is that all I will leave my family with?* it said in bold letters.

The next line said, *Enjoyed watching Sneakers with Max today.*

Max smiled. *Sneakers* was one of her favorite films. How delicious was Robert Redford in it? She tried to recall the day she and Mama had seen the movie. But it just wouldn't come to mind. She could remember them watching *My Fair Lady* together. Tons of times. It was their favorite film to watch. But *Sneakers* she had always associated with her father. They had watched it a few times after Mama died.

Hmmm.

Max shook her head. Was she looking for mysteries where none existed? This whole business with Lars and Papa's research had done her in. A seemingly innocuous—albeit odd—entry in her mother's book of accounts was sending her into a tizzy for no reason.

Still.

She turned on her computer.

There was that new movie database. What was it? Oh yes, imdb. com. She checked when *Sneakers* was released.

1992.

But that was impossible.

Mama had been gone for ten years by 1992! Was there another famous movie by that name? There wasn't.

She looked through the other entries in Mama's book. Nothing stood out. They were all correctly dated and had no noteworthy information. All except this last one. Dated wrongly and with an impossible movie reference.

Max went to her movie collection and pulled out the VHS tape of *Sneakers*. It had been a while since she had seen the movie. At worst, she'd enjoy watching it again. At best, well, maybe it would mean something.

She turned it on and found herself getting lost in the adventures of Robert Redford as Marty Bishop and his motley crew.

The credits started to roll. Usually she never watched the credits of familiar films. This time she did, her heart beating hard, not knowing what to expect, but expecting something anyway.

In the middle of the music acknowledgements, the tape became fuzzy and her father's face came on screen.

"I knew it!" Max exclaimed, pumping a fist in the air. She leaned forward.

"Hey there, Max," her father said, looking animated and handsome in jeans and a purple rugby T-shirt. He was sitting where she was on the couch. "Looks like you found the entry in your mother's diary. If I am around, talk to me when you find this. But there's a chance I may not be. If I'm not, honey, I want you to know that I love you. I also want you to do something for me."

Max felt her throat grow thick and her eyes sting.

"Tell Ernst that I love him," her father was saying, his face beaming, his large eyes dark and alert. "And his matzo ball soup. It was awful, but I loved it. And if you see Kevin, ask him if he still likes pea soup. Despite everything, I miss the chap. He meant well. I know this now."

Papa held up his hands in a peace sign and said, "I'll love you Max, forever in time." He leaned forward and switched off the camera.

The tape became fuzzy again, and the credits continued.

How very odd, Max thought, wiping away her tears.

But instead of being overcome by gloom, Max felt recharged. If she had found this tape before she met Lars, she'd have thought nothing of it. Well, she'd have cried an ocean of tears, but other than that, nothing. She'd have definitely told Uncle Ernst that Papa had loved his matzo ball soup. Uncle Ernst always lamented that he could never make it good enough for Papa.

She dialed his number.

"Uncle Ernst," she said when he answered. "I just found the strangest tape made by Papa. He asked me to tell you that he loved your matzo ball soup. Do you think it means something other than that? It's such an ordinary thing to say, but given all that has happened…"

Uncle Ernst let out a gasp. "Oh Max, Max!" he cried. Remember I told you Hiram was supposed to give me a copy of his research in case something happened to him? He told me that this would be his code word if you ever needed it! That he liked matzo ball soup." He started murmuring something unintelligible.

"Wait a minute, you were supposed to have a copy of the research?"

"Yes, which is why I was surprised that Lars Lindstrom had it. I told you that, didn't I?" His voice had started shaking.

"I guess you did. I didn't mean to upset you. Should I come downstairs?"

"No, no, I'll be fine. I was just going to the library and later to the store to pick up some fruit. Now, about Hiram, what were you saying?"

"It's all right, dear. You go do what you need to. I'll call you later." Max hung up.

She went back to the tape, rewound it, and watched her father's message once more.

Kevin Forsyth. Pea soup.

Max called her father's lawyer and got a number for Kevin Forsyth from him.

She dialed. "Here goes nothing," she muttered to herself.

"Hello," a female voice said, "Allied Research partners. How may I direct your call?"

"I…well, I need to speak to Kevin Forsyth."

"He is in India, I'm afraid."

"It's urgent; I need to speak to him immediately. My father Hiram Rosen used to be his business partner. Could I call him in India?"

"Please hold for a minute." Muzak poured into Max's ears.

Max waited for several minutes with the phone held away from her ear, her excitement growing with every second.

The woman came back on. "I have a cell phone number. He can take your call in India if you call right away."

Max hung up, suddenly realizing that she had used her home phone to make the call. Could the Berliner people still be listening?

Damn. Uncle Ernst's phone might be tapped, too.

What a pain.

She made her way to the main apartment office on the third floor. The building manager was a nice enough guy. He might let her use his phone.

Thankfully, he was in. Max told him her phone wasn't working and that she needed to call someone urgently in India.

He graciously agreed and left her alone.

Max dialed Kevin's cell. Voice mail. She hesitated. Should she hang up? Quickly she said, "Mr. Forsyth. This is Max, Hiram Rosen's daughter. He asked me to call and ask you if you still like pea soup. I have a feeling this might be important." She hung up. There, that was enough information but not too much.

Now what? She returned home and tried to work on her menus but just couldn't. She watched her father's video message a few more times.

The ending was odd. The peace sign. Papa was not the sort to do that at all. The various movements of the sixties and seventies had escaped him completely, he had often said proudly. And "forever in time." He would never say something soppy like that.

Max picked up a pen and paper.

She wrote down *mother's diary* and *matzo ball soup* and made check marks by them. Next she wrote *pea soup* and *peace*. Finally, she wrote *forever in time*. Her mother's diary had done its bit, Max suspected. Matzo ball soup had been addressed. And pea soup. Well, when Kevin called, that would be taken care of.

Peace.

With a loud whoop, Max jumped up. She rushed to her desk and picked up her copy of the Gita. Of course. *Peace* had been underlined and Papa had said he hoped she would never have to find out why.

This meant that the key to decoding the papers must have something to do with the Gita.

Max closed her eyes. She needed lunch.

And she craved Julian.

An hour later, she and Julian were huddled with Max's Gita on the table between them at a *taqueria* just outside the University of Chicago campus.

"So," she said, biting into a savory beef taco, "what do you think? Kevin hasn't called back, but the word peace must have something to do with this." She patted the Gita.

"Maybe your father wants us to find a certain chapter and verse," Julian said. "That may be a clue."

"But there are so many." Max put her hands on her cheeks and leaned forward on her elbows.

Julian nodded. "No more clues anywhere?"

"Forever in time," Max said. "That might mean something."

Julian checked his watch. "Speaking of time, I need to get back, I'm afraid."

Max grabbed his wrist. "Time! A specific time, maybe?"

"It's possible. But what?"

"No idea," Max said. "Could I wait with you while you finish your work?"

Julian smiled. "That will not do at all. Come on." He took her arm. "My work can wait."

They went back to Max's apartment.

Julian started looking around.

"What are you looking for, Sherlock?" Max chuckled.

"Clues, Watson," he said. "I have a feeling this is right under your nose and has been for a while."

Max glanced up as she closed the door to the apartment. Right above her was the cuckoo clock, frozen at 11:32.

"Julian," she whispered. "11:32 mean anything to you?"

He went to her. "Your father did this?"

Max nodded. "It was his clock."

"It must mean something." He opened the Gita.

Max's phone rang. "Hello?" she said.

"Kevin Forsyth here," a deep voice said.

"It's Kevin," she whispered to Julian.

"Hi. Let me call you right back," she told Kevin.

"Okay. On my cell please."

Max and Julian ran down to the building manager's office and used his phone to dial Kevin. "I'm going to get evicted when he gets the phone bill," Max said once the building manager left them.

"Mr. Forsyth, Max here. My phone may not be safe, so I needed to find a different line to call from."

"What's this about?" he asked politely.

"Did you get my message?"

"Yes."

"Does it mean anything to you?"

"It might."

Boy, he was being cagey. Max spent a few minutes telling him about Lars, the papers, and her fruitless trip to London.

Kevin sighed. "Oh dear," he said, his voice becoming friendlier. "I'm afraid you'll have to come to India to see me."

"I can't do that," Max said with a laugh. "I'll just wait until you get back."

"I'm here for the next six to eight months."

"You have the papers?" Max said.

"I do."

"But father didn't trust you," she blurted.

"Your father didn't want to do business with me, Maxine," Kevin said. "But he trusted me with his life. Hiram was a painfully honest businessman. I, on the other hand, was more grounded."

"He said you cheated him," Max said flatly.

"I doubt he used those words," Kevin said, completely unruffled. "Let me tell you what happened. Our company had run into trouble with clients not paying on time, and we had cash flow issues as a result. I wanted to deal with the problem by greasing a few palms, using tougher collection methods. But Hiram would have none of it. He and I started arguing about it. Finally, Hiram decided he could not stomach the life of a businessman and walked away. That's it."

"I see," Max said acerbically.

"Look, we were both upset. I lashed out at him, accused him of being a naive fool and of leaving me alone in a burning house of cards. But Hiram didn't yield. He was disillusioned. I was forced to declare bankruptcy. We didn't speak for a while after that. Some years later, Hiram called on me. He wanted me to have his research. He was able to get me a copy before I left for Kenya, but he didn't give me the key and pill samples. Things suddenly started getting more difficult for him. Now I was still in Kenya, so I asked him to wait until I returned for him to give them to me, but he said he couldn't risk waiting that long. He had to send them someplace safe. I gave him the address of my PO box in Manhattan, but the package never reached me. Luckily, the research is still safe with me. Hiram asked that I keep it until you called for it."

"If I didn't call? What was supposed to happen then?"

"Eventually, I'd have called you. Hiram left that bit to me."

Max was impressed with Kevin's no-nonsense manner. It made sense that her idealistic, often emotional father had admired this man for his worldliness. "So, does 'pea soup' mean something?" she asked.

"Yes!"

"Is that the key to decode the research?"

"It could be. But I suspect that the key that never reached me may be a different one. Look, I don't want to discuss this any more over the phone. Maybe I'll see you in Hyderabad."

"Hyd—" Max began but Kevin hung up.

She looked at Julian, who had turned pale.

"I know what 11:32 is," he whispered. "It's a chapter and verse reference from the Gita. This one."

श्रीभगवानुवाच
कालोऽस्मि लोकक्षयकृत्प्रवृद्धो
लोकान् समाहर्तुमिह प्रवृत्तः ।
ऋतेऽपि त्वां न भविष्यन्ति सर्वे
येऽवस्थिताः प्रत्यनीकेषु योधाः ॥ ३२ ॥

"Okay." Max sat down beside him.

Julian's face seemed tense with unanswered questions.

"Get your grandfather's diary. First page." Julian's voice turned soft. "It's the same verse, Max. I've been an idiot."

Max looked at the verse written in her grandfather's diary.

"This verse has been translated many ways, but given the context, I think this might be the translation we want," Julian said. "*I am become death. Destroyer of worlds*," he read aloud from her Gita.

"It's what J. Robert Oppenheimer said when he witnessed the Trinity nuclear test."

"That doesn't sound very promising," Max said.

"The joint work of the scientists at Los Alamos resulted in the first artificial nuclear explosion near Alamogordo in early 1945, on a site that Oppenheimer codenamed Trinity," Julian said. "Apparently, Oppenheimer quoted this verse during an interview later on when he spoke of the incident. Point is, he knew he had been responsible for something that could destroy the world."

Max lifted her tear-filled eyes to the ceiling. "It's what I suspected." Julian took her hand. Max went on, "If...if Opa had this verse on the front page of his diary, he must have believed he had done something really bad. He found heroin instead of aspirin."

They sat still for several minutes.

"So is this the key to decode the research? The key that Lars never got?" Julian asked.

"Papa sent it to Kevin, too," Max said. "The key and pill samples. But he didn't get them, either. Berliner must have stolen his package, too." She got up, put her hands on her hips, and exhaled deeply. "I have to go to India."

She looked at Julian. His mouth tightened, his eyes narrowed and darted all over the room. Max could almost hear him thinking hard. About what, she wondered.

He went to her and brought his forehead close to hers. "I guess we both do," he whispered.

She pulled away and looked at him sharply. "Julian, I need to know something. I couldn't bring myself to ask before—I was afraid of your answer, but I need to know. Are you seeing someone else? Because if you are, leave now and never see me again."

After a moment's hesitation, he looked straight into her eyes. "I'm coming with you," he said firmly.

Max wondered for a second or two about his hesitation and his oblique response but decided to put it out of her mind. She threw her arms around him and kissed him. "Be careful, Professor McIntosh," she said. "I'm very fragile right now, and I may be falling in love with you."

CHAPTER THIRTY-ONE

Rajiv Gandhi International Airport
Hyderabad, India

Aaron stood close to the airport exit and watched Max and Julian climb into the shuttle for the Hyatt Regency Hotel. He had been cooling his heels in Chicago, trying to accept that he may have lost the chance for some big bucks, when he had been asked to make preparations to leave for India. Max was going there. The papers were sure to be there, his employer had said. *Double pay*, Aaron had repeated to himself like a mantra. He had failed in London, but he was not going to be made a fool of twice.

The German. Aaron hadn't seen *him* yet. He looked around, half-expecting him to leap out from behind every potted palm and stone sculpture. Blondie would definitely be here. His employer had told him to expect it.

He stepped out of the airport, his fist wrapped tightly around the strap of his backpack. A gush of hot air hit him and, for a few seconds, half his body was in the cool comfort of the air-conditioned baggage area and the other half engulfed by Hyderabad's intense heat. He had expected to be greeted by cows and snake charmers. Instead the airport looked like most airports in the States. Globalization, he thought with a grin.

His shuttle arrived. The ride to the Hyderabad Royal Star Hotel was a short one. It wasn't much better than staying at the Y, but it was a stone's throw away from the Hyatt where Max and her boyfriend were staying.

CHAPTER THIRTY-TWO

Max put down the receiver. She had just informed Kevin that she and Julian had landed in Hyderabad.

"See you in two hours," Kevin had said. Two hours was a long time. Her nerves were frayed and raw. She wanted *and* didn't want to know the contents of the research. She wasn't sure which desire was stronger. All she knew was that the two feelings were tearing her apart. She had pumped herself up about doing this, finishing what she had started, but part of her still wished she were back in her kitchen in Chicago.

Julian pulled her close. "We should be singing a Bollywood song and dancing around those beautiful trees. You'd look perfect in a wet red chiffon sari, gyrating your hips against mine—"

Max let out a grunt of irritation.

Julian held up his palms. "Okay, okay. They say we have to try the lamb biryani here."

Max kissed his palms and nuzzled her face against his. "It's frightening how well you know me," she whispered.

Julian kissed her forehead. He said in a low, seductive voice, "Garlicky. Spicy hot. Meat that melts like butter in your mouth. Fragrant with saffron…"

Her mouth started to water. She moaned. "Oh, baby…how can I say no? And after, I want to buy the beautiful Indian outfit I saw in the hotel boutique."

"Which you will wear and do a Bollywood dance with me on the lawn?"

Max leapt at him and smothered his face with kisses.

Seated by a small rock garden in the Hyatt's Khazana restaurant, Max and Julian ate the spicy, savory lamb biryani with their bare fingers, just as the server had recommended.

After, they waited for Kevin in the lobby.

A plump, bearded man with a pleasant face entered and looked around. He was dressed in jeans and a plaid shirt. Upon seeing Max, his face broke into a huge grin. He strode toward her and held out both hands.

Max felt a sense of relief upon seeing Kevin. He was her father's old acquaintance, even if he had been an estranged one.

Max extended a tentative hand toward Kevin. He grabbed both of her hands and encased them within his own. "Thanks for coming, Maxine. And thank you for trusting me. Helping you won't wash away my sins as far as your father was concerned. But I'm hoping it might at least make them fade a little."

Max nodded, not knowing what to say. "Dr. Forsyth, this is my… uh, this is Julian McIntosh."

After exchanging introductions, they walked toward a sofa by a large window.

"You remind me of Hiram," Kevin said to Max.

"I'll take that as a compliment." Max smiled. "Thank you."

"Hiram was brilliant, but not a risk taker," Kevin said in a conversational tone. "Perhaps he was too honest for the business world."

"I think it's only right to run a business honestly," Max almost snapped. Normally she would have only thought such a thing. She was surprised the words had actually come out of her mouth, and with such force.

Kevin turned beet red. "Of course. I suppose I deserve that."

"I'm sorry." Max put a hand on his arm. "I don't know what came over me."

Kevin was perspiring. He took out a large handkerchief and wiped his face and neck with it. "Hiram always said it is unfortunate that kids have to bear the burden of their parents' actions. He bore his father's, and now you are bearing his. Which is why he chose to be ethical in all his dealings. There's no gray area in ethics, he said."

Max nodded with a sad smile.

"He once told me how strong he thought you are." Kevin put a hand on Max's shoulder.

She flinched a little. "It's a fleeting strength, I'm afraid," she said.

An awkward silence ensued. Julian nudged Max.

"Shall we look at the document?" Max said.

Kevin looked around. "Ah, there he is." He raised his arm and waved. A young man glided toward them.

"You said you have the key," Kevin said to Max.

"Well, we think so," Max said with a glance at the young man at their side.

"This is Rishi, an encryption expert. He will help us."

Rishi shook their hands and led them to an empty conference room in the hotel. He set up his laptop and looked at them expectantly.

"The research document is on this laptop," Kevin said. "Shall we try your key?"

Max showed him the verse and its translation. She explained how they found the 11:32 and connected it to the verse in her grandfather's diary.

"It would make sense," Kevin said.

They typed the English translation of the verse into the computer. A while later, Rishi turned the screen toward them.

The document looked less like gibberish. Clear language started to emerge.

Kevin scrolled to the top.

"Hiram has written to you, it would seem," he said.

Max peered at the screen.

My darling,

If you are reading this, it means I'm no longer in your life. It probably also means that Lars has failed.

I have made many mistakes, but leaving you alone is not one of them. I say that because I know that if I am gone, chances are you may never know why. The enemies I've made at Berliner are smart and they are cautious.

But now that you are involved, I wish you luck and send you blessings in this difficult journey. I hate that you are the one bearing this burden, but it seems there is no other way.

I want you to know this, sweetheart—if being your father was the only thing I accomplished in my whole life, believe me, it would be more than enough.

All other successes are miles behind you in their importance to me. And my failures meaningless and shallow compared to the joy of knowing you.

I cherish you more than anything. Now go, run with this, and change the world.

Max gave a shudder. Luckily she was able to compose herself and not give way to torrents of waterworks. "Did the verse decode the whole document?" she asked, filled with a renewed sense of purpose.

"Only partially," Rishi said, "Seems we need a second key."

Kevin smiled and shook his head. "Dr. P.S. Oup," he said. "Hiram was a clown. Pea Soup!"

"What does that mean?" Max asked.

"Your father was a clown *and* a geneticist. Gregor Mendel is the father of modern genetics. His groundbreaking work was based on the common variety garden pea. Hiram and I often talked about the ordinary pea soup with much respect because of this."

"So the key is pea soup?"

"Possibly. Or some combination of pea soup and Mendelian traits, another term we used often. There are a few different phrases that come to mind."

Max shuffled her feet and looked around the room.

Kevin smiled. "It'll take us a while to do this. Besides, I'll need some time to make sense of Hiram's research once we get it decoded."

"Of course," Max said. She and Julian left the room.

CHAPTER THIRTY-THREE

Hans considered his reflection in the hotel room mirror. There were deep lines under his eyes that had appeared as if overnight. His hair seemed to be thinning, too, or was he imagining it? He moved closer to the mirror and looked with a grunt of dissatisfaction. His roots were starting to turn their natural dirty brown. And he had neglected to bring his—some said unusual, but he maintained striking—shade of hair dye.

He rubbed his eyes. The dry Hyderabad heat was leaving him exhausted and irritated. At least his room in the Hyatt, three floors below Max's, was air-conditioned.

Hans had left London and returned to Germany knowing that no matter what Max and Julian decided to do, he would be able to take action. Herr Schultz had hoped that with Lars gone, Max might call upon Kevin for help. Ernst Frank couldn't be useful to her other than serving as a sympathetic ear, they had decided.

Still, Hans hadn't figured on Max making this much progress so quickly.

Hans left his hotel room, closing the door lightly behind him. He stepped outside the hotel and waited for his taxi to take him to the airport, where he knew Kevin and the others would soon be headed.

They would probably discuss the papers before they left for Karachi. There wasn't enough time for much else; their flight was in a few hours. He didn't need to listen in on their discussion. The content of the papers was well-known to Herr Schultz.

Hans planned his moves with caution. The Pakistani and Indian police were known to be ruthless. Being thrown in jail to languish for months, even years, without a trial was not unknown in these parts. The last thing he wanted was to be arrested in a place where Herr Schultz's influence held little value.

His wife had asked him how far he was willing to go for Herr Schultz.

Hans was starting to wonder about it, too.

CHAPTER THIRTY-FOUR

Max and Julian waited for Kevin in the hotel lobby.

A couple hours later, Kevin came to them. "It's done," he said.

Julian, Max, and Kevin settled themselves in a booth in the hotel coffee shop. There were a few families scattered around. No blond men. No suspicious men in baseball caps, either. Max's stomach did somersaults.

Kevin put his palms on the table and looked at Max. "Here goes. As early as the sixties, Hiram started thinking about going into genetics. It was cutting-edge work. He had his PhD, and he had worked at a couple major pharmaceutical companies. He told me he always kept Samuel's work in the back of his mind. Hiram knew the facts about the bacteria in the pill—that it affected thyroid activity, resulting in lowered metabolic rate and, theoretically, longer life. Then there were the unexplained symptoms like the fevers." Kevin raised a finger. "He also knew that the bacteria was contagious, that it caused elevated blood pressure in the lab animals, and finally, that there had been unrelated symptoms in the control group monkeys of high cholesterol, heart disease, weight gain, et cetera."

"It worried Opa because animals showing high BP almost always have something else going on," Max said. She became thoughtful. "Papa often asked Opa to go back to the lab—to work on what he had left unfinished. But Opa made excuses. Perhaps he was afraid of what he might find."

Kevin nodded. "Samuel should have swallowed his fears and found out what he had unknowingly unleashed."

Max stiffened. "Unleashed!"

Kevin held up a hand. "Sorry, I shouldn't have used that word. I'll come to it in a second." He licked his lips a few times and shifted in his seat, finally settling on a spot. "Hiram started working on the genetics of heart disease in the mid-eighties. Our business," he made a wry face, "was ancient history by then. For both of us. I started Allied, which took off in a big way."

"That failed business did a lot of damage to my father." Max tried not to sound accusing.

"Maxine, I admit I wasn't very honest, but I did what I had to do to keep the company afloat," Kevin said sympathetically. "Hiram preferred to let it go under rather than cut any corners. I even offered to do all the dirty work myself, but he chose to leave. When he left, I decided to end the business. Without him, we were severely handicapped. I begged Hiram to give it another shot, but he had lost faith in me. He went on to work at a safe and uneventful job after that. When Allied started doing well, I even invited him back, but he wouldn't give me a second chance."

They were all quiet for a while. Her father had not dealt well with failure. He was even less patient with others' failures and flaws. Rather than trying to forgive Kevin, to understand why he had done what he did, her father had just lost faith in the ways of the world.

If things had turned out differently, Papa might not have taken refuge in alcohol. He might have been alive today. If Berliner hadn't pushed Opa so much, he may not have been so blindly ambitious. Perhaps, he might have escaped Germany in time to pursue a career in another country, live a normal life.

Julian asked Max if she was all right. Max nodded. She looked at him with warm affection. If he hadn't offered to help that night after dinner, would she have called him after Lars died? Would she have been able to come this far?

A waiter arrived at their table. They ordered a large pot of tea and a plate of cashew cookies.

Kevin looked at Max. "After we parted ways, Hiram really needed validation," he said cautiously. "When the chance to work in genetics and heart disease finally came along, he was ecstatic."

"Papa wanted to be a cardiologist, but ended up pursuing bio-chemistry and genetics. He hoped to understand the heart's mysteries and find cures."

"Turned out that one person in his group of test subject volunteers was an 80-year-old man who had been an inmate in the Krippenwald camp around the time Samuel was there," Kevin said. "He had diabe-tes, but was otherwise healthy. Hiram found out that this 80-year-old man had gotten a fever at the camp after ingesting the Indus pill. But it had been a mild one. Some of them had mild fevers, others had high fevers. Some of his friends from the camp were not healthy. They had severe heart disease, fatty liver disease, some were obese, others had cholesterol problems and diabetes."

"Is that significant?" Max asked. "These are all different diseases."

"True. However, they are all diseases that result in people who show a certain set of risk factors. This group of risk factors is called metabolic syndrome. A person who shows at least three of the follow-ing risk factors is said to have metabolic syndrome." Kevin counted them off on his fingers. "A large waistline, which is related to obesity; high blood pressure, high triglyceride levels—triglycerides are a type of fat found in blood; low HDL, which is your good cholesterol; and lastly, high fasting blood sugar. The term metabolic syndrome was not coined until recently. This set of risk factors was connected to a poor lifestyle and heredity. Hiram saw no real reason to link any of this to his work. So he filed the information away, and nothing more came of it. That is, until he got a phone call from a scientist who had worked for Berliner in the forties and fifties."

Their tea arrived. Julian poured everyone a cup. The sweet fra-grance of nutmeg rose from the steaming tea.

Kevin dropped his voice. "This scientist claimed to have worked on Samuel's research in a secret lab until the late fifties. That was around the time Watson and Crick won the Nobel Prize for their DNA double helix discovery. It was a time when the world started looking at the human body in a different light. Turns out this lab run by Peter Schultz made some disturbing discoveries about Samuel's pill. They found diseases in lab animals that Samuel and Lars had perhaps not discovered. They also realized that the diseases were not random. They were related. They were all, as we know now, diseases under the metabolic syndrome umbrella. This meant that somehow the bacteria was causing a family of diseases. Before they could find out why, Schultz shut the lab down. He chose to bury it in order to avoid public embarrassment, rather than take responsibility. Because this former Berliner scientist had reached out to him, Hiram was interested once again in Samuel's work. But he did nothing about it." Kevin took a sip of his tea.

"What happened then?" Max said.

"Hiram finally plunged into Samuel's work when a new member joined his group. A volunteer who happened to be from the Greek island of Ikaria."

"What was special about him?" Max asked.

"Indeed," Kevin said with a grin, "His origin was a random piece of demographic information, until Hiram discovered something strange."

Max and Julian leaned forward.

"As part of his research, Hiram had conducted routine blood tests on all his volunteers. In these blood tests, Hiram found that the people in his test group all had memory cells showing a bacterium."

Max frowned.

"And because of the old concentration camp inmate, and the phone call from the Berliner scientist, Hiram thought of Samuel's pill and its bacteria," Julian said excitedly.

"Exactly," Kevin said. "It was an odd coincidence. Hiram studied both bacteria—the one from his volunteers and the one in the pills. He found that they were the same."

Max held up her hand. "One second, sorry. I'm losing you. What are memory cells?"

Kevin shifted his body a few times more. "Can't sit for too long in one place at my age. When a body gets a disease—a fever for example—it develops antibodies and memory cells which stay in the body to deal with that disease at a later date. Let's say you get a viral fever, your body develops antibodies so you are better able to fight it if you should get it again. That is how a vaccine works as well."

"Okay. So what did Papa do when he found that people carried memory cells of the bacteria that was the same as the one in the pill?" Max said.

"Hiram had started studying heart disease in the context of metabolic syndrome—or MetS as it is called—even before this term was officially coined. Among his volunteers were some people without MetS who turned out to not have any of this bacterium's memory cells. And there were some who had the memory cells and mild-to-severe diseases such as heart disease, diabetes, obesity, et cetera—all diseases related to the metabolic syndrome risk factors."

Julian looked baffled. "Does that mean the bacteria caused the MetS?"

Kevin shook his head. "The presence of the memory cells indicated only that the bacteria from the pill had invaded these people at some point in their lives. That meant that they had had the fever that Samuel had correctly associated with the bacterial invasion from the pill."

Max said, "I still don't understand what memory cells have to do with MetS. The bacteria doesn't cause MetS, just the fevers, right? And so having the memory cells should mean the body can fight the fever if it occurs again. What does that have to do with MetS? I'm confused."

Kevin smiled at her. "You hit the nail right on the head. The link between the bacteria and MetS-related diseases was the one Hiram was struggling to make, too. However, what he was finding was that people with metabolic syndrome, at least in his group of volunteers, seemed to have those specific bacterial memory cells. Many of these people hadn't ingested the pill, remember? They had got it because of its contagious nature. There *was* a link between the bacteria and therefore the pill and Metabolic Syndrome, however tenuous it may be. And the link was what Hiram had to find. What was known, what

Samuel had discovered, was that this Indus Valley pill and its bacteria lowered metabolic rate and increased life spans on one hand, but also caused metabolic syndrome on the other."

Max pulled out her grandfather's diary and began flipping the pages.

"Back up to that volunteer from Ikaria." Julian said, "Was there something special about him after all?"

"Yes!" Kevin said. "This Ikarian had the memory cells, which meant he had also been affected by the bacteria. But unlike the others, he showed absolutely no risk factors for MetS. He was very healthy. Hiram started conversations with scientists and doctors in Ikaria. He also continued speaking to the former Berliner scientist who had called him. Hiram even paid a visit to Ikaria and found, upon testing a wide sample of people, that the people from Ikaria have the memory cells of the bacteria but are somehow immune to MetS and live very long healthy lives, free of any metabolic syndrome-related diseases. The Ikarians are known for their longevity."

"Sort of like places in Italy and Japan?" Julian said. "Inexplicable reasons why people live really long lives there."

"Yes, although their familial structure and social habits gives them longer lives, too," Kevin said.

"Mind over matter," Julian said. "Ohmm…" he hummed and closed his eyes.

Kevin smiled. "In our case, though, it was much more tangible. It was genetics."

Max was fidgeting with her hair, her other hand holding a spot in her grandfather's diary.

"You have something you want to tell us," Kevin said in a fatherly tone.

Max showed them Samuel's diary. "Their guide at the dig, Abdul Chapar, gleaned from the writings that the pill was from Ikaria. The Ikarians had asked the Colossus not to take it out of the island because of the curse. And he stole it anyway. Looks like the Ikarians knew something was wrong with the pill, even then. It helped *them* live longer. But outside the island, somehow, the pill failed."

Kevin took the diary from her. "That certainly is interesting," he murmured. "Anyway, Hiram put on his geneticist cap, did DNA sequencing, and found something these Ikarians could never have known all those centuries ago."

Max realized she was holding her breath. "What?" she whispered.

Kevin said, "Time for a short science lesson." He looked at Max and Julian in turn. "DNA is the basic building block of life. All life. DNA is made up of sequences called genes. These genes carry the blueprints to build life—plants, animals, humans."

"Right," Max said.

"Did you know though that only about 2 percent of our own human DNA is responsible for building all the cells in our body?" Kevin said.

"I had no idea." Julian said.

"The rest, until recently, was called junk DNA," Kevin went on. "We now know that this 'junk' plays a part in human development. Scientists now call this part of our DNA, very imaginatively, non-coding DNA.

"Man has traveled to the moon and back, and yet we know little about our own bodies. Non-coding DNA contains many mysteries. Pseudogenes are one of them. These genes have lost their ability to produce cells and proteins, possibly because of mutation. In layman's terms, they have lost their work skills. These genes, however, can actually retain function for several million years and can be reactivated into working genes. And that brings us to what Hiram found."

"My head is spinning." Max put her hands over her cheeks.

Kevin put a hand over hers. "Stay with me." He went on eagerly. "Hiram discovered that one particular pseudogene sequence was missing in the Ikarian Greeks. His discovery of this is nothing short of a miracle. Talk about a needle in a haystack!" He let out a laugh. "Hiram found that all his test subjects carried the fnkL_ps pseudogene. His group was pretty diverse." Kevin looked down and checked Hiram's papers, "He had Caucasians, Asians, Africans."

Kevin went on, "Hiram found, however, that the Ikarians did *not* possess this particular pseudogene. The question was this: Was the missing gene sequence making the Ikarians somehow immune to some commonplace and yet potentially lethal afflictions?"

"And what was the answer?" Max took a sip of her tea.

"Of course, now he had to test the DNA of the people not from Ikaria to make sure he had concluded correctly. He checked the genes of his volunteers and compared those profiles to the Ikarians'."

"And?"

"And that is when he found what he was looking for," Kevin said. "The link!"

CHAPTER THIRTY-FIVE

Kevin almost jumped in his seat. "Hiram found the link between the bacteria and MetS. The pseudogene he found was an endogenous retrovirus!"

"And what in Vishnu's name is an endogenous retrovirus?" Max leaned wearily back into her chair.

Kevin chuckled. "ERVs or HERVs—human endogenous retroviruses—are fascinating. The majority of ERVs that occur in vertebrate genomes are ancient! Most of them have been inactivated by mutation. They are extremely unlikely to have negative effects on their hosts."

"But…" Max said.

Kevin held up his hand. "Nevertheless, it is clear from studies that ERVs can be associated with disease."

Max let her head drop to the table. "Now I have a headache."

Kevin smiled. "Max, this is fascinating stuff. Your father was a genius. What he discovered was that the ancient bacteria from the pills produced an enzyme that triggered this endogenous retrovirus. I won't go into the details of how." Max let out a sigh of relief. "But this virus caused the risk factors for metabolic syndrome in humans, and it turns out it did so in the monkeys as well, since they are so closely related to us."

Max stared at Kevin.

"Okay, okay," Julian said, holding up his hands. "Let me see if I understand this. Everyone, or I should say people not like the

Ikarians, has this retrovirus embedded in their DNA. And if they have been affected by the bacteria, the virus is activated in them—and as a result, they will have some form of MetS."

"Yes!" Kevin said.

Julian shook his head. "Come on, how could he conclude something so drastic? I mean, it's a big leap from a test group to, well… everyone!"

"A big leap, yes, but Hiram found the ERV in people not just in his study. He found it in people with and without MetS. He checked over a thousand volunteers from all over the globe. He spent a lot of time and a lot of his own money on the tests. He concluded that everyone who has that pseudogene sequence—which is most people outside Ikaria—has the virus."

"So why are Ikarians," Julian said, "the only ones without this gene sequence?"

Kevin shrugged. "There are probably regions all over the world like Ikaria with millions of people who are missing that gene sequence."

"So if most people outside of Ikaria have the virus in their genes, why don't they all have MetS?" Julian said.

Kevin raised his finger and stabbed the air with it. "Not everyone who has HIV develops AIDS. The truth is that every body is unique. Some people can fight the disease with good eating and living habits. Others just cannot, no matter what they do. Everyone reacts in a different way, but the common thread of the retrovirus is there. Funny, isn't it? That makes MetS a viral condition." Kevin became thoughtful.

Funny wasn't the word, Max thought. She was the one who would always have the extra weight on her, no matter what she did. What a thought—a bacteria Opa had unleashed had made her the way she was. Well, that and her sweet tooth, to be fair.

Kevin went on. "What Hiram found was that the virus had, in all probability, remained dormant in people for centuries. When it encountered this particular bacterium, it was reactivated, thus causing metabolic syndrome in the host. And the bacterium was introduced into the world by Samuel's pill. As I said before, our bodies are still enormous mysteries."

"I don't know," Max said. The weight of the accusation Kevin was making—or rather her father was making—was too much. "This is a rather rash conclusion to draw—that Opa's bacteria caused worldwide MetS. People have been obese for centuries."

"You must remember that MetS isn't only about obesity," Kevin said. "MetS is a collection of risk factors. Low HDL, heart disease, diabetes, et cetera. People have died for centuries of all sorts of causes that were never diagnosed. A skinny man with high cholesterol dies suddenly. No one knows why. A sudden heart attack."

Max pouted. "I still think it's far-fetched."

Kevin went on. "Think about when this happened. In 1945, after the war, what happened to the surviving camp inmates who had taken the pill—the ones who had lived with very low nutrition and whose lives may indeed have been extended because of the lowered metabolic rate?"

"They went to America and Israel," Max said.

"Possibly POWs were given the pill, too," Julian said.

"Ah," Kevin said. "Perhaps some went back to fight the war in other parts of Europe. Asia, even. Meaning, dear Max, that they went all over the world, taking with them the bacteria that activates the retrovirus in our genes."

Max dropped her head into her hands. It certainly was possible. But probable?

Kevin went on, "It's only since the fifties that commercial airlines became the more accepted mode of international travel. Travel started to become easier, faster, and more affordable, and as a result—"

"The bacteria moved easier and faster, too," Julian said, his face now somber.

Kevin nodded with a sigh. "Slowly people started being affected by it. Their dormant ERV was triggered. Over time, peoples' habits became more sedentary, they ate more. They developed MetS—mild or severe."

"Habits! Exactly. What about the fast food phenomenon?" Max said. "Maybe fast food, the bane of the US, is now affecting the whole world."

"I love a devil's advocate!" Kevin refilled his cup and bit off a chunk of cookie. "Over the years," Kevin said with his mouth full, "as people's lives grew more sedentary and their diets grew more and more processed, especially in the US, their bodies—which were fertile ground for MetS already, due to the retrovirus—were very badly affected. In the US, it has reached pandemic proportions. Max, I agree, it's not all one cause. Samuel is not to blame for the enormity of what this has become. These things go hand in hand. Let's say Samuel started the fire and modern times and habits fanned it. And so, as prosperity grows, as people become more sedentary and eat less and less healthily, MetS is and will be on the rise. It would have happened anyway, but perhaps not in the pandemic proportions that we see today. The virus has acted like an accelerator that is making the fire burn harder and faster."

Max didn't speak. Her eyebrows were still furrowed.

"Remember how bird flu and later swine flu spread from literally one guy to all over the world?" Kevin said.

"The Spanish flu spread like that in 1919," Julian said. "It was carried back home by soldiers returning from the first World War. Almost 40 percent of the world fell ill. Millions died."

The three didn't speak for a few minutes.

"You said groups of people might be immune," Max said. "Could the groups belong to the same race? It's possible that some people in Abdul's tribe are also immune. Which is why some believed in the curse while others lived long lives."

"Abdul?" Kevin said, puzzled.

Max held up her grandfather's diary. "Abdul Chapar—the guide who insisted that a part of their tribe had enjoyed longevity because of the pill."

"It's certainly possible," Kevin said. "The bacteria in the pill also lowers metabolic rate, remember. The camp workers and others lived longer because, with lower metabolic rate, they needed less nutrition to survive. In ancient times, nutrition was key. People who had lower metabolic rate and possibly the absence of the ERV lived exceedingly long lives. As long as they ate reasonably healthy food and remained active."

"What do you think actually happened to the Colossus?" Max asked. "He was imprisoned in his home toward the end."

"There's a story I read about a man in ancient Greece—yes, Greece again," Kevin said. "He became very obese, and morbid obesity as we know it today didn't exist in those days, at least not in abundance. He was considered so diseased and shameful that he stayed locked inside his home. He was fed through a window. No one really saw him, for he was too self-conscious to show himself. They may have even thought he was contagious. It's cruel, but there you have it."

"That might explain the name Colossus!" Julian said. "They probably just didn't realize that he became a really overweight guy."

"That would explain the social ostracizing," Kevin said. "But it's also possible that he developed diabetes. And as a result, perhaps he developed a gangrenous foot. Or a nasty skin condition that can result from advanced diabetes. Lots of things could have happened. Or maybe he just got very large, like Julian said. Any one of those might frighten others into thinking he was contagious. In someone else it would just be bad luck. In him, they immediately linked it to the pill and the curse it came tainted with. Turns out they were right. Just that the curse was a disease, not some higher power's whim."

"But his descendents, the Chapars, seem to be immune, so this guy just got unlucky," Max said. "Poor man."

"This may or may not be relevant," Julian said, "but the Indus civilization lasted from 3300 until 1300 BCE. Their decline began around 1800 BCE. Various reasons were cited—flood and drought being the chief ones. Perhaps this whole business with the Colossus was part of the reason for people leaving, unexplained deaths, and disease. Drought or floods, too, but I wonder if this pill had something to do with the demise or disintegration of these peoples."

"Could be," Kevin said.

"Kevin," Julian went on, "Are any races immune to other diseases? Have there been studies?"

"Genetic immunity isn't new," Kevin said. "A small percentage of people descended from Northern Europeans are virtually immune to AIDS. Swedes especially."

"I had no idea," Max said.

"Now," Kevin said cautiously, "the reason all this is so problematic for pharmaceutical companies."

"I was wondering about that," Max said. "Why should they be concerned? No one is killing scientists who discovered the HIV thing."

"Exactly," Kevin said. "So what do we have here? A disease that is caused by a bacteria and a retrovirus."

"Meaning?" Max said.

"How do we prevent many bacterial and viral diseases?" Kevin asked.

"By immunization—good heavens, a vaccine!" Max offered.

"A vaccine is possible, as is an anti-retroviral drug," Kevin said. "Once we find the mechanism to block the enzyme produced by this bacteria, someone could produce a vaccine to prevent MetS."

"What about those people who already have the disease?" Max said.

"An anti-retroviral drug like the ones used for AIDS could slow down the impact of the virus," Kevin said. "Good habits can keep the effects of the retrovirus in check, too."

"Don't we need the pill to make this vaccine?" Julian said.

"I don't think so," Kevin said. "But we do need the pill. Peer reviews and third party tests are essential for Hiram's work to be accepted."

"So if a vaccine happens, would it be given to all babies?" Julian said.

"If it happens, it would be a miracle," Kevin said. "But yes, I'd say a baby given this vaccine would have increased immunity to MetS."

"That would mean the slow death of many drugs," Max said thoughtfully.

Kevin nodded. "Many drugs may become obsolete if we attack MetS at birth or even with a retroviral drug. There would be some demand, but not nearly as much as it is now, and the demand might only decrease over time as immunity increases. But that could take decades to happen."

"Is that why Papa was killed?" Max asked after a long pause. "It was too big a risk, his bringing this discovery out?"

This was what the whole thing had been about, after all. The research was important, but so was the consequence it had brought upon the man who had made the breakthrough.

Julian and Kevin exchanged a look.

"This cannot just be about Berliner's drugs becoming obsolete over time," Julian said. "They can easily make the vaccine or develop a retroviral drug and make millions. They have the knowledge and ample time to do it. MetS won't disappear overnight. So why are they so keen on hiding this?"

"Why indeed?" Kevin said softly.

"The whistle blower!" Max said suddenly.

"Berliner's lab discovered that the pill was causing MetS," Kevin said with an emphatic nod. "They didn't have the knowledge to come up with the genetic explanation. But they knew enough, and they weren't given the chance to study it further. *That* is what the scientist told Hiram." Kevin pointed to Hiram's papers. "Labs in those days were gaining access to DNA information. It is possible that they might have eventually made the genetic link Hiram did. Instead, Schultz decided to shut down the lab and cover up its findings."

"Why did that scientist come to Papa?" Max said.

"Perhaps he had an attack of conscience, perhaps he was curious about the connection between the bacteria and MetS," Kevin said.

"Berliner would have a lot to worry about," Julian said. "This was the huge cover-up. They could have told the world what they had found, but they chose not to. There was the Nazi connection, the fact that they had dispensed a potentially dangerous drug to labor camp workers as part of disgusting human experiments. Bad PR, not to mention lawsuits from MetS sufferers, perhaps even prison time for the executives. Gigantic fines at the very least."

"All those are good enough reasons to kill," Max said.

Kevin looked at Hiram's notes. "I wondered why Hiram decided to code the document. He was protecting not only himself and you, but also the whistle blower."

"Good enough reasons to kill," Max repeated dully.

"It's probably not a good idea to dwell—" Kevin began.

"Really?" Max cried. "What am I supposed to do? My father was killed by Berliner, who is so powerful that I can do absolutely nothing about it. Isn't that the truth?"

Kevin said nothing; neither did Julian at first.

"And we are going to have to accept that," Julian said at last in a firm voice.

Max was enraged. Her eyes grew large. "Easy for you to accept. You didn't spend years hating your father for killing himself, only to find that he hadn't. And now I have to spend the rest of my life knowing that his killers are out there."

"We will have revenge in a manner of speaking." Kevin pointed to Hiram's papers. "Behemoth pharmaceutical companies have great influence over the journals. But our case is strong, and if we can get some pills that can be dated and analyzed in an independent lab, we can make Hiram's dream come true."

Max turned away. She didn't want the two men to see her show any sign of weakness, not after all she had been through, not after all they had managed to achieve together.

But retribution seemed impossible. Berliner was a Goliath she could never take on.

"Maxine." Kevin put his hands on the table. "Berliner may not have actually harmed Hiram, even though they were the ones who threatened him," he said.

"How did they even find out?" Julian said.

"Perhaps Hiram told them," Kevin said. "He was an emotional man. I can see him asking them to take responsibility."

"What can we do, even if we knew they did it for sure?" Max said.

They sat in silence. The answer was unsaid but loud enough to be deafening.

Absolutely nothing.

Max realized the two men were waiting for her to regain her composure. "What do we do now?" Max asked.

Kevin smiled and checked his watch. "We leave for Karachi in a couple hours. We may have a way to get our hands on some Indus pills."

Max looked at Kevin. There was a hope in her eyes, she knew, and it was a naked hope that was making him uncomfortable. Kevin squirmed. "Max," he began, and hesitated. "We...we can hope for the best, but..." He trailed off.

Max knew she had no business feeling the sense of hope she did. The journey of bringing her father's work to the world was only just beginning. But she felt so lucky to have these two good men by her side. She put a hand on each of theirs.

"I know, don't worry. And I don't think I have said this enough. Thank you. Both of you. Thank you, thank you."

CHAPTER THIRTY-SIX

Jinnah International Airport
Karachi, Pakistan

Stern-faced military personnel at the airport exits smoked and laughed, largely ignoring the passengers streaming by. Basking in the tropical heat were potted palms and hibiscus flowers in shades of vibrant yellow, orange, and red.

A gigantic Sikh in an elaborate red turban was summoning cabs. "We'd like a taxi, please," Kevin said. The Sikh lifted a dinner-plate-sized hand, and a taxi peeling yellow and black paint glided to a halt in front of them. Kevin, Julian, and Max got it.

The taxi reeked of sandalwood incense and old sweat. The driver was a handsome, freckle-faced young man. "American!" he drawled, taking one look at them. "Going where?"

"The Karachi History Museum, please," Kevin said.

The driver stomped on the accelerator and the trio collectively hit the back of their seat as the taxi took off.

"A camel!" Max exclaimed. The scraggly creature was walking along the street side. Atop it sat an old man with spiky white hair and large gold hoops in his ears. Perched behind him, a little girl undulated back and forth with the camel's movements. She was dressed in bright reds and blues. The camel too was decked out in mirrored fabric and bells galore.

It started to drizzle. Max strained to look outside from behind the rivulets of raindrops that curtained her tiny window. The rain stopped and the sky was a clear powder blue. Max rolled down her window and a cool, moist breeze wafted in.

On the streets, brightly colored art deco buildings were flanked with huts and bustling shop fronts. Women wearing burkas were everywhere, but so were women in modern clothing—almost all of them dressed in embroidered tunics and loose pants. The men wore anything from jeans and T-shirts to elaborate traditional dress.

"When Opa was here, this was still India, wasn't it?" Max asked.

"Yes," Julian piped up. "Until 1947, when the British left. The separation of East and West Pakistan from India was a painful one. East Pakistan became Bangladesh and West Pakistan remained Pakistan." He turned to look at her. "Did you know that before the British took over, India was a collection of princely states? And they were all more or less independent and very competitive. In fact, that is one of the reasons a handful of Brits were even able to take over India. Divide and rule was their motto."

Max suppressed a smile. Julian could never resist the opportunity to deliver a history lesson.

"One day," Max said, "I want to return to India to visit Coorg. My mother's people were from there originally."

"When did they emigrate to the States?" Kevin asked.

"Her parents moved to New York, I think, before she was born. In the forties, maybe."

The taxi stopped at a light, and a grimy peddler boy sauntered by with bright red roses. Before Max could make up her mind about buying them, the taxi took off once more. Ten minutes later, they glided to a halt.

In front of them was the Karachi History Museum, a modern building with some minarets to give it Islamic flavor.

"This museum is a treasure house for Indus and Islamic artifacts," Kevin said. "They have a few Indus pills, salvaged from age-old digs, the curator told me."

Max sighed. For a few moments, the flight and taxi ride had felt like ordinary vacation activity—albeit with one near-stranger and the other…a friend.

But no, Julian was becoming much more than that. J. How nice that sounded. Julian. J.

Her J?

Perhaps.

The excitement of a new place, taking in the sights, the smells, and the sounds had all overshadowed the apprehension she was sure they all felt.

"Let's go get us some pills," Kevin said cheerfully.

They walked along a brick path, then through large wooden doors to the front desk.

"Welcome," an attractive middle-aged woman said.

"Hello," Max said. "We're here to see Dr. Karim. I'm Maxine Rosen. This is Kevin Forsyth." She pointed to Kevin.

The woman looked startled. "The curator just met with Kevin Forsyth!"

"What?"

A tall, thin man walked toward the front desk, looked at them, and smiled.

The front desk woman stood up. "Dr. Karim, this man claims to be Kevin Forsyth, too."

Dr. Karim frowned.

Kevin went to him. "Dr. Karim, I am Kevin Forsyth. We spoke earlier. These are my friends. Someone has been impersonating me."

Dr. Karim's hand went to his chin. "I wondered why he sounded different. But thought nothing of it since he knew so much about the pills and its background. He recalled our conversation vividly. We spoke of my grandkids, remember? My goodness, what have I done?"

Max let out a shrill cry and sank to the ground. "How did they find out?" she said over and over again.

Dr. Karim came over to Max and kneeled beside her. Yes, a heavy-set German was the one who had pretended to be Kevin Forsyth, he told her. Max nodded, her mind in a haze. "He said the pills carried a contagion," Dr. Karim was saying, "and insisted that we give him the entire lot. He had a letter from a renowned contagious diseases expert with him asking that we release all the pills. Well, we only had a few to start with." Max let out a low groan. Dr. Karim sounded flustered. "I'm so sorry. But he was convincing. He brought a biohazard box and an expert with him to take the pills away. He even insisted that we have health check-ups immediately." With that Dr. Karim apologized once more and left.

Max got up and walked out of the museum. She, Kevin, and Julian sat on the museum lawn for a while, watching the erratic traffic go by.

"Let's go," Kevin said. "Nothing left here for us."

He hailed a cab. "Airport," he said to the cabbie.

"No!" Max cried, turning to him. "I'm not giving up yet. Please, let's stay for a day more. Let us think this through."

"As you wish. I'll change the flights," Kevin said tersely.

Their taxi cruised along the busy Karachi streets, but this time no one was interested in the odd camel or even elephant walking by.

Max scowled. "I've been an idiot," she said. "I called you on your cell phone, didn't I?"

Kevin nodded.

"I made sure I was calling from a safe phone. But not once did I think Berliner may have tapped your phone, too. Why would I? I mean, it was only after I found Papa's tape that I even thought to call you."

"They've been ahead of us all the while," Julian said. "Weren't they watching Lars for years? They might well have been watching Kevin just as long. He was once close to your father."

Max let out a grunt and began twirling a lock of hair. Julian gently pried her hand away from it.

Kevin closed his eyes. "I'm so sorry, Max," he whispered.

Max shifted her gaze outside the window, her hand defiantly back at her hair.

The taxi drew to a halt in front of the Holiday Inn.

Julian checked them in while Kevin changed their return flight. Kevin tried calling the Karachi History Museum. It was no good. The curator wasn't sure whom to trust anymore. The German even had identification, he said.

At Max's insistence, they agreed to look at every single paper they had collected since the saga had begun. Everything was brought to Kevin's room. Max pored over Samuel's diary, Julian looked at the papers from the DANK Haus on the dig, and Kevin looked over Hiram's research.

"What are we looking for, anyway?" Julian asked.

"A way to find the pills," Max murmured under her breath.

At around 4:00 a.m., when Max was about to give up, Julian closed his file. "This DANK Haus info is useless. Only factual—names, places, dates, times," he said.

"Wait," Max cried. "Did you say factual?"

"Yes." Julian yawned. He went to the kitchenette and started a pot of coffee. Their fourth.

"Are there any addresses?" Max said.

"Yes, but—" Julian suppressed another yawn.

Max went to him. He still had some papers in his hand. She took them from him.

"They're old." Julian threw up his hands and sank into a sofa.

Max began reading. Most addresses listed were in Germany. There was a page full of names in present day Pakistan. And addresses. None of the names were familiar. These were all the people involved one way or another with the dig—archeologists in Pakistan, some in Europe. All dead, most likely.

There were some names in Karachi for advisors on the dig. "We're going to check the local names," Max said.

"Max, you know how old this information is," Kevin said. "It's no use going around trying to track these people down."

Max gave him a look of disbelief. "I am not giving up after having come this far."

"Maxine, look at me," Kevin commanded. "It's time for us to go home. I'll try and get Hiram's research published in a respectable publication, and I'll find a way to get it noticed. I'll do what I can with what we have."

Max made a sour face.

"Uh-oh," Julian said. "Look at her eyes, they have that steely glint in them."

Max grinned.

"I know that look," Kevin said tiredly. "Hiram would often get it."

Max picked up a phone directory.

"Max," Kevin said, "stop this madness. Most people didn't even have phones then."

Julian nodded. "And even if they did, those numbers would be long defunct, not to mention that all of these people are probably dead by now."

Max stared at the list of names Julian had given her. The names began to blur. Her eyes closed. She let them. *I'll sleep for ten minutes, no more*, she promised herself.

Two hours later, she got up. The two men were fast asleep, sprawled on sofas.

She looked at the list of names once more. *Fardoon Chapar*, it said. *Interpreter*. With an address in Karachi.

Kevin stirred a little.

"Kevin!"

"Huh?" Kevin slurred.

"Fardoon Chapar was the guide's great-grandson! He was only a teenager back then. He could be around."

"Who?" Kevin mumbled as Max dashed out.

CHAPTER THIRTY-SEVEN

214 Rashid Minhas Road
Karachi

This time the fly wouldn't escape. Fardoon Chapar raised his arm and brought the swatter down with a crack. Missed. Damn. He looked at the fly, now safe on the opposite wall, and threw away the swatter. This lack of work was like a slow death.

"*Aajaa*, grandpa, chai!" Zeeshan, his grandson, entered the store holding two cups of tea in his hands and an oil-stained bag between his teeth. "And *pakoras*, fritters," he said.

Fardoon stood on tiptoe. A small window connected his store to the tea shop's kitchen next door. "Hey Khan, maybe someday we will make this hole bigger so you can pass the eatables through here."

He heard a chuckle from the other side.

Fardoon smiled at Zeeshan. "This gives you an excuse to go next door and admire the female customers, I'm sure."

With a wink, Zeeshan placed the snack on the table. He picked up a wooden stool and took it outside. Perched on it, he began adjusting the signboard.

"*Arre,* hey, don't bother," Fardoon said.

It had been weeks since they'd any clients.

"A lopsided signboard says we don't care," Zeeshan said. "Someone will come. Today, perhaps."

"I should never have asked you to join this business," Fardoon said. "Your wise father stayed in the village and has earned respect as a schoolteacher. Look at us!"

Zeeshan went to his grandfather. "One day we will go back there with money and fulfill our dream of making the lives of our people better. I spoke to some hotels yesterday. They will send some people our way."

Fardoon shook his head. "They take so much commission, the thieves!"

Zeeshan took a bite of a fritter. "Eat, or they'll get cold."

Fardoon took a sip of his tea and, with a satisfied sigh, surveyed the busy street a few feet away. A goatherd walked by, leading a flock of goats for their grazing session. Fardoon looked this way and that until his eyes settled on a young woman. Dressed in a sea blue *shalwar kameez* of chiffon, she had wondrous dark brown curls. A modern girl, Fardoon thought, but modest, for her head was covered with a scarf. She had the curves and creamy complexion that poets wrote verses about. *Mashallah!* Wonderful.

"If only I was a young man again! Zeeshan, soon it'll be time to find you a girl as beautiful as...wait...wait a minute." She was scanning the store signs. Her eyes finally rested on theirs—'*Chapar Interpreters—only English-speaking people in Karachi you can trust.*' She started moving toward their store. "Bring that chair! Not that one! The one with the cushion."

CHAPTER THIRTY-EIGHT

Oozing charm, a young man greeted Max. "*Aadab,* or shall I say, how do you do?"

"Hello, I'm Maxine Rosen. Here to see Fardoon Chapar."

An old man pushed his chair back. There was a look of intense curiosity on his face, and something else Max couldn't quite put a finger on.

He leaned forward, his eyes narrowing. "I'm Fardoon Chapar; this is my grandson, Zeeshan," he said. "How can we be of assistance?"

"My grandfather was Samuel Rosen," Max said. "You met him in 1935."

For a few seconds, Fardoon seemed lost in thought. "Of course, in Mohenjo-daro," he said. "Those were interesting times. I was so very young. I had just started interpreting. I remember that expedition well."

He said the last part with bitterness in his voice, Max thought.

"Would you like some tea?" Zeeshan offered.

Max wanted to say no, but had been told that in this part of the world, it was rude to refuse refreshment.

"Sure," she said. She turned to look at the street. There was no sign of anyone remotely dangerous. These people seemed nice and the street was busy. Zeeshan rushed out to get tea.

Briefly, she told Fardoon the story of the pills, their journey from India to Berlin, and their effect on the world, and about Berliner and her father's murder.

Fardoon's jaw had dropped halfway during the conversation. He stayed speechless. Sometime during Max's monologue, Zeeshan placed a cup of tea in front of her. Max absent-mindedly sipped it. Now done with her tale, Max finished the last of her tea and sat back, waiting for a reaction, and possibly a miracle.

Fardoon dropped his eyes to the table.

Max glanced at Zeeshan. His face was frozen. She turned around.

The blond stood behind her with a gun pointed at Fardoon. He put a rock-like hand on her shoulder. "Nice to see you again, Fraulein Rosen," he said. To Zeeshan, he ordered, "Close the shutter."

Zeeshan promptly obliged.

Max closed her eyes. The enemy had arrived here, too. Damn him, the bastard. She began shaking with rage.

"Everyone sit so I can see your hands," the blond said politely. "You, Miss Rosen, over there, please. *Gut.* Good. Now old man, where are the Indus pills?"

"I have no idea what you are talking about," Fardoon said. A trickle of sweat traced the curve of his cheek down from his temple.

The blond man cocked his pistol against Zeeshan's temple. "Want to think about it again?"

Fardoon jumped up with remarkable agility. "I remember now. I may have some."

Max let out a cry. This couldn't be happening. Fardoon was avoiding meeting her eye. The blond extended his hand, palm open.

"Not here," Fardoon said with disdain. "Besides, they aren't free."

The blond's eyes narrowed. He smiled thinly. "How much?"

Fardoon didn't hesitate. "One hundred thousand US dollars!"

"Aajaa!" Zeeshan cried.

Fardoon ignored him. "This is my chance to do something good for my son and his village. Let the pills bring some happiness to my people. By Allah, it is time."

The German laughed. "You're a funny little man," he said. "Maybe I should shoot this handsome young fellow and get you to talk without making any more jokes."

Fardoon was enraged. "If you harm a hair on his head, I will kill you."

"You forget I'm the one holding the gun here."

"And you forget where you are holding that gun. Zeeshan here is well connected with the Taliban and al-Qaeda. Haven't heard about them? Well, all you need to know is that they hate you. I'd remain very cautious if I were you. Some of Zeeshan's Talib friends visit us everyday around noon." Everyone turned to look at a clock on the opposite wall. It was 11:20. "The store hasn't been closed at this hour for over sixty years. They will know something is the matter, and before you know it, your head will be decorating a stake in the town square." The German frowned. Fardoon seemed to be enjoying himself. "They love European heads here—it makes a statement about infidels!"

The German seemed to hesitate. He glanced at Zeeshan, who promptly narrowed his eyes. He was looking over Zeeshan's clothing now, probably concerned that Zeeshan might be concealing a weapon, Max thought. It wasn't uncommon in these parts.

Finally the blond said, "I'll need to check on the money."

Fardoon said, "Go ahead. I know why you seek the pills. You have no idea how easy it would be for me to raise an alarm and have your head sliced away. Besides, it's getting close to noon. The Taliban have many faults, but they are punctual. They'll be outside in no time, wondering if they should break in. All we need to do is make a noise."

The blond raised his weapon. "You wouldn't dare."

Fardoon said, "We know who you are, we know about Berliner."

Zeeshan smiled. "You are from Berlin, yes? I'm sure you know this new group al-Qaeda is starting to have a presence there. What is a mere hundred thousand dollars compared to your family's safety?"

"Shut up," The blond said, but his voice was less cocky than when he had first walked in.

"Come Zeeshan, let's start shouting," Fardoon said.

The blond held up his hand. "I'll make arrangements. But if I don't get the pills, Tali-whatever or not, I'll finish you all off."

Fardoon nodded. The blond took a cell phone out of his pocket and made a call. He spoke clipped sentences in German. The person on the other side was brief. The blond hung up.

"You'll have fifty thousand dollars," he said. "Now the pills."

This couldn't be happening again. "No!" Max cried. "No! Please don't."

"First the money," Fardoon said, ignoring her.

The blond shook his head.

"No?" Fardoon raised his palms in the air, "Fine. I'm just trying to save your skin."

The blond hesitated for a few seconds before speaking. "He goes with me." He took Zeeshan's arm. "Your phones, please." He took Max's and Fardoon's cell phones and checked the place for a landline. There was none.

They started to leave. Max, no longer afraid and realizing the futility of her situation, leapt at the blond and managed to scratch him deeply across his cheek. "I need those tablets!" she screamed. "You cannot take away everything. I'm sick of you and your threats."

The German easily peeled her off his body and threw her onto the floor. He brought his gun to her temple and pressed hard. "I should have done this a long time ago. One less Jew in the world is one less problem, my father always said."

"Do it. I dare you," she hissed. "Just do it."

Fardoon stepped between her and the blond. "Let her go."

The blond shrugged him aside, his face fierce, his eyes determined.

"I'm asking nicely," Fardoon said. "We do not treat women this way. If you value your own life, you will let her go."

The blond let out a laugh. "You love to slaughter your women. Stonings, vigilante justice. This place is known for them."

Fardoon looked livid. "Perhaps. But if you kill her for these tablets, it means they're valuable, which in turn means you'll have to pay for a lot of people's silence. We may look it, but we're not a lawless land. Just like these groups I told you about, the police also love making examples of your lot. I'm merely trying to help you. It's costing you fifty thousand dollars now. With her blood on your hands, it'll cost you a lot more."

The blond dug his gun deeper into Max's temple, hit her hard with it and pushed her away. She fell to the floor. Pain shot through her head like a bolt of electricity.

The German said to Fardoon, "When your grandson and I return, you better lead me to the pills." To Max, he said, "Do not interfere where you don't belong."

Clutching her head in her hands, Max turned away.

The blond and Zeeshan left through the tiny back door.

Fardoon let out a sigh upon hearing the door being locked from the outside. The front shutter too was locked.

Max slowly got off the floor and went back to her chair. She held a handkerchief to her temple to stop the bleeding. "Thank you for saving my life," she said.

Fardoon waved her thanks away with a swift movement of his hand. He opened a first aid kit, found Max some antiseptic, and applied it to her gash.

"Don't you want the story of the pills to come out?" Max asked, wincing with pain.

"What story?" Fardoon said distractedly. "That the pills are making everyone sick and fat?"

"It's so much more than that," Max said. "With the pills we can get the bacteria in it and use it to make a vaccine. Heart disease, obesity, diabetes, high blood pressure—so much could be prevented in the future."

"All rich people's problems," Fardoon muttered, glancing up at the connecting window to the tea shop.

"Are you saying no one you know, no one in your village suffers from diabetes or high blood pressure?" Max said, tears starting to run down her cheeks.

"Child, what do you know about my people?" Fardoon said kindly. "Maybe they do have these diseases. But what they suffer from is a lack of basic resources. This money will give them that and more. And let me tell you one other thing. In Mohenjo-daro, all those years ago, numerous promises were made by your grandfather's friends and never kept. A school and hospital were started and left half finished when their work was done. Our graves were desecrated during the war. Some Germans came and emptied the Colossus's grave of the urns, with not so much as a *paisa* in return. This is the time for payment. If I give you the pills, what do we get? A small mention in a newspaper somewhere. Maybe."

"I'm so sorry about all that happened, but my grandfather had nothing to do with it," Max began.

Fardoon raised his hand. "It is possible. And maybe all I am is an old, ignorant man. But what I see here is a chance to make things right." He paused. "Or perhaps I just don't believe you. You must understand it is all rather far-fetched."

"Don't you see? That sort of thinking is exactly why it's so important for me to have the pills." Max said with passion. "Please, why don't you do both? Get your money and give me a few, just a few pills."

Fardoon stood on tiptoe at the window. "Khan, are you there? Khan?" To Max he said, "And risk the wrath of that monster? *Nah, nah.* I have Zeeshan to think of. It's not worth it to be a hero. No madam, I plan to hand over every last pill to him."

Max wrung her hands. "Damn, damn, damn," she said over and over.

"Khan!" Fardoon called. "Khan! For God's sake, is everyone asleep?"

"*Kya baat hai bhai?*" Max heard a soft voice say. "How much chai will you have in one morning?"

Fardoon spoke in hurried Urdu.

"Brother, you are becoming senile," the man on the other end said in English when Fardoon had finished.

Fardoon sat down across from Max in silence, drumming anxious fingers on the table.

CHAPTER THIRTY-NINE

Outside, Julian was on the street not far from Fardoon's shop. Half frantic, half irritated, his shoulders slumped. He wished he could have the old Max back—sweet, dithering Max who needed him to take charge. Here she had gone off all by herself doing heaven knows what. If it weren't for Kevin, he wouldn't even have known where she had taken off to!

He stopped outside Fardoon's shop. Closed. Great. Now what? He thought about Raquel. He really should call her. They had spoken a few days before. He told her he was visiting a colleague in India. She had believed him, since as far as she was concerned, India was in Asia. It would not occur to her that his area of work involved East Asia and not South Asia.

Still, he did feel guilty about misleading her. And at the same time, he was merrily leading Max on. He was turning out to be quite a nasty piece of goods overall.

The phone rang.

Raquel.

"Hi," she said in a tired voice. "I just got back home."

"I see," Julian said, his eyes scanning the street for Max.

"I'm fine, Jules, and how are you?" Raquel said.

"All right, I guess," Julian said, not taking the bait. "Why aren't you in bed?"

Raquel sighed. "I'm working. Always working. And I'm getting sick of it. Tomorrow I turn thirty-four, Jules. Thirty-four."

He had almost forgotten. "I would've called." He knew how lame he sounded. All he wanted to do was hang up and look for Max.

"Yes, well. I know you're busy, too. But I wish you were here."

He felt a pang of affection for Raquel.

But where the heck was Max? His heart starting pounding hard against his ribs. What if something happened to her? He would never forgive—

"Jules," Raquel said. "I'm tired. I want to settle down. I can't go on like this. Let's get married, let's have a baby, and after a year or so, I'll be recharged for this mad world."

Wow, really! "This is hardly the way to discuss this," he said and looked back at Fardoon's store. No sign of anyone.

"We never seem to have the time to talk anymore," Raquel said in an uncharacteristically vulnerable manner. "What are you doing in India, anyway? Weren't you just in London? What's with all the travel? I miss you. When are you coming back?"

"I'm not sure," Julian said.

"Am I boring you?" Raquel said sharply. How did she always know when he was distracted?

"No...it's just that my friend, uh, colleague is in a little bit of trouble, and I'm trying to help, but she—"

"What sort of trouble?" Raquel said tartly.

Julian was silent.

"I can see you are otherwise occupied. And maybe it's my fault. I'm here. I'm ready. Call me when you get back."

Silence on both sides. Julian was about to speak when, unexpectedly, Raquel said, "I love you," before she hung up.

Julian sank down onto the sidewalk, drained. Should he ask the tea shop if they knew where Fardoon had gone? Max seldom answered her cell phone these days. Still, it was worth a shot. He got her voice mail. He crossed the street and paced, keeping his eyes on Fardoon's store.

CHAPTER FORTY

Inside the store, Fardoon and Max stared at the walls for what seemed like ages when Zeeshan and the blond finally entered through the back door.

Excitedly, Zeeshan said, "The money will be transferred into our account in a few days as long as we give him what he wants. The bank manager assured me that the transfer has been initiated. She demanded that I buy her wedding trousseau, now that I'm going to be rich." Zeeshan plunked himself down on a chair and stared at his grandfather in joyful disbelief.

The German was starting to look nervous. His hair looked even more horrific than usual, Max thought with a grimace. Half yellow, half brown. Ugh. She'd had enough of everything. All she wanted to do now was leave this place in one piece.

"Can I go now?" she asked him icily.

"Not yet," he snapped, pointing his gun at her.

There was a knock on the back door. Zeeshan opened it. Three bearded men in traditional dress stood there, one of them armed with a large, ancient-looking rifle.

"Aah, Zeeshan *bhai*, Aajaa. There you are," one of them said. "Everything all right?" He glanced at the German.

Fardoon looked delighted.

The men gave the blond disapproving looks. One of them winked at Max. She pulled her scarf tightly around her head and chest in response.

The German spoke to Fardoon while keeping an eye on the newcomers. "Now the pills. If I don't have all of them, the transfer won't happen." He pulled Max by her arm, and Fardoon led them to his apartment above the store. Fardoon opened his closet. Nestled among his clothes was a wooden box. Inside were a few small pieces of jewelry, an Indus seal, and a small bottle of pills.

Max felt desperation rising in her chest. She was so close, so very close. With a cry, she leapt toward Fardoon and grabbed the bottle.

The blond slapped her hard across the face and snatched the bottle back from her. "Fräulein, my patience is wearing thin."

She tried to claw at him, but he held her away with minimal effort.

"I hope there are no more of these," the blond said to Fardoon.

Fardoon shook his head, avoiding Max's glare.

The German went through the entire apartment with quick nervous movements. He seemed to want nothing more than to leave this place. The presence of the men downstairs was unnerving him, Max thought.

Fardoon led them back to the store.

Max noticed that the man who had winked at her was trying to load the rifle. Oddly, he didn't seem to know how or where the bullets went.

The German handed back Max's cell phone. "Don't bother calling the police, not if you want that lily-faced boyfriend of yours to live. Or your old Jew in Chicago."

He quickly left.

The minute he was out of sight, the Chapars and their extremist friends let out a loud cry of joy. The three men peeled off their traditional clothes and threw them up in the air. They were wearing jeans and T-shirts. Except for their scraggly beards, they looked like college kids in any part of the world.

"Aren't you glad we didn't shave today, Aajaa?" one of them said.

Fardoon slapped them on their shoulders. "How did you get these clothes?"

"There are four people at Khan's tea shop sitting practically naked! There was no time for them to take our clothes, so we just wore theirs over ours!"

"And the rifle?" Zeeshan asked.

"It belongs to the security guard at the jewelry store next door. He was asleep, so we thought we'd borrow it. Nice touch, no?" The man who had winked at Max now smiled at her. She returned it with a small smile of her own. They were harmless.

She sighed. Seemed everyone but her was capable of outsmarting her adversaries. She got up and left the store through the back door.

Julian rushed toward her as she crossed the street. He grabbed her by her shoulders. "What happened? I was so worried." He touched her temple. "My goodness, you're hurt! Why didn't you tell me where you were?"

"Julian, you're hurting me." Max broke free from his grasp.

"I'm sorry," he said. He was shaking. "I was so afraid for you."

Max turned to look at the store. "The Germans have bought the pills for fifty thousand dollars," she said.

"That monster is in there, too?" Julian clenched his teeth, his voice frantic. He took her arm again. "Did he do this to you? Should we call the police?"

"What is the matter with you?" Max said. "You sound like Uncle Ernst! Anyway, I don't see how the police can help. Let's go." She pulled her arm away from his too-firm grip. "We're done here."

They walked in silence, Max fuming. "I wish I had found out nothing. Then I wouldn't have to live with this utter and humiliating defeat."

"Kevin will publish the report," Julian said.

"But without the pills, there will be no impact," Max said.

"The research community will look into it…eventually."

"And Papa's death? Who will look into that?"

"We have done quite well, considering. We got our hands on the papers, we figured out how to decode them. Surely you can feel some sense of peace that your father didn't commit suicide." Julian sounded irritated.

Max turned to look at him. Julian ought to know that his choice of words had been a tad callous. "Peace! There's no peace for me. Guilt. And failure. Those are the feelings I foresee for the rest of my life. Seriously, Julian."

Julian looked slighted. They walked a few steps further. "Look, I realize this might not be the best time to do this. To tell you this. But these past few days have changed me. I—" He looked away from her. "I have not been honest with you because I wanted so much to be part of this." He stopped and held out an arm to stop her, too. He turned her toward him and took both her hands in his. "Here's the awful truth. I was bored out of my mind when you came along with your story."

Max let out a low moan.

Julian's face and eyes showed naked, honest affection. "But now, I realize how much I'm starting to care for you."

"What are you trying to say, exactly?"

He swallowed hard. "There's someone in my life. Her name is Raquel."

Max pulled her hands away. "I knew it. I knew it!" She began walking away from him. "I should have known you were lying to me. I mean, why would anyone be attracted to *me*? It was this Indus pill business the whole time. Well, the adventure is over now, you can go home. Thank you for everything, Professor McIntosh!"

Julian kept pace with her. "Today," he went on calmly as if Max hadn't even spoken, "I found out that Raquel wants to get married, and I just couldn't—"

"*Mazel tov!*" Max shouted, throwing her arms up.

"Max," Julian said softly. "Don't you see? I couldn't tell her, 'Yes let's get married.' I just couldn't."

Max stopped walking. "What do you want me to say? Thank you? I'm so grateful that you find yourself attracted to dumpy old me, after all? Is that what you want? Damn you." Anger flared inside her with renewed vigor as a realization dawned. "That's why you didn't sleep with me, that's why you've kept your hands off me. Not because you didn't want our relationship to start this way. It was because of Raquel. You've been feeling guilty about cheating on her." She slapped Julian hard across the face.

Julian looked stunned.

"I'm sorry, but you deserved that," she said. "Look, it's best if you go back to your girlfriend. The rest of this great adventure won't be very pleasant for you, I'm afraid. I have a lot left to do."

Julian took her hands and kissed them. "You have done enough," he said softly.

He had chosen the absolute worst moment to reveal his lies. She was so mad she could hardly speak. And yet, she had fallen for him. Badly. "Tell you what," she said as calmly as she could. "Why don't you go home and get married? Forget all this ever happened." Julian's cheek had grown bright pink and still showed her finger marks. He rubbed his hand against it.

Max felt herself thawing a little. *Stop talking. Bite your tongue*, she tried telling herself. Julian had been honest, at least. Better late than never, right? But her mouth was on a roll. All her frustration, her anger, her exhaustion, and her deep sense of betrayal were pouring out as harsh words, and she could not stop them. "Have a dozen children who will be as gorgeous as your wife and you. This Raquel must be gorgeous, no? Have a great life. Send me Christmas cards."

"What are you going to do now?" Julian said meekly. "Let me help." He didn't sound very enthusiastic.

Max heard the doubt in his voice and responded to it. "You don't really want to help anymore, buddy."

He moved closer to her. "It's not that. I'm just…tired, I guess. It's time to go home. To the people who love you."

Max looked at him. One step closer and she could kiss him. The tropical sun had tanned his skin to a peachy brown. His shirt was not fully tucked in. He looked like he had come here straight from bed. And he looked like he wanted to take her in his arms. His eyes were full of concern. He was so sweet, so achingly handsome. He had admitted that he loved her. Incredibly sideways, but he had. She took a step toward him.

"You can't change the past," he said coolly. Too coolly.

Max turned and walked away in a huff.

CHAPTER FORTY-ONE

Aaron folded his newspaper and got up. He had been seated in the tea shop next to Fardoon Chapar's storefront for a while, polishing off cups of tea and pastries. His stomach was starting to feel a little queasy.

He was getting tired of all this travel—London, Hyderabad, now Pakistan. The food in London was all right, but why did the locals in these parts like to set their tongues on fire at every meal? He rubbed his sleep-deprived eyes. They felt like they were on fire, too.

Now Aaron watched the German leave the store holding a small bag. Blondie seemed to know where Maxine and her companions were at all times, just like his client did. Aaron wondered if his client and the German knew each other. Obviously they didn't care for each other, since Blondie had been anything but friendly.

It helped that Aaron wasn't the curious sort. The German, the papers, their importance, the girl—none of it was of interest to him. They could be spy secrets, chemical formulas, or secret love letters from centuries ago, for all he cared. His eyes were on the sack of gold at the end of this tunnel.

The blond took a taxi. Aaron followed it with one of his own and watched him enter his hotel and take the elevator. Aaron watched the elevator light. Fourth floor. He took the next elevator there. There were eight doors.

Aaron called the front desk. "Hello," he said, "I just got in from New York and was supposed to give a message from a friend to her boyfriend. She gave me his room number on the fourth floor, but I can't for the life of me remember it!"

"I cannot give out room numbers, sir," was the polite reply.

"Well, could you call him and tell him to expect a message in the lobby? I'll be there in a few minutes."

"His name?"

"This is the problem!" Aaron laughed. "My friend just started seeing him. German guy, heavy-set. She told me…it's Peter or something. Gosh, I wish I hadn't agreed to do this—"

There was a long pause. Aaron figured the desk clerk was checking to see if a German was staying on the fourth floor. Despite being so vague, he was sure she would call him.

"Please," he said. "It's just that my friend and this fellow had a big fight and he is traveling here on business, so when I told her I was going to be here, she begged me to—"

The voice softened. "Give me a moment."

Aaron hung up and waited behind a pillar. Opposite was a mirror. He could see some of the doors reflected there. Aaron realized he had made a big mistake. Whatever Blondie had received from the old man, there was no way he would leave it unguarded in his room. Aaron cursed. His harebrained scheme had backfired.

As he had suspected, the German quickly left his room with a plain black briefcase. Aaron took the stairs down. The blond was at the front desk.

"Please hold this for me until I check out," Blondie said.

"Very well, Mr. Altgeld," the receptionist said.

A mobile phone rang. "Hans *hier*," the German answered. He turned away and covered his mouth so his conversation was inaudible.

Aaron grinned. *All right, Hans Altgeld*, he said to himself. *It's down to the last lap of this race.*

Aaron didn't want to risk breaking into the hotel safe. The briefcase must contain what his client was seeking. Maybe his scheme hadn't been quite so harebrained after all. But it might also be a red herring. There was no way to be sure. Aaron watched the fourth floor for several hours. Hans left, presumably for dinner, around 6:00 p.m.

Aaron had to take the chance that whatever Hans had left with the desk clerk was important. He was sure the briefcase Hans had handed the clerk was the same one he had carried in London. He had a good eye for bags.

Aaron found a luggage store nearby and looked for a briefcase similar to Hans's. He didn't have much time; Hans might leave at any moment now that his work was done. He found one close enough and returned to the hotel. He spent the next few hours nursing a drink in the lobby. Hans returned around midnight, checked out, collected his briefcase, and left. A taxi was waiting for him. Aaron was prepared. His return ticket was an open one. He was ready to leave when Hans was.

"Time to rock and roll," Aaron whispered to himself.

A rickshaw he had arranged for earlier picked him up, and as per his instructions, followed Hans's taxi. Rickshaws were slow, but they had the maneuverability few other vehicles did. And he could stay hidden inside one. Not burdened with more luggage than his backpack, Aaron was all set to return home.

Triumphant, with any luck.

At the airport, Hans got off and briskly made his way to the Lufthansa check-in desk. Aaron checked in, too, and began following him through the airport.

Aaron held his knife, the source of his livelihood for years, inside his pocket. And now, maybe, just maybe, it would help him start a new life.

Hans stopped at a coffee shop close by. There was no one behind him. The briefcase was handcuffed to his wrist. Aaron made a wry face. Not that his knife could have cut through the thick handles anyway.

He put on a baseball cap, keeping it low so his face was mostly covered. He waited for the coffee shop to get busy, but apparently not many people were craving caffeine. An attractive woman with a large bag walked by, speaking on a cell phone. Aaron approached her from behind and expertly made a long tear in her bag. Books, CDs, make-up, and more started to spill out. The woman gave a little cry and leapt to the floor. Aaron had hoped Hans would move to help her since she was only a few feet away from him, but he didn't. He did, however, turn around to look. That was all the time Aaron needed. He got close to Hans for a second, and then walked quickly away.

Aaron kept Hans in sight as he approached the security gate. *Please God, let this go well. This one last time.* He looked at the ceiling and crossed himself. He stayed behind Hans with his head covered, making sure there was always one person between them.

Hans started to walk through the metal detector with his briefcase attached, but the security personnel asked him to un-cuff it and put it on the belt. He made a fuss, but they stood their ground. Aaron waited and let people pass until Hans had put his bag on the belt. Hans glanced around, and Aaron bent down to tie a shoelace. When Hans's back was turned once more, Aaron stood up.

Hans was about to pass through the metal detector. Aaron put his backpack and his newly bought briefcase filled with magazines and books on the belt. His bags were two bags away from Hans's and about to enter the X-ray machine. The person in front of him had a large handbag and was rather slow getting it on the belt.

Come on, Aaron prayed.

Hans passed through the detector and it began to beep. An attendant asked him to step aside.

Large handbag man was passing through the detector now. Aaron held his breath. It was his turn next.

A muscular guard patted down Hans, and when he reached his buttocks, his placid expression changed. He straightened himself and calmly asked Hans to empty his back pocket.

"There is nothing there," Hans said.

"Now, please," the guard said.

Hans put his hand on his back pocket. His face went into a frown. Aaron had passed through the detector with his face turned away.

Hans's briefcase was waiting to be picked up. Aaron pushed his own briefcase close to it. Not identical, but close enough.

"I need to get my bag." Hans moved towards the belt. He was several feet away from it. Aaron had collected his backpack and was pretending to have trouble with his shoes.

"Please do not move, sir," the guard said. Three other guards surrounded him.

One of them pulled Aaron's knife out of Hans's pocket. "Sir, you cannot carry this on board," he said politely.

"That is not my knife. I need to get my bag now!" Hans made a dash for the belt, but was quickly restrained by the guards. For a brief moment, his face was turned away, and Aaron swooped down on Hans's briefcase. He slipped it under his arm, swung his jacket around it to hide it, and began to calmly walk away. Behind him he could hear shouting. "My briefcase! Someone stole my briefcase!"

"Sir, it is there on the belt. Please calm down."

Aaron turned to watch. Hans hesitated. He was staring at the briefcase Aaron had bought.

Finally, he said, "I need to get it. I need to be sure."

"Sir your briefcase is safe." The guard gestured to the X-ray security man, who set the briefcase aside.

Aaron turned slightly to see a guard taking Hans to the briefcase. "Please open it," the guard said.

Yes! Aaron pumped his fist. He couldn't resist. He peeled off his cap and tried to catch Hans's eye.

Hans looked at him.

Aaron waved and gave a little bow.

"That rat—he has my briefcase! Look!" He pointed in Aaron's direction. A guard held him back from running towards Aaron.

"Is this not your briefcase sir?"

"*Nein!* He…he has my briefcase." He pointed in Aaron's direction. "That isn't mine. *Dum Kopf,* fool!" He lashed out at the guard. Promptly, he was handcuffed and led away.

Aaron was sure Hans would be detained for several hours, if not the whole day. At least that is what he had managed to glean from the desk clerk at his hotel. Pakistani security didn't like people who carried knives. There had been a surge of terrorist types trying to pass through their airports ever since the 1998 bombings of the American embassies in Africa. Terror could come in all colors and shapes, Aaron supposed. The fact that Aaron had filled his briefcase with extremist literature wasn't going to help Blondie's case, either.

Aaron rushed to his gate.

He landed in Chicago and promptly handed over the briefcase to his partner Geoff, who that same day handed him a cashier's check for $31,200.

Aaron booked a one-way ticket to Rio de Janeiro.

His new life was about to begin.

CHAPTER FORTY-TWO

Lufthansa's First Class Lounge
Schönefeld International Airport
Berlin

Max checked her watch. She had landed in Berlin three hours earlier and contacted Berliner. Chairman Peter Schultz had retired a while ago, they said. She asked them to call him and let him know that she was waiting for him at the airport. If he called, good. If not, well, at least she'd tried. Minutes later, she got a call asking her to wait for him here in the lounge.

She had eaten every single offering on the refreshments table. She was tired, but a nap was out of the question. He would be here. Any second. She could feel her heart thumping against her chest as if waiting to jump out and fall by her feet, a ragged lump of angst-ridden flesh.

Half an hour later, an elegant old man pushed open the lounge door and scanned the room. That suit, that hair, and those laser eyes. Max knew it had to be him—Peter Schultz.

His eyes finally landed on her. His first steps faltered, but he steadied himself and walked toward her. By the time he reached her, he seemed to have composed himself fully.

"Fräulein Rosen," he said in a honey-smooth voice.

He looked so elegant. His eyes were soft up close, but there was an uncanny alertness about them she had seldom seen even in younger people. He was groomed to perfection and smelled of cloves and vanilla. Max stood up.

"Thank you for coming," she said, but not politely. She cocked her chin at him. "You killed my father," she said. "After all that my grandfather did for your company, how could you go and kill his only son when all he wanted to do was the right thing—reveal the truth?"

Schultz looked unfazed, even a trifle disappointed. "Child, you are old enough to know that the truth can be a very dangerous thing." He pointed to the sofa she had been sitting on. "Sit, please. Let us talk like civilized people."

Max sat on the edge of the sofa. "So you don't deny it."

Schultz looked at her, his gaze unwavering. "Fräulein Rosen, we didn't kill anyone." Max started to speak again, but he held up his palm. "Do you know how many people work in our headquarters alone? Five hundred. In our factories—15,000 worldwide." Max couldn't help but notice how seductive his voice was. If she looked too deep into his eyes, he just might hypnotize her. "Our revenues are close to 900 million Euros a year. We make some of the leading drugs in the market today. Do you have any idea who we are?"

Max bit her lip.

A waitress stopped by. Schultz spoke to her in German. After she'd left, he continued. "Maxine," he said. "May I call you Maxine? You are so like Samuel."

"I know," Max said drily.

Schultz smiled. "I used to call your grandfather Herr Doctor even though he was my friend, because I respected him so much. But Hiram's work would have done us much harm had it come out in the open. "He shrugged. "Now the chips may fall as they may. Know this, however. I'll use all my power to ride out the storm that is sure to come." He leaned forward, his face earnest. "But I didn't kill your father. Ahh, tea!"

The waitress returned with a tray of tea. Schultz poured a cup for each of them. Seeing her suspicious expression, he said, "Oh, we watch the movies, do we? Very well. I will do what they do in the movies." He exchanged cups. Seeing her head go askance, he laughed and exchanged cups one more time. He raised a finger as if asking her to watch his next trick. He moved the cups many times so it was hard to know which cup belonged to whom. He ended his little drama by raising a cup and, with a small wave, indicated that Max should drink her tea, too. "It's from the Chengdu province. A special blend for me."

Max was disgusted. How could he be so flippant? He had ruined her grandfather's life and later her father's, and he was sitting there like a peacock, vain and detached, sipping his specially blended tea!

"You cold bastard!" She leaped at Schultz. A few security guards materialized by her side and pulled her away.

"Leave us alone," Schultz said. "It's fine." When everyone had left, he said, "We are too big to go around finishing off people. Sit, please." He resumed drinking his tea.

Max closed her eyes. Quietly, she said, "But he was murdered."

Schulz shook his head. Max looked at him, realizing that although he was smug, he definitely didn't show any signs of culpability. "All right, I'll play along," she said. "Tell me what happened."

Schulz looked at her with approval. "I knew Hiram was working on heart disease. I had kept an interest in his work. I even asked him to come work for me, but he declined. My company had too many bad memories associated with it. Of course, I understood. I had no idea about his work on Samuel's old research. One day, one of his test subjects called me, asking for money." He looked put out. "I paid him off and managed to get one or two telling memos related to Hiram's work. I begged Hiram not to publish the work. But he was determined to tell the world our ugly truths." Schultz looked thoughtful.

"I know about your secret lab," Max blurted. "The one you shut down after you discovered what the pill had done."

There was a pitcher of water on the table. Schultz poured himself a glass. "It's debatable how much harm the pills actually did. But the fact is my company would have been buried under frivolous lawsuits and preposterous claims of diseases we had let spread. As for Hiram, I promised him money. But he refused. He owed it to his father to publish the work, he said. He called me the worst friend anyone could have for abandoning his father. Many other unflattering names, too." Schultz took a deep breath.

Max was becoming more and more convinced that Schultz truly had no need to kill her father. He had billions of dollars worth of motive, but he was right. He could quash her comparatively small-time father and his work in a matter of days, even hours, with a few phone calls. Without harming him.

"I warned Hiram I'd discredit his work," Schultz spoke wearily. His eyes grew wide, reenacting his emotions from years ago. "I said I'd even discredit him personally, make him out to be a depressed alcoholic. Once that happened, the journals wouldn't bother with his work."

Max bit her lip. What Schultz was saying was despicable, but Papa *had* resorted to drinking heavily towards the end.

"But Hiram was dogged," Schultz said. "He rode out his period of disfavor and even managed to regain some friends in the research world. But I was prepared. I made sure he lost friends quicker than he found them. It wasn't easy or fun, but it had to be done. Soon he started gaining support among some alternative theorists. But before I could worry, I heard about his suicide." He looked at her as if waiting for her to contradict him. "I might have hated his guts, but I knew Hiram was a brilliant scientist. In my darkest moments, I'm ashamed to say, I was relieved that he was no longer a problem for us."

Max winced.

Schultz went on. "In my business it's easy to forget that we are trying to help people."

Max leaned back and closed her eyes. "Who, then? If not you, then who?" she said softly. "Who had as much to lose?"

Schultz shrugged. "Perhaps the people who have the pills now. Whoever has them probably has the same interests as ours."

"Whoa," Max said, sitting up straight. "You don't have the pills?"

Schultz smiled, as if he was welcoming the challenge of having to fight for them once more. Max wondered why he was looking so pleased if he no longer had the pills. Unless he was lying. "That's impossible," She exclaimed. "Your assassin stole them from under my nose with your dirty money."

Schultz now looked relieved almost. "You know, I could not rid myself of the nagging feeling that you were the one who had masterminded it all. Staging your elaborate game about finding the papers, then arranging to have them stolen from you. Same with the pills in Karachi. I was absolutely amazed. I thought how truly worthy you were of being Samuel's granddaughter."

"Sorry, I'm not that smart," Max said wearily.

"The pills Hans procured were taken from him at the Karachi airport by the same crook he had encountered in London. I would like to know who this very worthy adversary is. So yes, the question puzzling me too is who else has as much to lose as we do?" He smiled a smile that didn't quite reach his eyes and stood up.

Max didn't want him to leave yet. She held out her arm and almost touched his sleeve. "Please. Who could have done it?" She hated begging him, but this man was her last link to knowing what had happened to her father.

Schultz gazed into her eyes. "I can't believe the competition would resort to killing Hiram either. Too messy and not worth their while. Of course I'm thinking of a competitor in our league with less to lose than, say, a smaller company."

Was that the best he could do? Max impatiently shook her head. "But why did Lars die? They said heart attack, but isn't that too convenient?"

Schulz shrugged.

Max felt so deflated. But she wasn't ready to completely exonerate Schultz. If she kept him talking, he might give something incriminating away. What would she do then? She hadn't thought that far.

Schultz extended his hand. "Goodbye Maxine," he said. Max looked up at him. He let out a chuckle. "Ach, look at you with those great big, sad eyes! You do so look like Samuel." He sat back down. "Had Hiram any enemies?" he said after a while.

Max ran her tongue over her dry lips and shook her head no. It was unimaginable that Papa would have any enemies.

Schultz made a smacking sound of irritation. "There must be some reason. How about love?" His voice grew excited. "A failed love affair. Something mundane like that. Too much love. Too much love breeds evil. My bet is on money, though. If I weren't as powerful as I am, I might have felt compelled to do something…shall we say, rash?" He gave her a smile that reminded her of a hungry fox.

He looked old and a bit tired. His smile now turned more sincere. "Before you go Maxine, I want you to know that I admired Samuel. And Hiram. And now even you, my dear. This has been most entertaining."

He held out his hand but Max did not take it. He shrugged. "Let the game continue. You do your best to get this research out. I will do my best to quash it. *Guten tag,* good day." The former chairman of Berliner turned around and left.

Max sat still, looking at the glass doors that swung shut behind Schultz.

Her mind went to Julian. He must be preparing to get married to Raquel in some exotic location. A castle in Scotland, perhaps.

Visions of an isolated castle at the end of a pristine lawn floated in front of her eyes. Guests streaming toward it. Pink and white balloons and flowers everywhere.

A torrent of jealous acid flooded her stomach.

Damn him. And damn that Raquel. They could get married on the moon for all she cared.

Like this airport, Max had been left in no-man's land—a place between places. She could never go back to her old self, where she had managed to find a modicum of stability. Where an acceptance of her past had taken hold with the will to go on and make her life a success. She might never be able to go forward, either. To a place where she could leave behind forever the dreaded questions of *who* and *why*.

And yet, here she was. In Berlin. Alone. She had just accused a very powerful man of murder, and although she had felt apprehension, she hadn't been seized with panic. She had not even thought about fidgeting with her hair, let alone fainting.

Maybe she would find a way out of this no-man's land.

She walked onto the plane with head held high.

CHAPTER FORTY-THREE

Julian warmed his hands with a cup of coffee and walked over to his living room window. He had landed in Chicago several hours earlier and was settling back in his small one-bedroom apartment on Southport. Raquel hated his place. The street crawled with yuppie drunks on the weekends, she would say. Well, there was a bar downstairs and, yes, young people did have a good time there. But Julian didn't hate them. He had even become friendly with some of the regulars. But Raquel was critical of everything.

Then there was Max. He sipped his coffee, wishing he had never met her, never gotten involved with her and her insane problem. And yet all he could think about was her face, now happy, now sad, her lips full and welcoming, her eyes filled with eagerness to make love to him.

Max wasn't like other women he had been with. She was so confident about some things, so diffident about others. So unsure, so unaware of her own voluptuous beauty. And yet so headstrong and impulsive.

After the Fardoon debacle, Julian had decided to let Max blow off steam. He needed to think, and Max needed to sort things out for herself. Their flight back to Chicago was early the next day. He figured she would calm down by then.

Back at the hotel, Julian had suggested some sightseeing, but Max wasn't interested. She just wanted to stay in her room, she had said. They had met for lunch but it had been eaten in icy silence. After, she had left him alone. He tried calling her, but she had left a recorded message saying she wanted to take a nap.

He had spent a few hours visiting Karachi's sights. When he returned, he had knocked on her door. No answer.

Worried, he'd gone to the front desk only to find out that she had checked out. He had imagined all sorts of awful things. She could have been drugged. Or kidnapped! Julian had called Kevin, but he had no idea where Max had gone.

Sick with worry and yet angry with Max for not keeping him informed, he called her cell phone. Voice mail. He tried calling her work number. He knew that Max had forwarded that number to her assistant's cell.

Kim answered. He started to introduce himself when Kim said, "Julian, hello. Max told me about you. She landed safely not long ago."

Julian exhaled with relief. "And?" he said hopefully.

"She's fine, but I'd give her some time." Kim told him that Max had stopped in Berlin to meet Peter Schultz but hung up before Julian could say anything more.

Julian felt a rush of irritation. Silly, silly Max. He put down his coffee. Why had she felt the need to traipse off to Berlin to confront this Schultz? That was foolish, not to mention dangerous. What if he had done something to her? In the midst of his frustration, he also realized that he felt great remorse for leaving her to go off on her own.

At least she was safe. And she was home.

The lack of sleep from changing time zones began to overwhelm him. In a few hours, he would go to her. Tell her how he really felt about her. And apologize. On his knees.

Then he would lecture her.

For that he needed energy.

Julian awoke with a start. It was 4:00 a.m. He picked up the phone. Might Max be asleep, though? Never mind. He wanted to see her. He called her apartment.

There was no answer. Where was she? He called three more times. Nothing.

He dressed, ran out, and managed to find a cab.

At Max's building, Julian hurriedly explained to the front desk clerk why he needed to let him in, reminding him who he was. Maxine Rosen's frequent guest, good friend, even. The man wasn't convinced. It occurred to Julian that he had only been to her apartment once.

The desk clerk called, but there was no answer. "She isn't home, sir," he told Julian.

"Try her mobile," Julian said. He waited while the man at the desk made the call.

A cleaning woman entered the building. The desk clerk greeted her while he waited for Max to answer. At the same time, he pressed a button and opened the glass doors to let her in. Julian dashed in through them.

"Sir!" the doorman yelled.

But Julian wasn't listening. He took the elevator to the 35th floor. He could hear the doorman summoning security.

He reached Max's floor and banged on her door. No answer. She had told him she was a light sleeper. Why wasn't she answering?

He pulled out his phone and called her again. Still nothing. He checked the time. 5:00 a.m.

Where are you, Maxine Rosen?

He paced in front of her apartment with a growing sense of dread that something was very wrong.

CHAPTER FORTY-FOUR

Ernst Frank's apartment
Chicago

The phone rang. Ernst picked it up slowly. "Hello," he said, rubbing his eyes.

"I read your email," his grandson said. "Max has managed to decode the research. It'll be published now, I suppose."

Alex had developed his mother's cutting voice ever since he had taken over her company years ago. Ernst bent his head down and listened patiently to his grandson's ranting. He couldn't help being amazed at how alert he sounded. Like his mother, Alex must have risen at 4:00 a.m. and done his five-mile run.

"Clients will leave us slowly but surely. Sally Hart Weight Loss will become obsolete." Alex's voice became a whine. "There are investors waiting in the wings. They will disappear at the slightest whiff of doubt. Without that cash influx, this company will be finished."

"Alex," Ernst said. "Hiram told me this before and I'm telling you now. This will take years to make a dent in the business. Your mother was unstable. She was unable to see that."

"Maybe," Alex went on, "but perhaps it's as good a reason as any to sell the company."

"Please, no!" Ernst cried. "If you sell the company now, you destroy Sally. She would have died for nothing."

"*Zayde,* grandfather, I took over the company because you begged me to. We'll keep my mother alive this way, you said. The truth is, she is dead. It's time to move on."

Ernst was livid. "But…but…that isn't what we discussed. What about everything I did for you? For Sally?"

"This company isn't your daughter. Sally Hart is gone."

Alex's words were stabs at Ernst's heart. He wanted to scream. The company was what had kept Sally in one piece. It was what had held her together throughout her unhappy marriage. It had been her support during and after her messy divorce. It had been her solace. Alex was wrong. The company *was* Sally Hart.

"We cannot let the company go just like that," Ernst begged.

"Max should have let sleeping dogs lie," Alex said and hung up.

Ernst felt a rash of anger at the events that had choreographed his actions thus far. The stone hand of defeat was pushing him against a wall, choking the life out of him. It was over. It had all been for nothing.

He had done what he had thought was right. He hadn't been able to prevent Sally's death, but he had kept his daughter alive through the triumphs of her company. He had done his part. And now, so easily, Alex was ready to throw it all away. It would all have been for nothing if Sally's company were sold.

Ernst sat on his couch and watched the lake for a while. A sense of calm descended over him. His decision was made. He got up, steadied himself, and opened his safe. A small bottle containing a deadly poison stared back at him. Samuel had given it to him decades ago to get rid of a mouse.

"We modified the botulinum toxin in the lab by spawning a rapid-acting mutation of the *Clostridium botulinum* bacteria," Samuel had said at the time. "They used it in covert Nazi operations to poison quite a few Allied officers. It brings on fatal paralysis in a human in less than ten minutes, but a mouse should be dead in seconds after ingesting this."

Ernst put the bottle in his pocket along with a small pistol from his safe. Just in case.

He needed some air. He walked to the front door and opened it. To his amazement, he found Max outside, asleep on the floor.

"Darling, I was expecting you for breakfast. What are you doing here so early?" Ernst bent down and helped her up. She fell into his arms and held him tight.

"I'll make you a nice cup of tea." He led her in and closed the door.

Ernst went into the kitchen. He opened a cupboard and took out a box of chamomile tea bags. He started a kettle and put a hand in his pocket. He took out the bottle of botulinum toxin and held it over one of the teacups. He hesitated for a few seconds before letting several drops fall. He then opened a packet of coconut cream cookies. "What's that? Did I hear you right? You just got back from Berlin? I thought the plan was to go to Karachi from Hyderabad, and straight back home."

"Yes," Max said, "But I…I had to see Peter Schultz, Opa's old boss."

Ernst poured hot water into the teacups with shaking hands and placed both cups on the tray.

"He looks quite amazing for his age," Max was saying. "He just might live forever."

Ernst stepped into the living room with the tray trembling in his hands, his face twisted in a frown. Max looked at him.

"Should I take that?" she said.

"No, I've got it," Ernst said. What had she learned? How much did she know?

"I accused him of killing Papa."

Ernst managed to slam the tray on the coffee table. He opened his mouth in surprise but could say nothing. Of course, she would think Berliner had killed Hiram.

"How silly of me," he said. "I left the cookies in the kitchen."

He leaned forward and caressed her cheek. She put her hand to his and their fingers met for a second before his hand left her face. Her fingers were cool. Just like they had been as a child. She had clung to him the day Hiram had been found dead in his apartment, face down in his own vomit with a bottle of whiskey beside him.

Ernst had consoled her—as well as himself—that in time all would be well.

After that, he had done right by Max. Taken over for Hiram. He had done his duty.

Ernst went into the kitchen and returned with the cookies.

"What's the matter?" Max said. "You don't look well." She stood up, her eyebrows scrunched together, and touched a palm to the side of his neck.

Suddenly Ernst couldn't bear her touch. "It's…it's nothing. I'm worried about *you*. Drink the tea. That cup. And try a cookie."

She picked up a cookie and took a bite. He sat beside her on the couch.

"Berliner didn't kill Papa," she said.

Oh dear, Ernst thought. How many minutes, hours, days before she realized the truth? How much time did he have?

Max smiled weakly.

"You haven't had any tea," he said.

"It's too hot." She grimaced, her pert nose wrinkling like a small child's.

He nodded. She was a smart girl. She would know before long. As they talked she would find out. His muscles relaxed at the realization. He had held his secret like a tense ache for years now. At the thought of sharing it with her, he almost felt young again.

It was a wonder she hadn't realized the truth already. It was because she trusted him completely. Like one trusted the sun to rise every day.

Ernst forced himself to think of the evening he had poisoned Hiram. He had added over 30 grams of aspirin to Hiram's bottle of whiskey, knowing fully well that Hiram was going to have several drinks that evening. In fact he had even stayed and chatted with him, encouraged him to drink more, leaving only when the stomach cramps had come on. The combination of aspirin and alcohol would cause severe gastrointestinal bleeding, and if ignored, Hiram would die. The dose Ernst had allowed him to ingest virtually guaranteed it.

Later, when he was calmer, he had tried convincing himself that he had done nothing more than bring peace to a troubled man, a man who was tottering on the brink of a messy end by drinking too much anyway. The police and medical examiner hadn't even considered foul play. They had found the aspirin in his system and concluded it was either suicide or accidental death, as Hiram drank too much and was known to be prone to depression.

After killing Hiram, Ernst held on to the botulinum poison for the day he would be caught for his horrible deed. The day he would have to use it on himself. But that day hadn't come.

Instead a day even more horrific had come. This one.

He had managed to go on by telling himself that he had done what was needed to avenge Sally's death. Hiram should not have laughed at him when Ernst asked him to not publish his work. "My Sally will die if you do," Ernst had pleaded. But all Hiram had done was rebuke him and Sally for being childish. "Tell her to see a doctor," Hiram had said. "It will be years before Sally's company is affected. And by that time she can make permanent changes, maybe even sell the company." Ernst had tried telling Sally all that, but all she had heard was the sound of impending doom. Her paranoia had taken over from there.

If only Hiram had taken him more seriously, if only Sally had been more stable. If only, if only.

Killing Hiram hadn't been easy. Living with it had been a nightmare. Not a day passed without him feeling a cool chill every time he set eyes on a bottle of whiskey or aspirin. It wasn't just the fear of being caught. He had been burdened with remorse watching his dear Max suffer because of her father's death. The poor child had struggled to understand the reason her father had left her.

He shouldn't have done it. It was rash and foolish. He had tried over the years to stop questioning his action, but it wasn't easy. And he hated how he was able to pass for a sweet old man now. Jagged shards of guilt had eaten away at him over the years.

Had it been worth it?

Not once was he able to give himself the answer he wanted.

CHAPTER FORTY-FIVE

Max wondered if Uncle Ernst was pondering over Papa's death, too. Was that why he was looking so agitated?

"I was thinking on my way back here, who could possibly have profited from Papa's death? It couldn't have been for money. Papa didn't have much. It had to be the document." She was rehashing her conversation with Schultz, but here in this familiar setting, it was easier to try and make sense of what he had said. She frowned. Schultz had said something vaguely significant. She looked around the room as she searched her mind for what it was.

On the dining table was a fruit bowl with some plastic-looking red apples. A stack of brochures was strewn on a chair. The colors were bright blue and lemon yellow—a stark contrast to the rest of the room whose colors had faded with time. *Sally Hart Weight Loss*, it said.

Max glanced at the brochures. They extolled the virtues of Sally's company. New food products were mentioned.

Uncle Ernst suddenly breathed in, a sharp intake that sounded like a wheeze.

"Are you all right?" Max was truly concerned now. She picked up a cup of tea and brought it to her lips when Uncle Ernst suddenly reached over and grabbed her hand. A few drops of tea spilled on her lap. "Oww, that's hot! What is the matter, Uncle Ernst? You're not yourself today."

"Not that cup, dear, no. This one is for you." He handed her the other cup on the tray.

She took a sip. Uncle Ernst seemed to breathe easier. The tea was bitter. It had been steeped for too long. She set it down, leaned back, and closed her eyes.

It came to her then. What Schultz had said. If Berliner was too powerful to need to kill her father, it meant that someone less powerful would actually need to kill him. But how would they have found out about Papa's work? Papa wouldn't go around telling people. She hadn't for a moment believed that he had been the one to tell Berliner about his work. Schultz had confirmed her belief by telling her about Papa's test subject who had called and blackmailed him. Had this person called other companies, too?

Think, Max. Think.

Max glanced at the brochures once more. Sally would have had a lot to lose. Hers was a small weight loss company. But Sally couldn't have done it. She was already dead when Papa died.

She drank some more of her tea and turned to Uncle Ernst. His jowls were shaking. His face was pallid.

"Uncle Ernst, how many people knew about Papa's work?"

Uncle Ernst's eyes were filmy. "No, no, no," he was muttering to himself.

That's when it hit her.

Like a hailstorm, pounding her mind with one icy realization after another.

What had uncle Ernst said once? "I was supposed to keep Hiram's research, not Lars." Uncle Ernst knew Opa's work. He was his closest friend. He was the one person to whom Papa would have told everything. In fact, Papa probably did give Uncle Ernst the research. He gave copies to Uncle Ernst, Lars, and Kevin.

She looked at him and she knew. There was apprehension in his eyes, but mostly there was immense sadness. Tears were streaming down his face.

But why? Why did he do it? For Sally. For revenge of course. Seldom sympathetic about weaknesses in people, Papa had been quite callous about Sally's suicide, she remembered now.

Uncle Ernst clenched his hands and gave a little sob.

Max's chest filled with a searing pain she hadn't known in years. She stood, tripped over the coffee table, and fell. Uncle Ernst tried to help her.

"Why did you?" she bawled. "Why? Why?"

"My child!" he cried, his tongue stumbling over his words. "You have no idea how relieved I am that you know. My sin has been gnawing upon me for too long."

Max moved away from him.

Uncle Ernst looked devastated. "Don't be afraid. You're breaking my heart." He held his trembling hands together. "I was beside myself when Sally died. When I told Hiram my Sally had died because of him, he shrugged. He was drunk. He laughed and called her a mad woman." Ernst began to sob. "Not his fault, he insisted. You have no idea how it feels to be helpless and watch your loved ones die. I've had to do it twice. I was helpless the first time. After the second time, I just couldn't let it go."

"And so you made me that helpless one?" Max sank down to the floor.

He bent down to be at eye level with her. She shrank against the wall. "All I wanted, all I ever wanted when I got out of that camp was to have a family. A daughter. After my wife and child were gassed, it was all I dreamed of for a happy life. How does one gas a baby girl? How can a God, if there is one, stand by and watch such a thing? But it happened. And this God watched it happen—over and over and over again!" He slammed his fist against the wall.

"Once I got over wanting to die myself, I swore I'd have a family again and when I did, I'd do anything to protect them," he said fiercely. "I decided that as far as my family was concerned, I got to play God. I was helpless against the Nazis. But I wasn't helpless after the war ended. I would show them and myself that I was capable of having a family I would do anything for."

He held his chest. The intensity of his words seemed to have taken his breath away. "Sally had been my golden child until she met James Hart," he growled. He straightened himself slowly. His back must be killing him, Max thought. Uncle Ernst walked away from her. "He was a gold digger. It takes one to know one, I told Sally. I had spent my youth taking advantage of rich women. But she became furious and didn't listen. James Hart left her alone with Alex—a baby. And still she stayed away from me. She held all that old anger against me even after the bastard I had warned her about had left her. She rarely spoke to me for years. Suddenly, one day she called. She wanted to give me a chance. All I had to do was help. But I couldn't. Instead I let her die."

Max was unable to form coherent thoughts. She wondered if Uncle Ernst might hurt her. She looked at the door. There were some fifteen feet between her and safety. And he was distracted. "So he did give you a copy of the research," she said. "You, Lars, and Kevin. If Lars failed, sooner or later I would have found that tape and asked you about the matzo ball soup. You did have the research!"

Uncle Ernst nodded. "Of course, I did. But I destroyed it along with the pill samples he gave me."

"I thought you loved my father like a son." Max edged toward the door.

Uncle Ernst put his palms over his face. "I begged Hiram not to release the work. 'Don't make me choose between a son and a daughter,' I said. But he became indignant. He didn't care that Sally had threatened to commit suicide. She couldn't bear the idea of facing ruin a second time. The first time she attempted suicide was when her husband left her. When that attempt failed, she threw her energies into rebuilding her company from the rubble he had left behind. When she heard about Hiram's research and his plans to release it, she attempted suicide again. I still did nothing. I hoped, fervently, that the threats from the Berliner people would stop Hiram, but he only became more determined. I asked him to postpone releasing the work, just until Sally was better and could be reasoned with. But he refused. And Sally, assuming the worst, took sleeping pills once more. This time she died. I hated Hiram then as much as I hated the Nazis." His clenched fists slammed against the windowsill. He turned suddenly.

Max stopped moving. Her face was covered with perspiration. Uncle Ernst came closer to her.

"Have you any idea how hard it was for me to do it? You were always my little angel, turning into a beautiful young woman," he said gently. "You were so dear to me." His voice suddenly grew animated. "I have something for you."

Max thought about the bitter tea. "The tea…was it poisoned?" If it was, she didn't seem to be feeling the effects yet.

"No! Never!" He turned away. "I thought I could, but I just couldn't. You're my Max. My liebchen."

Max scoffed at this. Uncle Ernst looked angry now. Max scrambled to her feet and made for the door, but Uncle Ernst was blocking it. In his hands was a small gun. His hands were shaking, but that only made Max more frightened that it might go off. "Sit! Please. I hate to do this but I need you to understand. Please."

Max felt a strange calm come over her. The events of the past few days had made her more capable than she had ever thought herself. Or perhaps she was standing outside of herself, watching the scene unfold. It was what she sometimes did to cope. She went back to the sofa but remained standing. She felt like she was losing control of her body—only her mind seemed alert. Her legs had gone wooden. Was it the tea or merely the shock of Uncle Ernst's betrayal?

Uncle Ernst went to the coffee table and picked up the second cup of tea. He took a sip and went on. "And in case you're thinking it, I didn't arrange to kill Lars. When you went to London, I placed a threatening call to him. That's all." His face took on an expression Max had never seen before. It looked like a death mask.

"Hiram could have helped Sally, but he didn't. He was too selfish. He had been waiting for years for success, he told me. 'I cannot wait until your daughter gets well to enjoy my glory. She may never get well,' he said. I know he had tried to reason with her, but in the end, he just didn't care about anyone but himself and his ambition. He deserved—"

"To die? You took a life, how is that fair?" Max cried.

"All's fair in a love like mine," Uncle Ernst said sadly.

Max felt her knees give way. If this was the way it was to end, so be it. Kevin would see that the research was published. She had done her duty. She had avenged her father.

"Today I'm torn," he said. "You see, you are the one I love most, you're my dearest. You have been the one true joy in my life. Only you. And so before I feel weak and change my mind, look here. I have something for you in this backpack. A thief, a man named Aaron West, has been working for me. He has been following you everywhere."

"What?!"

Uncle Ernst gulped down his tea and sent her a sad smile. "Darling Max. If you only knew the pain I have felt every time I looked at you. I realized too late that you were the one I loved most. And now that you know, I cannot go on. I love you, my darling. You've been all the family I ever wished for."

Max squeezed her eyes shut, feeling love and hatred for Uncle Ernst all at once—an emotion that was tearing her apart. Seconds later, a shot went off. Max slumped to the ground. Seconds later she heard a groan followed by a dull thud.

She opened her eyes. How was she alive when he had used the gun on her? Or had it gone off by mistake? There was a desperate knocking at the door. She somehow got to her feet and opened it.

Julian threw himself at her and squeezed her so tight she could barely breathe. "Are you all right?" he took her face in his hands. "I was mad worried about you," he said. "I then remembered that your Uncle Ernst lives here. I'll call an ambulance." He stumbled over Uncle Ernst. "Did he shoot at you?" He picked up the gun. "Did he shoot himself, too?"

Uncle Ernst's fist was clenched. Julian pried open his hand. There was a bottle. He looked at the cup of tea on the table and at the bottle.

Max was shaking.

"And what's this?" Julian opened the backpack that lay beside Uncle Ernst. "There's a vial of pills here! Two vials. These aren't the Indus pills, are they?"

Max couldn't respond. She was drowning under a tsunami of feelings—anger, love, sympathy, grief. A flood of icy reality washed over her. She had lost everything. Everyone she held dear was gone. She looked at Uncle Ernst lying on the floor—misshapen, flabby. In his tattered, ugly wool sweater. Poor darling Uncle Ernst. How much harm he had done in the name of love. The only thing she could feel good about, the one thing she could hold on to, was that he had said he loved her.

Julian was calling the police in a voice that sounded drugged. The world around her dimmed. Julian became a smudge.

Max slumped to the floor.

CHAPTER FORTY-SIX

Max tore open a new bag of whole-wheat flour. She was about to make a batch of chocolate chip cookies for a client. With maltitol, 80 percent cacao dark chocolate chips, egg substitute, and a combination of applesauce and a brand new olive-oil-based butter substitute, Olicol. It didn't smell appetizing, but she had been assured in a secretive whisper by the product demonstrator, that the end result, if not buttery, did not taste like cardboard.

As long as the money was good, she'd make them.

Max creamed the maltitol and the butter substitute then added the egg substitute. Kim giggled, seeing the faces Max was making as she added every ingredient. Max exaggerated her horrified expressions, encouraged by Kim's delight.

And since it was inevitable, Max began thinking about him. She thought of him once every hour. At least once every hour.

More than three weeks had past since she had last seen Julian. A lifetime ago.

She had fainted, of course, and missed all the police action. When she came to, she was home and there they were—Julian holding her hand and Kim fussing about the room.

She ought to be grateful that Julian had walked in—blundered in, really—with noble intentions. But as she sat up in bed and tried to explain how complicated things were, he just hadn't gotten it.

"I thought your uncle loved you so much," he had said. "Why the poison and the gun?"

"He couldn't bring himself to poison me," Max said. "I think he planned to drink the poisoned cup himself from the start—"

"Perhaps," Julian almost snapped. "But he did try and shoot you."

"I don't think he intended to shoot me, either," Max insisted, irritation rising like a ribbon of fire within her chest. "The gun just went off."

Julian scoffed. "That shot was meant to kill. You got lucky, Maxine Rosen."

As Max's annoyance grew stronger, Julian went on, working the story out like Hercule Poirot on speed. All this when Max was only just coming to terms with the painful reality of losing Uncle Ernst and finding out that he had killed her father, had even contemplated killing her.

Max finally lost her temper and began shouting, asking Julian to just shut up. She didn't remember her exact words, but she had ended her rant by calling him cold, unfeeling, and insensitive.

"You should consider it a favor that I even came looking for you after the inexcusable way you left Karachi," Julian had said.

"You used me!" Max responded harshly. "I fell in love with you, Julian McIntosh. You lied to me. You used me for thrills. Thanks for the favor!"

Julian got up. "That's how you see it, do you?"

That was when Kim entered the room bearing smiles and a tray full of fresh-baked chewy oatmeal chocolate chip cookies and home-made thick-cut fries, both of which Max loved.

Julian gave Max an angry look, said goodbye, and stormed out of the apartment.

Max sighed. What a way to lose a great friend and possible lover. She should write a book. *How to meet a beautiful, sweet, kind man, give him a great reason to have dinner with you, embark on an adventure, fall in love, solve a mystery together. And instead of thanking him for looking for you in your hour of need, insult him and drive him away.*

Nice work, Max.

"It's time you stopped beating that batter," Kim said.

Max smiled sheepishly. She arranged lime-sized balls on cookie sheets and put them in three layers in her immense oven.

"Want some coffee?" Max said.

"Sure, but I can go get it," Kim said and left.

Losing Uncle Ernst and Julian in the space of a few weeks was more than Max could bear.

But she hadn't had Julian to start with. It had all been a sham. Max sat in front of the oven and watched the cookies bake. Thirty minutes later, she removed tray after tray of thick, chewy chocolate chip cookies that for once made her stomach turn.

"My life has become like these cookies," she said aloud. "Sweetened by an artificial sugar and full of an unspeakable fat." She had to taste one before she made another batch. It was for good luck. She always tasted one small piece, although her pastry teacher at the culinary school had said, "Never eat ze product."

"Ohh," she cried aloud, holding her hand over her stomach. Missing Julian had become an intense ache. She turned the hot cookie over in her hands, took a bite, and pronounced sadly like he might have, "Not bad, lassie. Not bad at all."

"Could I have one?"

"Not yet," she said automatically, "They're too hot." She didn't look up. The cookie blazed into her hand, but she couldn't put it down.

Surely it wasn't his voice. Not in her kitchen. That familiar, soothing, deep, delicious, sexy voice. "Julian," she whispered, putting the cookie down with a wince.

Julian peeled a hot cookie off the sheet. "Ouch!" he cried.

He was dressed in a crisp blue linen shirt and khakis, looking so very, very…

Max felt her mouth go dry.

Julian bit off some of a cookie, swallowed and clutched at his throat. "What the devil are these? Vinyl chocolate chip?"

She started putting the cookies on cooling racks.

He dusted crumbs off his hands. "*How urr ye?*" he said in Scottish.

Max didn't speak.

"Nice kitchen you have here."

Max mumbled a thank you.

"Thing is," he said, "are you free for a project? A research project?"

Max turned to him with hands on her hips and an "are you out of your mind" expression.

Julian's face took on an apprehensive look. The Scottish lilt in his accent became more pronounced. "It's…it's food related. It's a historic food thing." He was looking at everything in the kitchen but her. He picked up a spatula and began picking at its silicone end. Max snatched it away from him. "Well, someone wants to write a book about ancient feasts from all over the world and, uh, I suggested adding recipes." He began running his fingers through his hair. "Of course, someone needs to test them because they want to market it as a cookbook, too, and I thought perhaps you might—" He looked at her with hope in his eyes. "Be interested?"

Max steeled herself. "No," she said more curtly than she had intended. He was being horribly insensitive. "I cannot work with you."

Julian seemed to have swiftly cast off his nervousness. He smiled a lopsided smile. "In that case, will you have dinner with me?"

"I cannot get over the fact that you lied to me," she said.

Julian sighed. "All right. If I had told you the truth about Raquel, you'd have stopped looking at me the way you did. Right?" He blinked his eyes a few times. "No one's looked at me like that, not since I was fifteen. I couldn't risk losing that even for the few hours I was spending with you. I didn't think I'd see you again. But you asked me to go to London and that seemed the worst time to tell you." He looked at the floor. "After that, in Chicago, I admit I wanted to go to India, but you said if I was seeing someone, I couldn't go with you. It was selfish and stupid. But I was falling for you, too."

Max tried not to look at him. "That's twisted," she said. But her anger had evaporated. And she knew she was blushing blotches of red. Only this time, she didn't care.

He was smiling broadly now. "Has anyone told you how incredibly beautiful you are? That they could lose themselves in that gorgeous hair of yours—quite literally?" He touched the ends of her hair.

Max's face was on fire. Julian stuck his finger out just close enough to touch her clavicle.

"What are you doing?" she said quietly.

He took another cookie, his manner quite nonchalant. He was having his intended effect on her, and she knew that he knew that she knew.

"Raquel wanted to get married, as you know." He pulled himself up on the counter and chewed on the cookie tentatively. "I was going to break up with her, but after our last fight, I tried convincing myself that I loved her. She started to plan the wedding in her usual style—alone. I was in the room, but it made no difference." His eyes turned to the ceiling. "I sat there, forcing myself to listen. She asked me if I could try and do more with my life—be more ambitious—she didn't care what I did, but her family did. Could I just look at my options, since we were going to be married and all. I told her I had to go, and I left. I don't think she even noticed. But Raquel is quite capable of going through with her elaborate wedding plans without me." He pursed his lips.

Max wanted to laugh, but bit her lip. "So you came here."

"Almost directly," he said.

Max started to giggle. He wanted her. He actually wanted her. *Where is your pride, Rosen?*

Julian came closer. She could feel his cookie breath on her face. Cookie breath mingled with something minty.

Max stepped back.

Julian pulled her curls away from her face and held them back, clasped in his hand. "Do you know how difficult it was for me to keep my hands off you in London and later in India?"

"That day, when you were at my apartment, you said something in Scottish," Max said.

"Don't remember," Julian said with a smirk, obviously remembering it clearly.

"I want to know what you said."

"*Dae ye?*" he said with a rakish grin.

"Yes."

Julian moved closer. "I said you are more beautiful than you will ever know."

Max fought the urge to leap at him with pleasure. "Do you like my cooking?" she asked calmly. She didn't want one more boyfriend who depended on her cooking to love her.

Julian put a hand on his chin. "I really didn't care for that butternut squash flan you made that evening. Too mushy. Or this horrendous vinyl cookie. Other than that, not bad, lassie. Not bad at all."

It was enough.

She grabbed his face in her hands and kissed him hard. Their lips stayed locked even as she wrapped a leg around his.

Kim entered, gasped, and dropped two cups of coffee on the freshly scrubbed floor.

Max threw her head back and started to laugh.

EPILOGUE

Two years later

Max opened an email from Kevin.

> It's been a long wait, dear Max. I have some news we have all been waiting for.
>
> The article I wrote in the **New Medicine** journal finally has gotten some attention. GenMed, that maverick new biotech firm, has started investigating the Indus pills. Thank heavens for the one right thing Ernst did before he died. Without him we wouldn't have had any pill samples.
>
> Anyway, GenMed wants to look into creating a vaccine or a retroviral drug! They sent out a press release some weeks ago. You were away in Scotland. It'll be a long, drawn-out process to make either of these, and after, to make sure they are universally accepted. But it's a start.
>
> Point is people are getting interested in what we have to say. Just yesterday I heard whispers about lawsuits against Berliner. One has already been filed in New York, I think.
>
> I hope you won't ask me how I managed to get the article noticed or how I got the Indus pills into the hands of the powers that be at GenMed, because Hiram may not have fully approved. Emphasis on the <u>may</u>.

But this time, my dear, my conscience is absolutely clear.
Love,
Kevin
P.S: What made you think of a remote Scottish castle of all
places for the wedding?

Whatever Kevin had done, Max didn't want to know. In this case, though, the means may have justified the end.

Julian burst in, threw his bag in a corner, and sank into a chair. "That Blake Jackson maybe the most boring man on the planet. I'm always falling asleep at our meetings." He looked at Max. "Are you all right, love?" He went to her.

Max fell into his arms.

He held her close and kissed the top of her head.

All Max could do was look up at him, shake her head, and blubber incoherently.

Too much happiness sometimes struck her dumb.

ABOUT
THE AUTHOR

RANJINI IYER HAS BEEN a business consultant, script writer, film producer, and importer of Indian silk bedding. She lives in Chicago with her husband and two sons. This is her first novel.

ACKNOWLEDGMENTS

This book wouldn't have happened if it hadn't been for the fascinating stories I heard growing up about Bayer AG from my father, Dr. S. Ramanathan Iyer. He worked for Bayer in Germany in the seventies and later in India. Bayer's Nazi connections, their connection to I.G. Farben, their powerful omnipresence in Germany, and more were all facts that stayed with me over the years.

The book *Aspirin* by Jeffrey Diarmuid added fuel to those memories, and the seed for *The Colossus* was sown.

Thank you, dear brother Ravi, for reading early drafts of the novel and providing me with much encouragement to keep going. To Madeleine and Amy, thanks for reading the first draft of the book. Thank you to my cousin Smridula Hariharan for working with me on the early scientific explanations for the bacteria in the Indus pill.

Amma, I am so grateful to you for being there when I needed you most, for willingly babysitting for hours while I wrestled with my manuscript and mainly, for your constant and calming presence.

To Renni Browne of The Editorial Department, thank you for teaching me how to edit a manuscript. Thanks to Hillel Black for his notes. To my editors Jillian Ports and Tequan Wright, I am most grateful. *Colossus* is a tight, fast-moving story thanks to you. Zach Vinson, thank you for a crisp line edit.

A great many thanks to Robert Astle, my former agent and now publisher. For your patience, your insights, and encouragement. And also for your kind indulgence/blind eye to my occasional email tantrum. Thank you for keeping the faith all these years.

Thank you Danielle Fiorella for a smashing cover design.

And finally, my best friend, strongest and most insightful critic—my husband, Amol, this book is for you. Thank you for reading countless drafts of this book with minimal complaint, all the while saying how poorly qualified you were to offer me meaningful feedback and yet managing to provide me with some wonderful and brave pointers. Without you, there would be no inspiration, no writing, and certainly no *Colossus*.

Author's note

This is a work of fiction. However, the following are the facts upon which this story is based. Some literary license has been used with the timing of the factual events as related to genetic discoveries.

Indus Valley Civilization:

This civilization lasted between circa 2500 and 1700 BCE. It was discovered in 1927 through excavations of Harappa and Mohenjo-daro (mound of the dead), both in present day Pakistan. The religious characteristics of its peoples may have continued to form Hinduism.

The script of the era hasn't been deciphered yet, although some believe it to be Dravidian based. Much about the civilization remains a mystery.

What is known, however, is that these were quite a modern people—their architecture, their granaries, and even their plumbing were all quite advanced for the time. The society was also probably democratic, and they conducted trade with other parts of the world.

(Source: Enclycopedia.com)

Why the civilization disappeared despite their advances also remains a mystery. Some experts say it may have been because their rivers ran dry. Others say the reason for their end may have been an epidemic of some sort.

The ruins of this ancient Bronze Age city, some of them remarkably preserved, are still in Pakistan. For more on Mohenjo-daro visit http://www.bbc.co.uk/news/magazine-18491900

Ikaria:

Ikaria is an island in Greece where people live very long lives. Some call it the place where people forgot to die.

(Source: http://www.bbc.co.uk/news/magazine-20898379)

I.G. Farben:

I.G. Farben was a German Limited Company that was a conglomerate of eight leading chemical manufacturers, including Bayer (makers of aspirin), Hoechst, and BASF, which at the time were the largest chemical firms in the world.

Prior to the First World War these firms had established a "community of interests—*Interessengemeinschaft*—hence the initials I.G., and they merged into a single company on December 25, 1925, thus constituting the largest chemical enterprise in the world.

Costly innovations such as the production of synthetic rubber (Buna) from coal or gasoline, persuaded IGF, during the economic crisis of the 1920s and 1930s, to establish close ties with Hitler and the Nazi Party.

In connection with the economic preparations for the forthcoming war against the Soviet Union, the IGF board, with government support, decided to establish an additional Buna works and installations for the production of synthetic fuels. The board decided on Auschwitz in Upper Silesia as the place where the new installation was to be located, not only because of the excellent rail links and the proximity of its coalmines, but primarily because the concentration camp being constructed offered IGF a considerable and cheap workforce, up to 10,000 prisoners to build the new plant.

At first, the plant managers protested against the maltreatment of the prisoners working in the plant and their poor physical condition, but eventually they went along with SS policy, in order to speed up the work.

There were five I.G. Farben owned or contracted manufacturing plants that produced Buna, most of which utilized slave labor.

The pesticide Zyklon B, for which I.G. Farben held the patent, was manufactured by Degesch (Deutsche Gesellschaft für Schädlingsbekämpfung), of which I.G. Farben owned 42.2 percent (in shares) and which had I.G. Farben managers in its managing committee. Today, the plant operates as Dwory S.A.

(Source: holocaustresearchproject.org)

History of Aspirin:

c400 BCE: In Greece, Hippocrates gives women willow leaf tea to relieve the pain of childbirth.

1763: Reverend Edward Stone of Chipping Norton near Oxford gives dried willow bark to 50 parishioners suffering rheumatic fever. He describes his findings in a letter to the Royal Society of London.

1823: In Italy, the active ingredient is extracted from willow and named salicin.

1838: Salicin is also found in the meadowsweet flower by Swiss and German researchers.

1853: Salicylic acid is made from salicin by French scientists, but it is found to irritate the gut.

1893: German scientists find that adding an acetyl group to salicylic acid reduces its irritant properties.

1897: In Germany, Bayer's Felix Hoffmann develops and patents a process for synthesizing acetyl salicylic acid, or aspirin. First clinical trials begin.

1899: Clinical trials are successfully completed. Aspirin is launched.

(Source: aspirin-foundation.com)

Endospores:

Certain bacteria, such as bacillus, clostridium, sporohalobacter, anaerobacter, and heliobacterium, can form highly resistant dormant structures called endospores.

Endospores show no detectable metabolism and can survive extreme physical and chemical stresses, such as high levels of UV light, gamma radiation, detergents, disinfectants, heat, freezing, pressure, and desiccation.

In this dormant state, these organisms may remain viable for millions of years, and endospores even allow bacteria to survive exposure to the vacuum and radiation in space. According to scientist Dr. Steinn Sigurdsson, "There are viable bacterial spores that have been found that are 40 million years old on Earth—and we know they're very hardened to radiation." Endospore-forming bacteria can also cause disease; for example, anthrax can be contracted by the inhalation of *Bacillus anthracis* endospores, and contamination of deep puncture wounds with *Clostridium tetani* endospores causes tetanus.

(Source: http://en.wikipedia.org/wiki/Bacteria)

Metabolic Rate and Longevity:

Genetic predisposition to elevated serum thyrotropin is associated with exceptional longevity. The precise mechanisms responsible for the effects of hypothyroidism on life span, however, have not been clarified, although multiple actions of decreased thyroid hormone concentrations (including lowering the metabolic rate, lowering core body temperature and oxygen consumption, and reducing reactive oxygen species generation and oxidative damage) may play an important role in longevity.

(Source: http://www.ncbi.nlm.nih.gov/pmc/articles/PMC2795660/)

Memory Cells:

A memory cell refers to one of a number of types of cells that make up part of the immune system. These cells are a vital part of the system that defends the body against bacteria or viruses that cause disease and infection.

(Source: http://www.wisegeek.org/what-is-a-memory-cell.htm)

Non-coding DNA:

The human genome is riddled with dead genes, fossils of a sort, dating back hundreds of thousands of years—the genome's equivalent of an attic full of broken and useless junk. Some of those genes can rise from the dead like zombies, waking up to cause disease in humans. One such disease is muscular dystrophy. Another that is caused by a virus embedded in the gene is schizophrenia (see below).

(Source: New York Times, "Reanimated 'Junk' DNA Is Found to Cause Disease," by Gina Kolata, published August, 19, 2010)

The culprit genes can be part of what was called non-coding DNA, regions whose function was largely unknown before until September 2012.

In September 2012, the ENCODE (Encyclopedia of DNA Elements) project, completed by hundreds of scientists from dozens of labs around the world, revealed that 80 percent of the human genome serves some purpose and is biochemically active, for example, in regulating the expression of genes situated nearby. What was labeled as "junk" DNA is now believed to be quite functional. The genes may actually be switches that trigger the body to act a certain way that causes it to function properly, as well as malfunction.

This study may lead to the understanding of various forms of cancer and other diseases that may be caused by the way these switches work in human bodies.

Retroviruses Embedded in DNA:

Schizophrenia has long been blamed on bad genes. Wrong, says a growing group of psychiatrists. The real culprit, they claim, is a virus (Perron's virus) that lives entwined in every person's DNA.

In the past few years, geneticists have pieced together an account of how Perron's retrovirus entered our DNA. Sixty million years ago, a lemur-like animal—an early ancestor of humans and monkeys—may have contracted an infection. It may not have made the lemur ill, but the retrovirus spread into the animal's testes (or perhaps its ovaries), and once there, it slipped inside one of the rare germ line cells that produce sperm and eggs. When the lemur reproduced, that retrovirus rode into the next generation aboard the lucky sperm and then moved on from generation to generation, nestled in the DNA. "It's a rare, random event," says Robert Belshaw, an evolutionary biologist at the University of Oxford in England. But such genetic intrusions stick around a very long time, so humans are chockablock full of these embedded, or endogenous, retroviruses. Our DNA carries dozens of copies of Perron's virus, now called human endogenous retrovirus W, or HERV-W, at specific addresses on chromosomes 6 and 7.

If our DNA were an airplane carry-on bag, it would be bursting with around 100,000 retrovirus sequences inside us; all told, genetic parasites related to viruses account for more than 40 percent of all human DNA.

(Source: June 2010 issue of *Discover Magazine*, published online November 8, 2010, by Douglas Fox)

Endogenous Retroviruses (ERV):

The majority of ERVs that occur in vertebrate genomes are ancient, inactivated by mutation, and have reached genetic fixation in their host species. For these reasons, they are extremely unlikely to have negative effects on their hosts except under unusual circumstances.

Nevertheless, it is clear from studies in birds and non-human mammal species, including mice, cats and koala bears, that younger (i.e., more recently integrated) ERVs can be associated with disease. This has led researchers to propose a role for ERVs in several forms of human cancer and autoimmune disease, although conclusive evidence is lacking.

In humans, ERVs have been proposed to be involved in multiple sclerosis (MS). A specific association between MS and the ERVWE1 or 'syncytin' gene, which is derived from an ERV insertion, has been reported, along with the presence of an MS-associated retrovirus (MSRV) in patients with the disease. Human ERVs (HERVs) have also been implicated in ALS.

In 2004 it was reported that antibodies to human ERVs were found in greater frequency in the sera of people with schizophrenia.

Additionally, the cerebrospinal fluid of people with recent onset schizophrenia contained levels of a retroviral marker, reverse transcriptase, four times higher than control subjects. Researchers continue to look at a possible link between HERVs and schizophrenia, with the additional possibility of a triggering infection, inducing schizophrenia.

(Source: http://en.wikipedia.org/wiki/Endogenous_retrovirus)

Enzymes:

An enzyme is a protein that acts as a catalyst. Enzymes are responsible for accelerating the rate of a reaction. Bacteria release enzymes.